THIEN - KIM LAM

Full Exposure

A NOVEL

AVON

An Imprint of HarperCollins*Publishers*

FULL EXPOSURE. Copyright © 2023 by Thien-Kim Lam. All rights reserved. Printed in the United States of America. No part of this book may be used or reproduced in any manner whatsoever without written permission except in the case of brief quotations embodied in critical articles and reviews. For information, address HarperCollins Publishers, 195 Broadway, New York, NY 10007.

HarperCollins books may be purchased for educational, business, or sales promotional use. For information, please email the Special Markets Department at SPsales@harpercollins.com.

FIRST EDITION

Designed by Diahann Sturge

Library of Congress Cataloging-in-Publication Data has been applied for.

ISBN 978-0-06-323729-2

23 24 25 26 27 LBC 5 4 3 2 1

To all my fellow children of immigrants, whose duties rest heavily on your shoulders: your dreams are important, too

ACKNOWLEDGMENTS

Writing one book—much less two—is a monstrous quest. This book wouldn't exist without the guidance and cheerleading of my badass party.

This book kicked my butt—in a good way. Thank you to my editor, Erika Tsang, for helping me whip it into shape. As always, Tara Gelsomino, your guidance keeps me grounded yet pushes me to shoot for the stars. Much gratitude to my publicist, Jes Lyons, whose astounding skills have gotten my books into the hands of so many readers.

I'm so lucky to have found a writing community who gets me. Thank you, Tracey Livesay and Farrah Rochon, for your wise advice for this new author. To my fellow Asian romance writers Jackie Lau, Cathy Yardley, Ruby Lang, and Julie Tieu: your work continues to inspire me. Thank you, Donyae Coles, for calling me out when I overthink things and for encouraging me to play with my art supplies when I'm stressed.

Shout-out to my local indie shop, Loyalty Books, for all of your support. Hannah, Christine, Gene, and the rest of the Loyalty crew are passionate about books and the people who read and write them. I was honored to be your guest bookseller for Indie Bookstore Day. (I still have my name tag if you want me back!)

I can't forget my Bawdy Bookworms community. You've supported my books every step of the way. I'm glad to have found my crew of romance readers who enjoy inclusive, spicy reads *and* love discussing our new favorite vibrator.

Jennifer Seneca, thank you for indulging me on a whirlwind (and very cold) weekend in New Orleans. We had a blast eating our way around town. Get yourself a friend who enables you to buy that fancy fountain pen while simultaneously pitching your New Orleans romance novel to the owner of a stationery store. We need to go back there and then hit up the Vampire Café for bottomless brunch again.

I can't forget my IRL Boss Babes, Leticia Barr and Lisa Frame. Your unconditional love for me keeps me steady. I'd be lost without you two.

Huge gratitude to my sister, Thien-Kieu Lam, who has taken on the role of family historian. Her research into my grandparents' and parents' journeys from Vietnam to the United States has helped me better understand what they went through and what they sacrificed to raise us. Cảm ơn Ba Mẹ.

To my husband: thank you for keeping me stocked with chocolate, coffee, and seltzer water. Most of all, thank you for believing in me and encouraging me to do what I love. Thank you to my teenagers who still think I'm cool—for a mom, at least. They slipped me meals and coffee as I tried to type out the movie playing in my mind. I love you all.

Last but not least, thank you to my readers, especially those who messaged me to share how much *Happy Endings* meant to you. I'm writing the Vietnamese American characters I wanted to see in my romances, and I'm thrilled that they resonate with you, too.

CHAPTER 1

Josie Parks looked down at her 30 by 30 list. *Attend a Mardi Gras parade* was something she had yet to do, but that was about to change. An impromptu solo vacation in New Orleans didn't land in her lap, well, ever. But it was the silver lining to the last-minute cancellation of her client's bachelorette party photoshoot. So for the next seven days, Josie was finally going to put herself first.

According to the official Mardi Gras website, a parade was rolling through the neighborhood where she was staying. The parade route was only a fifteen-minute walk according to her map app. New Orleans's city blocks were nothing like the quiet, sepia-toned DC neighborhood she'd grown up in. Half the homes lining the street were painted in several bold colors each.

It'd taken her twenty minutes to walk three blocks because she kept stopping to snap photos with her camera, which she'd lovingly dubbed Ruby. Josie never went anywhere without its well-worn strap around her neck. Each house was full of personality. Some were decked out with Mardi Gras decorations, including in the front yard. She remembered reading how "house floats" became popular a few years ago.

Josie was already falling in love with the city. Music greeted her everywhere she turned. The city's energy seeped into her bones. She caught herself nodding along to the jazz music drifting from the bars she walked past. Though a different musician's touch flowed out of each bar, they harmonized in their own magical way.

A few yards after she passed the bars, a different kind of music tickled her ears. A mix of blues and—was that notes of Caribbean beats similar to what her mom listened to? Of course! This was zydeco, New Orleans's special blend. She tucked her list into her oversized purse before rushing toward the parade.

"Wow." Josie stopped short at the street crossing. Her jaw dropped. The photos from her quick online search didn't do the parade justice.

The music and cheering drowned out everything around her. Crowds of at least six or seven people deep lined both sides of the street. They held up their hands and yelled at the people on the floats. One person managed to catch something without spilling their drink. Beer in a giant plastic cup, it looked like. That must be the "cheap-ass beer" that Trixie Nguyen, one of her best friends, had warned her about. Josie had no plans to buy watered-down booze from sketchy vendors.

Zydeco blared from floats, drawing her attention to their bright, flashing lights illuminating the night. She increased her pace to get a closer look at the giant sculpted dragon on the float closest to her. The wings extended from the side of the float and flapped. She half expected it to lift into the sky. The details on its six-foot head were impressive. The horns shone with pinpricks of light and its eyes glowed red.

The dragon's mouth opened, and smoke billowed from it.

Josie clapped and reached for her camera. Her head spun from the glorious colors and creativity in front of her. Calling them floats seemed like a disservice. These were moving works of art. This was nothing like parades back in DC, which comprised mostly local marching bands and politicians waving from convertibles.

"Beautiful, ain't it?" someone next to her asked.

Josie turned to a Black woman wearing the largest green, gold, and purple hoop earrings she'd ever seen.

Josie could barely hear her over the cheering and music. She nodded.

"First time?"

"Yes!" Josie shouted above the noise. "It's amazing!" She couldn't hide the excitement in her voice. Who cared if it branded her as a tourist? She was finally checking a Mardi Gras parade off her list.

The woman grabbed her arm, and Josie froze, her entire body tensed. What did they do to first-timers at Mardi Gras parades? As if sensing Josie's unease, the woman loosened her grip and placed a sisterly hand on Josie's shoulder to guide her deeper into the crowd. Josie quickly pulled off her camera and tucked it into her purse. She didn't want it to get bumped as they walked through the dense crowd.

"Hey!" the woman hollered at the people in front of them. "It's her first time!"

What was even happening? Josie's fear from earlier had been replaced by curiosity. She knew now that this woman wouldn't let anything bad happen to her.

"Make some space!" Hoops Lady cried out again. She had an extremely commanding voice.

Slowly, the crowd parted as the woman pulled Josie closer to the parade. She didn't stop until they reached the metal barricade that kept people off the street.

"Now you can catch better beads!" Hoops Lady's mouth was right next to Josie's ear.

The people who'd parted to let them through smiled at Josie. Then they bombarded her with, well, Southern hospitality.

"Welcome to New Orleans, sweetheart."

"Raise your hand up high like this so they know you want some beads." Several people reached up to demonstrate.

"As soon as you catch it, put it around your neck so no one tries to rip it out of your hands."

"Never bend down to pick up beads if you value your hands. People will step on ya to catch beads."

Josie chuckled and bobbed her head at each person who graciously gave her tips. After reading about crowds and parade pickpockets on travel sites, she'd been super vigilant about people walking up to her. But everyone she'd met so far had been friendly and helpful. Josie pulled out her phone to capture as much of the parade and people as she could.

"Here's your chance to catch your first set of beads!" Hoops Lady pointed to the next float heading their way, a locomotive with a smoking chimney. The wheels were an illusion made from lights that were programmed to make the train look as if it were traveling on train tracks. Standing on the float were costumed and masked people. Each person had one arm weighed down with giant necklaces while the opposite hand grabbed and tossed them into the crowd.

Josie's body vibrated with anticipation. Here was her chance to take home a special souvenir! She thrust her open hand into the air, grateful that her five feet eight inches gave her an advantage over the people around her.

"Attagirl!" Hoops Lady shouted encouragingly. Josie should have asked for her name, but she liked the mystery and spontaneity of it all. Boring, responsible Josie would have walked away and missed a front-row spot. Not to mention meeting all these kind people.

She kept her eyes on a man with a blue mask and engineer's hat. He'd been swinging his beads low, closer to the front. If she leaned to the left just a little at his next toss, she could—

Josie closed her fingers into a fist as soon as the cold plastic touched her palm.

"I got it! I can't believe I caught—" She turned to Hoops Lady to celebrate, but the woman had disappeared. Maybe she'd moved behind her. Forgetting that the beads were still in her hand, Josie spun around to look for the woman.

The heavy beads gained momentum and flew into the air.

And right into a man's head.

"Oh my God!" Josie gasped. She nearly dropped the beads but

for some reason remembered the advice to hold them tight. "Are you okay?"

"Watch it, lady!" the Southeast Asian man hollered, bent over with pain. "Fucking tourists."

She looked at the hand that was holding his temple. Then back down to the large, pearl-like lavender beads she'd whacked him with in her excitement. The necklace's beads started at around marble size but graduated all the way to the size of a Ping-Pong ball. Even if there was no blood, beads this big could have done some major damage.

"I'm so sorry. It's my first time at a Mardi Gras parade, and I saw those gorgeous beads. They weren't gaudy like the other ones and—" Great, now she was babbling to a stranger whom she'd almost knocked out with some stupid plastic necklace. She took a deep breath to calm her racing heart. "I'll take you to urgent care. You could have a concussion."

She had no clue where the nearest one was, but she couldn't just leave him on the sidewalk like this. The parade was going strong, with no end in sight. The paradegoers, who had made an opening for them at first, had pushed forward to fill the space up front where Josie had been standing. The front row was always prime real estate during a Mardi Gras parade.

"I'm fine," the man grumbled. He'd straightened up and dropped his hand from his face.

Well, butter my biscuits as her friend Reina Guidroz would say. He was hot. Like Marvel superhero hot.

His straight black hair fell over his eyes, which held something that could pass as amusement. Was she staring too hard? She didn't think so. She pressed her lips together in case her jaw had dropped. Nope. She hoped whatever she thought about his looks wasn't telegraphed in her body language.

His jaw was set as if he was trying not to smile. The rest of him was just as pleasing to the eye. His black leather jacket molded around his shoulders, and under it he wore a fitted navy T-shirt. Oh, yes, her imagination had plenty to work with.

Suddenly, he started laughing. Not the funny kind of laugh but the sort an evil villain gave after confessing their maniacal plan to take over the world. The cheery zydeco music pumping from the floats mixed with his laughter gave her the chills. Maybe the beads had hit him harder than she'd thought. Was that the beginning of a bruise on the side of his head? She squinted. Was there a welt, too?

So much for relaxing during her impromptu vacation. Instead, she'd probably cracked the skull of an extremely attractive local. What if he called the cops on her and pressed charges? Her best friends would bail her out, but she'd never hear the end of their teasing.

She took him by the arm and pulled him away from the crowd to where she could hear herself think over the loud music and screams of "Throw me something!" Behind them was a bar. She maneuvered his laughing ass to the side of the building. He tugged himself out of her grip.

"Hey." She looked into his eyes and spoke slowly. "Are. You. Okay?"

His laughter stopped. He stared at her long enough that she began to slide into worry mode. Before she could panic about his head, he opened his mouth.

"You're gorgeous." He smiled dreamily at her.

"Look who's talking. You're pretty hot yourself." Josie clamped her hand over her mouth. She never flirted with strangers. Except now she was. Maybe she should add it to her 30 by 30 list and check it off. No, that would make it a 31 by 30 list, which didn't have the same ring to it.

"Are you real or did I die after being clobbered by giant beads?" He tilted his head, studying her.

Dammit, she must have hit him harder than she'd thought.

"You're alive. And I'm real." She touched his arm to ground him to reality.

He placed his hand on top of hers and squeezed it as if to test her assertion. His touch sent a surge of electricity through her body. Even though she'd met him only five minutes ago, she was drawn to him.

"Beautiful and not a dream." His thumb rubbed circles on the back of her hand as he continued to stare into her eyes.

She jerked away, the back of her hand still tingling from his touch. She wasn't the type to be instantly attracted to a stranger. All her previous relationships were with people she'd become friends with first. Maybe it was the guilt from hurting him even though it was accidental.

"It's my first Mardi Gras parade," she repeated in case he hadn't heard her the first time. "And the first beads I've ever caught and I—"

"Hey, it's okay. I'm fine." He smiled and opened his arms wide to prove his words.

Good grief, how could this man's eyes sparkle from a mere grin? Josie wanted to pull out her camera. Something about him begged for her to photograph his captivating energy. Then she'd take him out for coffee so he could tell her why the hell he'd walked through a Mardi Gras parade without paying attention to the people around him.

"I guess the universe wanted us to meet in the most dramatic, most New Orleans way possible." He winked, grimacing slightly before covering it up with another smile.

"I don't know about the universe, but *you* could have a concussion. *I'm* trying to take you to urgent care." Josie pulled out her phone to search for one. Her friends constantly told her to stop trying to save everyone she met. But this was different. He could be *physically* broken. And that needed fixing.

"I'm fine. I don't need a doctor." He attempted a few steps but wobbled until the brick wall caught him. "Okay, maybe I do."

Josie grabbed a chair from the bar's outdoor seating. He didn't fight when she sat him down.

She tried to remember her first aid training. How long did you have to watch someone for signs of head trauma? She could remember only the TV medical dramas her mom loved. Usually head traumas didn't go well on those shows. Hopefully that wasn't the case with this man.

If this were an indication of how the rest of her vacation would be, Josie was better off researching and planning the rest of the week instead of being spontaneous.

CHAPTER 2

Spencer Pham tried to remember what he had been doing before—before *her*. He'd been holding something, but what? He scanned the sidewalk in front of them hoping it would jog his memory. It was right there on the edge of his mind, but the pounding in his head pushed it away. At least he had a beautiful woman to distract him from the pain.

Her thumb was a blur as it swiped through her phone. The weapon still dangled from her arm.

"You should wear the beads. The color looks good on you." He didn't come home to New Orleans to hit on tourists, but he couldn't let this opportunity pass him by. The way she'd taken charge of the situation was hot.

She was hot. Her dark jeans accentuated all her curves. The neckline of her loose, green top drew his attention to her collarbones. Damn, since when did he find collarbones sexy?

From the low vantage point of his chair, the streetlights combined with the flashing lights from the floats to create a halo around her black afro. Her cheeks were slightly flushed. To borrow a phrase from his sisters, this woman glowed. The universe had sent him an angel as if to reaffirm his decision to move back home after losing his job in DC.

"What?" She looked up from her phone.

"At least put them around your neck before some jerk swipes them."

He nodded gently at the beads. The throbbing veins in his forehead refused to be ignored. Even through his haze of pain, he couldn't help but notice how the iridescent light purple beads highlighted her warm brown skin. She was right. They weren't gaudy like most beads caught during the parades. These were the prized ones that people fought over. They would look radiant around her neck.

"I can't do that!" Guilt shadowed her face.

What a pretty face she had. What would it feel like to kiss her full, lush lips? Maybe he'd been hit harder than he thought. Now he was imagining kissing this stranger. A tourist.

"You should have them." She nearly ripped the necklace off her arm and thrust it at him.

He shook his head quickly. Both to clear the image of kissing her and in response to her offer. Bad idea. He stifled a groan and grabbed his temple.

"You caught them, so they're yours. Mardi Gras etiquette." He gently pushed her arm to offer the beads back. And tried to ignore how soft her skin was. "Besides, I have lots of beads already. It's a perk of growing up around here."

She bit her lip as she considered his words. "Fine. But you have to tell me why you were so close to the barricade if you're not here to catch beads."

As a New Orleans native, he'd caught plenty of beads over the years. He used to thrive on the adrenaline rush from snatching them out of the air. Though not extremely tall, his five feet ten inches gave him a slight advantage over most parade-goers.

The last time he'd done that was ten years ago, though he was pretty sure he still had the hand-eye coordination and timing to grab the best beads. Of all the parades he'd attended, he'd never been taken down by a strand. Until today.

Even if the strand was in the hand—um, on the arm—of this glowing woman in front of him.

"I'm waiting."

Her demanding tone didn't faze him. He'd grown up with a Vietnamese mother and grandmother. Not to mention three younger sisters who weren't afraid to ask for what they wanted.

"It's kind of embarrassing," he finally admitted.

"Try me." Her face softened.

"I got swept into the crowd."

She raised an eyebrow in skepticism.

"Fine." He sighed. "I wasn't paying attention. During Mardi Gras the crowd has a mind of its own. Like waves in the ocean. You live here long enough, and you can see it start to happen. The crowd hits critical mass and starts to move as one unit. Anyone on the fringes gets swept in and absorbed into it."

Great, now he was babbling about crowd theory. Way to impress her with nerdy facts. His cheeks grew warm.

"Wow. I have no idea how critical mass relates to Mardi Gras, but it makes sense when you put it that way."

He was relieved to hear amusement in her voice.

"I was deep in my thoughts, and next thing I knew I was pushed up front. The rest you know." He'd had an urgent need to escape New Orleans East, so he'd made his way into the French Quarter to clear his mind. He'd forgotten that the parades drew huge crowds and clogged traffic.

"Right. I really should take you to urgent care. I'd feel better if you took the beads."

She also happened to have a very soothing voice.

"Keep them. I don't need a reminder of how I got taken out by giant beads my first Mardi Gras back in ten years."

"A city can change a lot in ten years. So technically you're a tourist in your hometown."

"What? No way. I'm—" He stopped when she began laughing.

"Kidding." She put both hands up in defense. "I couldn't help it since you were so anti-tourist earlier."

"You'd be anti-tourist, too, if that happened to you." He pointed at her beads.

"I can't say I've been in that position," she tossed back.

That word conjured images of her full hips and round ass in many different positions. He cleared his throat and tried to focus on other things, like how he should call his grandmother to tell her he'd be late for dinner.

"You know what I mean." The way her tongue darted out to lick her bottom lip, her mind might have wandered in the same direction as his. So the attraction was mutual.

"So what you're saying is that you're inexperienced when it comes to interacting with native New Orleanians?" he teased.

"Maybe it's just one particular native who got in my way." She pressed her lips together as if hiding a smile.

"Oooh, touché."

"Seriously, though, my first day in New Orleans has been one thing after another." She shook her head. "I was trying to be spontaneous, since there was a parade blocks from my rental. Instead, I almost killed a man."

Her face contorted. Was she going to cry?

"Whoa. That escalated quickly. I'm still alive and mostly well." Suddenly he wanted to make her laugh again to stop her from being so hard on herself. He hooked his foot around the leg of a chair nearby and pulled it over. "It was an accident. I know you didn't mean to hurt me. Why don't you sit a minute?"

To his surprise, she dropped into the chair.

"Sorry, I didn't mean to unload on you. We don't even know each other's names."

"That's an easy fix." He held out his hand. "I'm Spencer Pham, hapless native."

"I'm Josie Parks, tourist and apparently a menace to said native." Her mood had lifted enough to make a joke. She shook his hand.

"I hope you have better weapons of mass destruction for your next trial run."

Josie mock gasped. "I'm concerned for your well-being, *Spencer Pham*. I'm not some kind of Mardi Gras vigilante trying to rescue the best beads from greedy paradegoers."

"Okay, okay, you're not a vigilante." He took the beads out

of her hands and slipped them over her head. "You make those beads look good."

"Since you're flirting with me, I'll assume you're not—"

"My phone! I dropped it when the beads—" Spencer smacked his head. "Ow! Fuck!"

"Wait, what?" Josie sat up straighter. "Why didn't you say something sooner?"

"I was a bit distracted, if you haven't noticed." He rubbed his forehead. "I was taking B-roll of the parade for my documentary."

"So you're telling me that not only did I smack you in the head, but I made you drop your phone over there?" She pointed to the sidewalk where they'd first met. It was as if they'd never been there. People jumped up and down as they fought over beads.

Spencer frowned and nodded. If his phone was still there, it was probably crushed. He should have bought the extended warranty.

Josie pursed her lips, ran her hand over the beads, and shook her head. Her eyes darted from him to the parade in front of them before her mouth opened and she began to chuckle.

There it was again. Her deep, unfettered mirth was music to his ears. Her shoulders relaxed as she let the amusement take over her body. She was absolutely stunning.

"You— I don't even know what else to do about today except laugh."

Her energy was contagious, and he joined her in laughing. What else could they do about this comedy of errors except laugh?

CHAPTER 3

Josie couldn't stop laughing. She didn't care that the few people who walked past them gave them a wide berth.

The more she laughed, the more her body relaxed. She'd shouldered so much stress over the past couple of weeks in preparation for what was supposed to be a work trip. It'd been easy to check off tasks on her Biggest Destination Photo Shoot Ever list, but an ink mark didn't indicate how emotionally challenging it'd been for her to step away from her studio for a week. Even if she trusted her sister to take care of things while she was gone, she couldn't help but worry.

All that work to come to New Orleans, and her trip had fallen apart on the very first day. She hated when things didn't go according to plan, no matter how good her backup plan was. But this time she had been caught off guard. She had focused all her energy on researching the location and logistics for the weeklong photoshoot that Josie hadn't had time to formulate a backup plan.

After the surprise cancellation earlier that morning, Josie had pulled up her 30 by 30 list. She hated not having something to do or things to mark off. Life was easier when she had a plan.

"I could use a do-over for this day," Spencer wheezed, once their laughter finally faded.

"Same. And what a terrible day it's been." Josie wiped the tears from her eyes. Her side ached from laughing so hard.

"There's gotta be a silver lining somewhere. No one is this unlucky," he joked, his eyes still soft from their shared laughter.

"I doubt it. It's my first day here, and my client canceled the entire trip. Why couldn't she cancel it before I left DC? But my mom and sister convinced me to stay and take time off. So I did. I tried to have fun and hit you instead."

"Wait, did you say today's your first day in town? And you're from DC? There's your silver lining!"

"How can you see one from"—she waved her hands—"this?"

"I lived in DC for the past ten years! Maybe we sat in the same train car and never knew it."

"You're kidding, right?" She'd flown almost a thousand miles to injure someone from her hometown.

"See? Universe." He crossed his arms and nodded. "Things happen for a reason."

"The universe wanted you to lose your phone?"

"Well . . ." He shrugged. "I wouldn't have met you. What are the chances I'd run into someone from the DMV all the way in New Orleans in this very spot?"

"And she'd knock you over so you dropped your phone?" Josie sighed. "Maybe it survived?"

He side-eyed her.

"Right. Highly unlikely." Josie sucked her teeth. "Sorry."

"And the hits keep coming."

"I'll replace it." Thank goodness for the nonrefundable deposit from her canceled photoshoot.

"You don't have to do that."

"I do, and I'm not taking no for an answer." Wait till she told the Boss Babes about today. They'd probably laugh at the ridiculousness of it. Then buy her several cocktails.

"I know how you can make it up to me." He pulled himself up and met her eyes.

She blinked but couldn't look away. His eyes shined with excitement, but there was so much more behind them. She needed to learn more about him and photograph all the different emotions in them.

"Josie, I think you're hot, and I'd like to know you better. Maybe over some café au lait and beignets?"

"Nope, I'm taking you to urgent care to make sure you don't have a concussion." She tapped on her phone. "The nearest one isn't too far away."

"Have you been to Cafe du Monde yet?" He ignored her very practical suggestion.

She rolled her eyes. She had a feeling he wouldn't stop until she responded. "It's on my list for tomorrow. Now can we focus on your head?"

"How about I take you there right now? On a date. I'd like to know you better."

Wait, he was asking her out. For some reason, she wanted to hang with him, too. So she could photograph him, of course.

Not because she found him attractive. Her first priority was getting him some medical attention.

"Come on. My treat." Spencer pulled himself up from the chair. He winced, and his hand flew to his head, which by the looks of it would sport a very nasty bruise tomorrow. "If we leave now, we can beat the drunk parade after-party."

Spencer took a step forward and swayed. Josie jumped up to grab him, but he held up a hand. She stepped back.

"I'm fine. Got up too fast."

She couldn't help but hover.

"But I wouldn't mind someone to keep me steady." He winked. "You up for the job?"

She raised an eyebrow but didn't argue. After everything she'd done to him, she'd let him keep his pride.

He wasn't too much taller than her. His muscular build could easily be mapped out through his thin T-shirt. Her imagination had been correct. She resisted the urge to squeeze his toned arm and see how fit he truly was.

He took her silence as an invitation to lean into her. She didn't mind. He smelled like—bread? She took a covert sniff. Yes, freshly baked bread. Maybe he'd spent the day in a bakery? His muscular arms could've come from kneading bread.

She'd known him for less than fifteen minutes, but he fascinated her.

They took a few awkward steps together until they found a rhythm.

"Let's make a quick stop at urgent care." She tried to steer him in the opposite direction.

"I'm *fine*. Cafe du Monde is this way." He pulled her back and grinned. "You know you want some fried dough. And spending time with you is making my head feel better already."

Josie's stomach grumbled. Now that her adrenaline rush had dissipated, she was starving. His expression was so hopeful, she didn't have the heart to turn him down.

"Let's go get some beignets."

"Yes!" He pulled her in tight for a hug that sent shivers down her body. "It's a date."

"It's not a date. If you show any signs of a concussion, we're taking a cab to—"

"Yes, yes, urgent care." He nodded. "I get it."

She couldn't let him roam New Orleans with a head injury, Josie told herself. She'd watch him closely in case he really did have a concussion. Not because he was handsome and charming.

CHAPTER 4

Spencer flashed Josie the most charming smile he could manage through his headache. He'd rather spend whatever brief time they had together doing something fun. Sitting in some beige medical waiting room was the opposite of fun. His headache wasn't anything that some over-the-counter meds couldn't fix.

"You wouldn't happen to have any ibuprofen in that bag of yours?"

"Oh! Why didn't I think of that sooner?" She guided him away from the foot traffic and extricated her arm from around him. Spencer instantly regretted losing her warmth and touch, but there was plenty of time for that later.

"Sorry I don't have any water." She handed him two pills from a container with labeled compartments.

"It's fine." He swallowed them dry. "Are you always this prepared and organized?"

"My friends say I'm the mother hen of our group. And I'm an older sister, so I've had lots of practice."

Sister! He was in so much trouble.

"Can I borrow your phone to text my sister? I was supposed to check on my grandmother a couple of hours ago." Bà Bà would either be worried or too consumed with her Viet action drama to notice he was late.

"I'd be a monster if I said no." She fished her phone out of the pocket of her jeans.

He hoped one of his sisters could stay with their grandmother until he could get home. His thumb hovered over the keypad. Nina, his youngest sister, was the safest bet. She wouldn't scold him like the others. After quickly orienting himself to Josie's phone, he sent the text:

Josie: It's Spencer. Got stuck in the Quarter & lost my phone. Can you stay with Bà Bà till I get home?

Nina: Seriously?! How the hell did you do that?

Josie: Long story. I'll explain later. I'm stuck in the city till the parade crowd clears out.

The little dots bounced as he waited for her reply. Even if he could catch a Lyft, surge pricing would be ridiculous. He was still unemployed and had to be careful with his finances. Finally, Josie's phone buzzed.

Nina: You owe me.

Josie: Thanks! Love you, too, sis.

She replied with the middle finger emoji. He chuckled. He'd made the right choice to ask Nina first. His two other sisters wouldn't have agreed until he explained in great detail why he was late. That was something he didn't want to do on Josie's phone.

"Everything good? Do you want me to get you a Lyft home?"

"No! I mean, everything is fine. My sister is gonna hang with my grandmother till I get home."

Josie's lips pursed in worry.

"It's not every day a smart, gorgeous woman hits me in the head and allows me to take her out for beignets." He winked and offered his arm like he'd seen guys do in the movies.

Her eyes narrowed as she studied him. "Remember, any sign—"

"I'm *fine*. Let's get some food. I'm starved."

Spencer hadn't had a plan when he jumped into the rideshare to New Orleans that morning. When his grandmother had reminisced about her early years in Louisiana during breakfast, he'd been inspired to create a short film about the krewe his grandfather had founded.

Why not attend a parade for B-roll and to give him more clarity on his new project? Ever since high school, he'd figured out how to succeed in almost everything he tried. His previous attempts were merely false starts as he found his footing, but he was determined to excel in filmmaking, too.

He'd studied his ass off to get straight A's and a scholarship to college. He was the first one in his family to graduate from college because that's what his parents expected him to do. His mom and dad had worked long days to provide for him and his siblings. The least he could do was keep up his end of the bargain and take care of his parents and grandmother now that they were older. They deserved to rest now that he and his sisters were adults.

Spencer might have lost his job and had to move back home, but he was going to make his parents proud of him on his own terms this time. Making this a film about his grandfather's legacy would redeem him.

He'd think about that tomorrow. The pain meds were starting to kick in, and he was able to walk without Josie's aid. All he wanted was to spend a couple of carefree hours with her. Now that she wasn't holding him up, she pulled out her camera. The gadget transformed her into a different person. It became part of her body as she looked through her viewfinder and snapped photos. It was fascinating to see New Orleans through her fresh eyes. She studied things he took for granted because they were always around.

Things like the trucks cleaning up the trash from tourists and parades. Beads abandoned in puddles of— Spencer grimaced— best not to think about that. The iron lacework that lined the balconies in the French Quarter. People laughing with their friends, beads of all sorts hanging around their necks.

He'd never actually stayed at a hotel here. Spencer wondered what the going rate was for a short-term apartment rental in the Quarter these days. Mardi Gras season was so lucrative that some residents rented out their apartments at the start of the season in early January and stayed outside the city for the next two or so months.

"Everyone is so happy and relaxed here," Josie said after zooming in on some women standing on the second-floor balcony above a used bookstore.

"They're on vacation in the best city in the world. Why wouldn't they be?" Spencer wasn't sure if he was trying to convince her or himself. He'd gone from living on his own in DC to sharing a home with his parents and grandmother again. With all the things that came with being the eldest Vietnamese child living at home.

"I'm usually the cruise director for my friends or family when we travel. The keeper of all plans and backup contingencies in case the weather doesn't cooperate. Kinda hard to relax," Josie countered without pausing from her picture taking. "Are you always happy on vacation?"

"If you consider 'in-between jobs'"—he used air quotes—"a vacation. That's what my mom tells her friends. Can't have an unemployed thirtysomething son at home."

He'd hated his old job. Taking time off was considered a sign of weakness. He'd kept his head down and rarely taken vacation time to see his family. He'd thought if he worked hard enough, his boss would notice. That might have worked in high school and college, but adult life wasn't that way. He hadn't been able to bring himself to attend mindless happy hours with his boss only to compete in ass-kissing contests with his colleagues.

"I can't imagine moving home after all this time. Though my

parents would take me in if I asked." Her shutter clicked several times. "What did you do back in DC?"

"Data analyst for a government contractor. The most boring job ever." He'd only taken it as an escape from his family. And for the pay. The salary was too good to turn down after his family had lost their jobs after the big oil spill. He promised his family that he'd send as much money home as he could until—well, until they were in a better place financially. Ten years later, they were the ones supporting him. "Enough about me. Tell me what else you have planned while you're here."

"To be honest, I didn't have much planned except work. This is the first true break in a long time. It's a weird feeling."

"You get to do whatever you want, right? Not planning for anyone, so you should be happy," Spencer pointed out.

"Theoretically. Though not having a plan makes me twitchy." She turned the camera toward him. "We should document what happened today."

"Hell no!" Minutes before, he'd caught his reflection in a window and grimaced. Spencer had no plans to preserve his bruise for all of digital eternity.

"Fine. But I'll get you to change your mind." She put her camera down.

His insides twisted at the thought of disappointing her. He wanted Josie to be happy and carefree if he could help it. Although, how could he be invested in the emotions of someone he'd just met? He'd dated women in the DMV but never truly clicked with anyone. He'd been home barely a month and found instant connection with a stranger—from DC of all places.

His stomach untwisted when she gave him a small smile. She wasn't upset that he didn't want his photo taken.

"Seriously, though, I hope we can both laugh about this someday. It's kinda funny, if you think about it." She shrugged before turning her camera toward another historic building.

Did that mean she hoped they would laugh about it in a future where they were together? As friends or something a bit more? He hoped for the latter.

"You know what would make me happy right now?" He changed the subject, not ready to think about the future. He wanted to enjoy her company for however long she'd give it to him.

"Hot, sugary beignets!" Her lips turned up into a wide, childlike grin.

"You read my mind." Spencer almost tripped over his own feet. He'd buy her beignets every day if she smiled at him with this much joy every time.

The mouthwatering fragrance of fried dough hit them well before the café was within sight. He inhaled, and all the weight on his shoulders fell away. The air surrounding them was warm and sweet, promising its patrons a moment of respite from their busy day. If Spencer squinted, he could see tiny flecks of powdered sugar floating in the air.

Thankfully, they'd arrived at Cafe du Monde during a lull. The line moved quickly, barely giving him a chance to ask for her choice of drink. He asked for two orders of beignets along with two steaming mugs of café au lait. It was his standing order whenever he stopped here.

"Let me pay for it. It's the least I can do after hurting you." Josie reached into her bag.

"No, it's on me. My hometown, my treat." He nudged her away from the window. "They only take cash, and I've got a twenty burning a hole in my wallet."

"Okay, but next one's on me." She took a deep breath. "Oh my God, this place smells amazing. Are you sure two plates are enough?"

"Let's see how you feel after the sugar rush." Spencer laughed as he soaked in her wonder. He didn't want this night to end.

Their orders came out through the tiny window on a dark green plastic tray. He grabbed it and motioned for Josie to find a table in the café's covered outdoor area. In his opinion, this was the best way to experience the French Quarter. They could people watch and absorb the pulse of the city. Like its music. There was always someone busking and serenading diners and folks passing by.

"Wow, that's a lot of sugar. Mind if I take some pics?" Josie said after they'd claimed a table. She'd already pulled out her camera and walked around their small table to take photos. She even turned the tray this way and that to find the best angles.

"You'd fit right in with my family. My sisters are always taking photos of their food to post on Instagram."

"I almost forgot about Instagram!" She swapped her camera for her phone. This time she took some video along with photos. "I promised to send pics to my friends back home."

If he still had his phone, he might have taken a picture of her taking photos of the food. But that would be weird. He didn't want to be weird around her. The best he could do was try to remember all the details of tonight. He had a feeling that meeting her had changed his life irrevocably. He wasn't sure how, but he felt it in his gut.

"I know you're a professional and all, but it's still January and our food is getting cold," he teased.

"You're right." She sat down. "Let's eat."

"Wait!" He stopped her as she reached for the food.

She froze with her hands in midair. Josie tossed him a *Now what?* look.

"Before you dive in, there are some rules to eating a beignet."

"Really?" She lifted an eyebrow. "For fried dough. I know how to eat donuts."

"These aren't just any donuts." Oh God, he sounded pretentious. He tried again. "Okay, so there're no real rules, but let's call them best practices. They're mine at least."

"Go on."

"First, you have to find the piece with the most sugar." He made a show of slowly turning the tray around. "Because some will inevitably fall off when you pick it up. You want the sugar to dust the other, less blessed beignets."

He settled on a piece that partially rested on two others. Grabbing it by the corner, he slid it away from its companions. Small, delicate landslides of sugar slipped off the chosen one onto the others.

When he looked up, Josie had her phone pointed at him. It was obvious she was in her element.

"Are you photographing me?"

"Is that okay?"

He nodded. This time he didn't mind being the subject of her pictures. "A good student always takes notes from the master."

"Your mastery still remains to be seen." Her eyes were on him instead of her phone screen.

"Oooh, a harsh critic." It had been years since he'd felt so—what? So alive. And silly. He was having fun.

"Now you eat it, right?"

"You have so much to learn." He held up his finger. "If you dive right in without the proper precautions, there will be a sugar calamity!"

Josie barked with laughter.

"What? I'm not being dramatic this time."

"Your old-timey vocabulary is endearing." She gestured to the fried dough in his hand. "Continue, wise one."

"Before you take a bite, you must hold your breath or the sugar will fly everywhere. If you breathe in, it flies into your nose. Breathe out and you dust your friends."

He made a show of holding his breath before biting off a piece, navy shirt be damned.

"Oooh, that's so good," he mumbled as he chewed the crispy, slightly chewy treat. The sugar melted in his mouth. He groaned. "Damn, I've missed this."

"Come on, you can find beignets in DC. It can't be that good."

"Try one and find out," he said before taking another bite. Big mistake. His words blew the sweet powder into the air and all down his navy shirt. Some flew into his nose and he coughed. Nothing a swig of café au lait couldn't fix.

She snickered.

"Look who's not following the rules. Let me show you how it's done." Josie grabbed several napkins out of the small metal holder. She unfolded the thin, flimsy sheets and tucked them into her shirt in some semblance of a bib.

"Nothing screams tourist like a napkin tucked into a shirt."

"I think we already established I'm a tourist when you became acquainted with my beads. Besides, I have a strategy. Inspired by your lack of one." She pointed at his sugar-bombed T-shirt.

"You wound me." He gasped and put his hands on his chest.

It was her turn to study her cardboard tray with its three untouched mounds of sugar. Her mischievous smile worried him. He hadn't known her long enough to figure out what she had planned, but he had a feeling this was a trick.

"I think I'll go with this one."

Like him, she reached for the piece with the largest mound of sugar. She wiggled it gently but dislodged a mountain of sugar. Not the best technique, but maybe she didn't have a sweet tooth.

She slowly brought the beignet to her lips. All night he'd studied those gorgeous full lips that easily turned up in a playful smile. He'd gotten shivers every time she'd graced him with one. It would be torture to watch her mouth close around— *Chill, Spence.* Just because he hadn't been with anyone in a while didn't mean he should get a hard-on for the first beautiful woman he'd met in New Orleans.

"Watch the expert"—she encouraged him to lean in closer—"show you how it's done."

That was a request he couldn't turn down. The chair scraped the concrete as he scooted it closer to her. Now he sat next to her instead of across the table. He was close enough to smell her perfume. Something spicy *and* sweet.

She brought the treat closer to her mouth. Why couldn't he keep his eyes off her mouth? He studied her dark amber eyes with flecks of brown that glinted with a splash of trouble. Good trouble, he hoped.

Right at that moment, she blew on her beignet. A snow shower of powder floated up, but most of it shot right into his face. He gasped in shock. Also a rookie error. The sugar coated his mouth. Flew up his nose. He coughed. She'd pranked him! And he fell for it.

"Oh, shit." She pulled the napkins out of her shirt and waved them in the air to dissipate the cloud between them. "I didn't realize it would fly everywhere!"

When his coughing didn't subside, she pressed the Styrofoam cup of milky coffee into his hand.

"Drink," she commanded.

He did.

"That's the second time you tried to kill me today," he said accusingly after he'd caught his breath.

"I did not try to kill—"

"You did! But I forgive you." He pinched some sugar between his fingers and tossed it at her face. "Now we're even."

She gasped but laughed with him.

"This is the most fun I've had in a long time. I'm glad I almost killed you with my beads."

"She has confessed!"

Josie stuck her tongue out at him.

"You have sugar on your—" He reached out to her slowly, giving her time to wipe her own face. But she didn't. She sat still, hands in her lap, and lifted her face to him. "Nose."

He rubbed the powder off with his thumb and slid it across her cheek. She leaned into the caress.

"I want to kiss you," he whispered.

Her eyes shined.

"What are you waiting for?"

CHAPTER 5

Josie closed her eyes as their lips met. After their flirting, his touch electrified her. Tingles like the ones she'd only read about shot down her body. She sighed into his mouth. Taking that as encouragement, he deepened the kiss.

She opened herself to him. Josie luxuriated in exploring his warm, firm lips that tasted of sugar and coffee sprinkled with fun and confidence. It had been a long time since she'd allowed herself to have fun and to go with the flow.

The noise around her faded as she pulled him closer and ran her fingers through his silky hair. He groaned. His mouth became more insistent, as if mapping every curve of her lips. She relished knowing that her touch affected him so strongly.

Here she was in a new city kissing a man she'd met only a few hours before. A man she'd wanted to kiss ever since she set eyes on his handsome jawline. The cloud of sugar surrounding them made the kiss even more magical. Was she hearing music? This entire evening was surreal, like something from the romance books the Babes passed around.

Wait, there *was* music. It was getting louder, as if someone was walking toward them. The tune was vaguely familiar. Was that a—

"What the hell," Spencer mumbled against her lips, and broke off their kiss. The blond busker wearing a cowboy hat whom she'd seen earlier was standing outside the patio area and serenading them with his acoustic guitar. The people around them clapped and cheered.

Josie sat back, embarrassed. Her heart was still pounding. She couldn't remember the last time a kiss made her feel so—what? Lost. No—free.

It was strange to feel so unburdened and currently be responsible for no one but herself. There were so many things she could do this week that the possibilities overwhelmed her. She distracted herself from those thoughts by taking a swig of her now-cold coffee. It was nothing a list couldn't fix.

"If I tip you will you stop singing 'Just the Way You Are'?" Spencer grumbled and stuffed some cash into the musician's hand, forcing him to stop strumming his guitar. The guy tipped his cowboy hat and walked off.

"You're an adorable grump. Who doesn't like Bruno Mars?"

"That was a cover. If it were actually Bruno, I'd let him serenade us while we made out all night." He blushed. "I mean if you wanted to."

Oh, she wanted to. But was it the best decision to have a week-long fling and then fly back to DC? It sounded like he planned to stay in New Orleans for much longer. There was no future here, and Josie didn't like unknowns. She needed lists and check boxes to stay focused.

"What are we doing, Spencer?" No point in beating around the bush.

"What do you mean?" He was taken aback by her question. "We're having fun. Two adults enjoying themselves."

"Sorry, that came out wrong." She avoided his eyes by dusting the sugar off her shirt. How could a grown woman like her be so awkward? "What I meant to say is that I don't usually kiss someone I've known for only an hour."

"Me neither, but we crossed paths for a reason. Clearly there's chemistry between us, so why not see it through?" He leaned back in his chair and propped a foot up on the railing that separated the patio from the rest of Jackson Square. "You can't deny that this is a little magical."

She bit her lip, annoyed that she agreed with him. He must have seen her wavering.

"I don't want you to do anything you're not a hundred percent on. Just say the word, and I'll walk away." He crossed his arms and tipped his chair back so it was balanced on its two back legs. "But you'll always wonder what could've been between us."

He was pretty sure of himself. But he was also right. She didn't want him to walk away yet. She didn't know how Spencer Pham fit into her life right now, but as her friend Reina often reminded her, Josie had to trust her gut more often.

"You're not showing any signs of a concussion, so there's no reason for me to stay." Her gut—and lower—desperately wanted him to stay. "But I can stay until we finish eating."

"I'll take it." This time he took a big bite out of his beignet, disregarding all the "rules" he'd taught her earlier. He didn't even look at the sugar raining down on his clothes.

"There's something called napkins, you know." She handed him some.

"I think I'm past the point of no return." He stood up and brushed off his shirt and jeans.

She couldn't help but snap some photos of him. Patches of white dusted his chest and sleeves. He looked like he'd lost a fight with Tinker Bell's cousin the Fried Bread Fairy.

"You're so comfortable with a camera." He sat back down and peered at her phone. "Any tips for an aspiring filmmaker?"

"I take stills, so I'm not sure how much of what I learned applies to filmmaking." She'd never taken formal classes but tried to remember what her mentor—her old boss—had taught her. "Tell me about your film. Is that what you meant by B-roll earlier at the parade?"

"My grandmother tells these fantastic stories about her life with my grandfather right after they immigrated here. He and his friends founded the Krewe of Saigon, the first all–Vietnamese American krewe in New Orleans!" He puffed out his chest proudly. "He passed away when I was little, so I don't remember everything he told me. People need to hear his story and how the Vietnamese people are a vital part of this community."

"Wow. He sounds like a trailblazer."

"He was. Can you imagine being a refugee starting over in a place where you don't know the language and founding a krewe?" Spencer's voice held awe and reverence for his grandfather.

"Sounds like my parents. No matter how hard life was, they managed to find joy in their lives."

Her mom and dad had worked their asses off to provide for her and her younger sister. Yet her mom always made time to bake cakes for neighbors' birthdays or church potlucks. She even started a spades club that turned into a weekly social gathering. Josie, who honed her card-playing skills by watching her mother, had recently been inducted into it.

"I have no idea how long my film will take to shoot, but maybe you could help while you're here. When do you turn into a pumpkin?"

"Seven days." She'd almost given up and taken a flight back home that morning. Instead, she went to a parade. And hit him. In return he gave her a little tour through the French Quarter and kissed her sugarcoated lips.

What if she found someone to have a little fun with? Just for the time she was here. Spencer could be that someone. It was obvious they had chemistry. And she had an entire apartment to herself.

She could write a list a mile long on why spending more time with him wasn't a good idea, yet none of the reasons was as compelling as checking *Help someone follow their dream* off her 30 by 30 list. Especially someone as hot and charming as Spencer.

CHAPTER 6

"Are you planning on exploring New Orleans all alone?" Even before their kiss, Spencer wanted to know everything about her. Maybe he'd learn something that could convince her to stay.

"How did you know that I'm here alone?"

"First, you told me your client canceled. And the entire time we've been together, you never once mentioned that a friend or companion was waiting for you. Or might want to join us for beignets."

"Oh, so now you're a detective. Where's your tiny notebook and spyglass?"

"You're not getting away that easily." He admired how she deftly used humor to deflect personal questions.

"Yes, it's just me on this trip, but you already know that wasn't my original plan. The entire thing has been a soap opera." She sighed and crossed her legs.

"Can't be anything as convoluted as the Chinese dramas my grandmother loves. Dubbed in Vietnamese, of course." He never turned her down when she asked him to watch with her. As bananas as the plots were, he couldn't pull himself away.

"The brides have known each other since high school, but both moved to DC separately for their jobs and became reacquainted," Josie began. She recounted their romantic proposal where both brides surprised each other at the National Zoo with a ring. Unfortunately, Josie wasn't sure what caused their last-minute broken engagement and now-canceled bachelorette party.

"Wow. So you've known them since they met?"

"Funny enough, they each secretly hired me to photograph the proposal." Josie chuckled. "You should've seen the look on their faces when they both pulled out a ring!"

"You win. That's almost as good as my grandmother's soaps."

"And that's how I decided to stay in New Orleans and finish checking off my thirty by thirty list."

"What's that?"

"A few years ago, my friends and I came up with a list of thirty things we want to do by the time we turn thirty years old." She pulled out a well-worn leather notebook and flipped it open. At the top of the page in neat handwriting was *30 Things to Do by the Time I'm Thirty*. As far as he could tell, all but a handful of items had been checked off.

"You're so close to finishing. When do you turn thirty?"

"I turned thirty last month." She shrugged. "Technically, the list says thirty *by* thirty. As long as I finish it before my next birthday, it counts." She crossed her arms as if daring him to contest her logic.

"Okay, chill. I'm not the list police. It sounds supercool, actually." He wondered if he would've done more meaningful things if he'd made a list like hers. "So what's on it?"

"It's private." She held the notebook to her chest.

"Come on, we shared one of the best kisses of my life. That's gotta mean something."

"Best kisses of your life?" She raised an eyebrow.

"Need a refresher?" He arched his in return.

Her lips twitched. Spencer leaned closer, hoping she'd close the distance between them. She did not.

"Number twenty-one was to attend a Mardi Gras parade in New Orleans." She pointed to a line in her notebook.

"Why did you choose Mardi Gras as opposed to Carnival in Brazil or the Caribbean? Besides New Orleans being the best city in the world, of course."

"DC is the best city in the world, I'll have you know. But I chose Mardi Gras because one of my best friends grew up here. I thought it would make for a fun girls' trip, but we couldn't make it work with everyone's schedules."

"See? New Orleans is better with company."

"I did a quick search on my phone to locate one near me," she continued, without acknowledging his last remark. "But I'm trying to be more spontaneous while I'm here."

He snorted. "Researching online isn't very spontaneous."

"Well, deciding to attend it at the last minute was! You already know what happened after that."

"How could I forget?" He slid his hand across his temple. It was swollen. "Is there a big project you're working on? Because of your list?"

"As much as I love my job and my boudoir photography

studio, it's become so mundane. Zoe, one of my best friends, says I'm burned out." Her shoulders sagged. "I think she's right."

"Most people wouldn't consider boudoir photography mundane. However, New Orleans will reawaken your muse. This city is full of history and so much culture to photograph!" Spencer cringed at his over-the-top sales pitch. When had he made himself an ambassador for the city? Maybe he did have a concussion.

"That's what I'm hoping. I want to cross off the number one item on my list. My plan for tomorrow is making a list of places to visit based on research and friends' recommendations."

"What's number one on your list?"

"Submit my photos to Stevens Art Gallery back home. As soon as I figure out what to include in my portfolio." His face must have been blank, because she added, "It's one of the top photography galleries in DC. Rumor is the majority of their customers are either celebrities or live on Capitol Hill."

"That sounds cool, but you must have a lot of photos already. Why not your boudoir photos?" He hadn't seen any of her work, but her talent was obvious in the quick shots she'd taken on their walk to the café. At least the ones he'd happen to peek at over her shoulder.

"I'd never do that without my clients' permission. I want to do something different. I've been photographing weddings and boudoir sessions for most of my adult life. Maybe surrounding myself with the history here will make my work more art gallery worthy. Once I figure out what that really means." Her fingers twitched nervously against her thigh as if she wanted to pick up her camera again.

"Maybe I can help."

Spencer needed to find a way to see her after tonight. He didn't like how she was making plans and he wasn't part of them. But what did he have to offer that she couldn't refuse?

"You don't even know me. Why would you help?" Josie asked.

For a second Spencer wondered the same thing. What the hell was he doing offering someone he barely knew help with her 30 by 30 list? Maybe he missed spending time with people who weren't his family. He'd gone from living alone in his tiny DC apartment to being back in his parents' three-bedroom duplex where his parents and grandmother followed his every move.

Or maybe he wasn't ready to let Josie out of his life just yet.

"Let's call it Southern hospitality."

"You said you grew up here, right?" Josie's eyes flitted left to right as if ideas were flying through her head at fifty miles per hour.

"Born and raised." Spencer nodded then straightened in his chair. She knew how to work a camera, and it'd been years since his last film class. Maybe—

"What if we help each other out?" they both said simultaneously.

Goose bumps ran down his arms. Could they be on the same wavelength?

"You first," Josie said. She was on the edge of her chair.

"What if I show you all my favorite places for your photos? The insider track."

"And I'll help you with your film while I'm here!" Josie flashed him another one of her beautiful smiles. "You'll talk to lots of interesting people for it, right?"

"I plan on it. I wouldn't mind borrowing your eye for composition. And maybe you can be my camera operator until I replace my phone?" It was a big ask, but they weren't strangers anymore after sharing a sugary kiss. Correction: a sugary kiss that rocked his world.

She bit her lip as she considered his request. He could feel her earlier excitement wavering, as if using her camera was a step too far.

"We can film on your camera until—"

"Spencer Pham, dude! I've been looking all over for you."

"Jimmy Bui?" Spencer jerked his head toward the tall Southeast Asian man standing where the busker had been not too long ago.

"That's Dr. James Bui to you," he said in a joking tone. He turned to Josie and offered his hand. "But the lady can call me Jimmy."

"Stop being an ass," Spencer barked before Josie could respond. He glared at his friend, then lightly punched him in the arm. They both laughed as if that's how they usually greeted each other. "Josie, this is my friend from high school, Jimmy. Josie and I met at a parade tonight."

"Nice to meet you. I was the scrawny kid that followed him and his sisters around back in the day." Jimmy smiled at Josie, then said to Spencer, "I can see why you skipped out on dinner with your grandmother."

"Shut up. I texted Nina about it. It's fine," Spencer retorted quickly.

"Speaking of your sister, I'm here because Nina called me. She said something about how you lost your phone and I should find your ass before she kicks mine."

Spencer bit back a laugh, even though he was annoyed at Jimmy's interruption. For as long as he could remember, his friend had crushed on his sister. Hard. Except Jimmy was a tiny bit afraid of Nina, the youngest but also the bossiest of his sisters.

Jimmy tapped his watch. "You better get home before your sister gets pissed and rats you out to your parents."

Spencer turned from Jimmy to Josie and back again. He groaned inwardly. Whatever magic they held had disappeared when Jimmy interrupted them. Spencer's shoulders drooped.

"I'm really sorry. I have to go."

"Oh." Josie's face fell.

The evening with her had made up for getting lost in a Mardi Gras crowd and being hit by beads. They'd had so much fun in the past couple of hours. Now it was ending before he'd convinced her to let him help with her list. She'd been so close to agreeing, but Jimmy was right. He'd promised his parents he'd take care of his grandmother this week.

"My offer still stands. Text my sister Nina and she'll give you my number. That's who I texted from your phone." Spencer downed the rest of his coffee. He gave her a quick kiss on the cheek as Jimmy dragged him away.

"Sorry, Josie. It was nice to meet you!" Jimmy waved. She

nodded and smiled. Not to be outdone, Spencer stepped in between them and waved at Josie, too.

"She seems nice," said Jimmy.

"Josie's more than nice. She's smart and gorgeous." Spencer had no idea if he'd hear from Josie, but if he did, he wouldn't waste any time asking her out again.

CHAPTER 7

"You interrupted us," Spencer grumbled as he followed Jimmy to his car. "Josie and I were having a moment."

"Sorry, Spence. I promised Nina I'd give you a ride home. She was worried after you texted her from someone else's phone." Jimmy's sedan beeped as he unlocked it.

Spencer slid into the front seat and buckled his seat belt. What's done was done now. He was grateful to get a ride back with Jimmy instead of shelling out for a taxi or Lyft.

"What happened to your head? Do you want me to look at it?" Jimmy turned on the interior dome light and peered at his temple.

His slacker high school friend had gotten his act together and become a freaking medical doctor. Spencer was only a little bit jealous. All Viet moms of single daughters must have rejoiced when Jimmy got his degree. Spencer was glad he wasn't a hot commodity in the Viet Auntie Network's informal matchmaking service.

"I'm fine except for the biggest headache ever." Spencer touched his head and hissed. "I lied. It fucking hurts."

"You should've gotten medical attention instead of flirting in the Quarter." Jimmy held up his hand and gestured toward Spencer's head. "May I?"

Spencer nodded. Jimmy grabbed some gloves from a bag in the back seat. "So how did you receive this beauty?"

"I was taking a video of the parade, dodging drunks. Then—*bam*—beaned in the head with beads." Spencer gritted his teeth as Jimmy pressed around the goose egg on his head. "Turns out the hottest woman in the universe was on the other end of the beads. So I asked her out."

"Did she agree because she felt bad about hitting your sorry ass?"

"Ha-ha. No. She said yes because I'm charming. Fuck that hurts!" Spencer gripped the door handle. "You did that on purpose."

"Sorry. I needed to palpate it." Jimmy leaned back in his seat and pulled off his gloves. "I don't think you have a concussion, as your ability to curse me out isn't impaired. But the bruise will look even nastier tomorrow."

"Thanks. I'm glad it's not serious." Spencer meant it. He hadn't stayed connected with a lot of friends when he moved to DC, but he had with Jimmy. Being able to hang with Jimmy made moving back home a little less depressing. "Sorry Nina made you hunt me down. How'd you know where to find me?"

"Dude, every time you ask for a ride into the city, you have me drop you off at Jackson Square. It doesn't take a genius to smell the beignets on your clothes. Text Nina and tell her we'll be at your parents' soon."

Jimmy tossed his phone to Spencer before easing the car out of the parking space. Spencer did as he was told while his friend maneuvered around tourists crossing in the middle of the street instead of waiting for the crosswalk like sensible human beings.

"Couldn't you take her somewhere with *good* beignets instead? Somewhere less touristy. Like Cafe Beignet." Jimmy shook his head.

"Hey, I like the beignets at Cafe du Monde! Besides, everyone should experience the rickety metal chairs and wobbly tables at least once."

Spencer preferred the anonymity of sitting among strangers who eagerly stuffed fried, sugary dough into their mouths and washed it down with café au lait. No one made fun of him for being Asian. No asshole classmates who muttered some fake Asian language under their breath when he passed them in the hallway. People assumed he was a tourist and left him alone.

"Those tables are still the worst! And the napkins are so thin, you need a giant stack just to fit under the wobbly leg."

"The more things change, huh?" Spencer smiled, glad that one of his favorite places in his hometown had remained mostly the same while he'd been away. "I took her there because it was on her list of places to visit. And I happen to be a regular."

Jimmy snorted. "Prepare yourself. Nina will read you the riot act when you get home. Apparently she had to cancel her date because of you."

Spencer frowned. Crap, he'd forgotten about that. "But I have a good excuse."

"It's gonna take us forever to get out of the Quarter with all the Mardi Gras tourists, so you have time to prepare your apology," Jimmy said. He added, "I'll vouch for your head injury."

It took them a while to navigate away from the French Quarter to the interstate that lead them to the outer suburbs. After the war, many Vietnamese refugees had gone to California or Florida. What many people didn't know was that some of them had made their way to Louisiana. Once they'd settled down, friends and family joined them. It was a familiar immigrant story, but he was proud of how his people thrived in New Orleans.

Many of them, like Spencer's grandfather, were able to continue their work as fishermen, while others embraced the opportunity to forge a new path in a new country. They were placed in Section 8 housing at the Versailles Arms Apartments. The community eventually was dubbed Versailles by its residents, whether they lived in those apartments or not.

"What's this about taking parade video? Are you working on another film?" Jimmy asked him once they were cruising at a steady speed.

"Bà Bà was talking about the Krewe of Saigon again, so I thought a short documentary about it would make a good present for her one hundredth birthday." Spencer hadn't considered it for her birthday that morning, but it seemed like a good idea now.

"What about your film about the Viet fishermen?"

"I got seasick."

"History of the church that sponsored our community here?"

"All the aunties brought their daughters to their interviews. It turned into a marriage mart." Spencer rolled his eyes.

"The V.A.N. strikes again. You're lucky you're not a doctor

like me. I run the other direction when I see the aunties dragging their daughters my way."

"Maybe they need medical advice?" Spencer chuckled, glad he had escaped what they jokingly called the Vietnamese Auntie Network since he'd returned home. No matter what happened in their community, the aunties managed to sniff out the latest gossip and kept tabs on who was dating whom. Spencer had not missed them while he was in DC.

"That's almost as bad!" Jimmy groaned. "You know how hard it is to tell an auntie or uncle that I don't want to look at their rash?"

"Gross."

"Exactly. So you gave up on the fishermen and church history films. What about the unknown Viet fusion restaurants one?"

"I need to be inspired. I saved the footage for all the other ideas, so they're not going anywhere."

"Are you sure that's why you keep changing your film topic?" Jimmy asked. "Maybe you should enjoy your time off awhile instead of cramming it full of projects."

"Is that what my family is saying about all my ideas?"

Jimmy's silence was the confirmation he needed.

"I'm going to prove to them that I can become a filmmaker." Making a film, even a short one, was a big commitment. He had to make sure he was passionate enough about the subject before he dedicated so much time to it.

"It's okay if you don't know what you want to do right now," Jimmy added.

"I do know what I want to do. I want to make this film for Bà

Bà's milestone birthday celebration. It's also the church's big Tết festival, so it's a gift for our community as well."

Spencer would finish the film by his grandmother's birthday. He'd prove to Jimmy and his family that he could succeed in something artistic and make them proud.

CHAPTER 8

A rumbling sensation in her abdomen stirred Josie.

"Five more minutes," she mumbled without opening her eyes. She pulled the blanket over her head and groaned. Her stomach was mad at her for eating only beignets last night instead of something heartier.

Josie's eyes flew open. Last night she'd kissed a man she'd only known for an hour. She touched her lips. Maybe it had been a dream? She unlocked her phone and scrolled through her photos.

Spencer—and that kiss—*was* real.

She had no regrets. He was attractive and more exciting than anyone she'd met recently, but she didn't come to New Orleans to hook up. Today she had a city to see and a list of items to check off.

She grabbed her notebook from the nightstand and traced the big teal circle around the first item on the list:

Submit my portfolio to Stevens Art Gallery.

Spencer did have a good idea. Capturing the lesser-known cultural history was a smart strategy to get her work accepted by the gallery. That meant exploring the areas of New Orleans most tourists didn't visit. The city was big, and she wasn't sure where to begin.

Time to call in the calvary—after she washed her face and brushed her teeth. Trixie Nguyen grew up here, and Reina Guidroz attended college in New Orleans. She sent a 911 text to the Boss Babes' group chat. Within seconds, her phone rang. One by one, her friends joined the group video call.

"How's New Orleans?" Reina exaggerated her Southern drawl and pronounced the city name as if it were one word. "Have you gotten laid yet?"

"She's there for work." Trixie chided the redhead but laughed. Reina wasn't known for her filter.

"All work and no play makes for a boring life," Reina shot back.

Josie pursed her lips. Life had been "exciting" twelve years ago when her younger sister, Tasha, was hospitalized after being struck by a hit-and-run driver. The accident and hospital bills had almost cost her parents their house. If keeping her family healthy and having financial security meant she was boring, so be it.

"It's only boring to you, Reina. Everyone has different priori-ties." Trixie shook her head at Reina.

"Tell us about your first day there," Zoe Tran asked, ignor-ing the other two's bickering. Zoe cleared her throat loudly. Her friends quieted down and smiled at Josie expectantly.

Time to spill the beans.

"I sort of met a guy during the Mardi Gras parade yesterday," Josie said sheepishly.

Her friends starting speaking all at once. Josie took the time to adjust her pillows and sit up in bed.

"Shush!" Zoe finally called out. "Let Josie talk."

"Wait, is that why you're still in bed past noon?" Keisha Walker asked. She co-owned a soul food restaurant, Hazel's Kitchen, with her brother, Andre, who happened to be Trixie's boyfriend. "This really is an emergency!"

"I did get up to brush my teeth before calling you. I still have my manners. You should be glad I thought of you as soon as I woke up." Josie smoothed the satin bonnet covering her hair and rubbed her eyes, which were still bleary from sleep. "I was out late with Spencer."

"Is he hot?" Reina craned her neck for a glimpse around Josie. "Is Spencer still there?"

"Yes, he's hot. You know I don't do one-night stands, but we did kiss at Cafe du Monde."

Reina applauded. "I'm proud of you!"

"Who are you and what have you done with Josie?" Trixie teased.

"Back up. I thought you were following a client around town for her bachelorette party," Zoe said, then quickly added, "I'm glad you're having fun."

"My plans changed as soon as I landed at the airport." She filled them in on her client's broken engagement and the canceled destination photoshoot. "She told me to keep the apartment since it was already paid for. Mom and Tasha convinced me to turn this trip into a vacation."

Everyone nodded in agreement. They knew Josie had been on the verge of burnout.

"I need your help." Josie squared her shoulders. "My plan is to eat, walk, and take photos that have nothing to do with work."

"I'm so glad you're putting yourself first finally." Trixie smiled wistfully. "I wish I was there to show you all my favorite places."

"If you need recommendations, I have a few restaurants you could visit and do some recon for me," Keisha suggested. She was constantly studying the latest trends to see if they'd be useful for her restaurant.

"I'm glad you're taking a break, Josie. You've been working super hard," Zoe said. "I'm envious that you're on an artist's vacation!"

"Yeah, yeah, creativity is great, but orgasms are even more relaxing," Reina said pointedly. "You should spend more time with that Spencer guy."

"So I need your help for something important," Josie repeated, ignoring Reina. "I need recs on what parts of the city to see. The less touristy the better."

Zoe gasped. "I know that look. What are you planning?"

Josie bit her lip, trying to rein in her excitement. She didn't want to get her hopes up before she'd even started. "I'm ready to build my portfolio to submit to Stevens Art Gallery and finally check it off my thirty by thirty list."

"Oh, how about a photo series about our regulars and their

favorite DC foods. You can do the shoot at the restaurant." Keisha's face lit up. "You know they have some good stories."

They all chuckled, having been subjected to many tales while dining at the restaurant. It wasn't a bad idea, but if Josie were to stay in New Orleans for the week, she wanted to make it a productive week.

"Your boudoir work *is* art. Even if you take other photos, you should include some boudoir stuff in your portfolio to show your range," Reina said.

"Reina's right," Trixie added. "Maybe you can do a collab with Zoe and her couture designs."

"I love that you love my boudoir photography, but I don't think the gallery will appreciate my current work. They probably want something more artsy? I was thinking something different. A change from my usual style. You know, people with more clothes on. Maybe some landscapes."

"If they don't like it, they don't deserve to show your work!" Reina tossed her hair. "We can make a fuss if they discriminate against your photos."

"Whoa, Reina." Josie chuckled. "You're jumping way ahead. I want to take this week to explore new subjects. Stretch my creative muscles a bit."

"I think it's a fabulous idea. I know how easy it can be to fall into a rut." As a lingerie designer, Zoe was familiar with the ups and downs of creativity.

"Maybe you'll meet a hot guy or gal to photograph—on the streets and in the sheets." Reina waggled her eyebrows and laughed at her own joke.

"You talk about sex more than me. And I sell vibrators," Trixie said, and rolled her eyes.

"It's because she hasn't gotten any in forever," Keisha teased.

Reina huffed before pressing her lips together.

"How can we help you?" Trixie asked Josie, ignoring Reina's dramatics. "Do you want me to catch the next flight to New Orleans?"

Josie laughed at their banter and suddenly wished they were here with her. Though she had a feeling Reina would lead them on a weeklong pub crawl and she wouldn't be taking many photo walks.

"No, I want to do this on my own." Trixie was right. It'd been ages since Josie had focused on her needs instead of taking care of her sister, Tasha, and mothering the Boss Babes.

Her friends nodded in encouragement.

"I need suggestions for some off-the-beaten-path places," Josie continued. She leaned her phone against the bowl of fake fruit on the coffee table and grabbed her notebook and fountain pen. "Give it to me."

They debated over the best places for Josie to explore. After fifteen minutes, the group had narrowed down the list to seven places. One for each day of her trip plus a few as backup in case of rain. There was nothing Josie loved more than having a plan and a list to check off.

A weight had lifted from Josie's shoulders after talking to her friends. The Babes' energy made her feel as if she could accomplish anything. She was determined to take the best photos of her life to get into that gallery.

"Now that you have your list, we have more important matters to discuss," Reina announced. "How did you meet this Spencer?"

"Yes, we need pictures," Keisha added.

"Last night was so magical. I'll never do that again, but at least I have memories and pictures." Josie's cheeks hurt, her smile was so wide. She texted pictures of Spencer to the Boss Babes. Appreciative murmurs circulated among her friends.

"I can finally check off the one item Reina made me add to my list," Josie said.

"Come on, kissing a hot stranger is fun!" Reina winked. "But tell us how you met."

She grabbed the giant lavender beads off the nightstand and explained how she'd hit him. Then dove straight into her spontaneous date.

"Well, that's a creative way to get someone to pay attention to you. And you kissed. It's like something out of a romance novel," Zoe said, and clasped her hands to her chest.

"Are you going to see him again?" Keisha asked.

"Of course not. He doesn't have a job and doesn't know how to do what he wants to do next." Josie didn't know what she wanted to do next, either, but that didn't mean she planned to sell her studio and run off to another state.

"We're not saying you have to marry him, Josie." Zoe chuckled.

"It's been a long time since you've been so excited about someone," Trixie reminded her in a gentle tone.

They were referring to her last relationship, but Josie didn't want to talk about the past. It was better to focus on the future, because she could actually do something about it.

"Think of it as a seven-day mindset experience. Like those books you have us read. See if you can spend the next week being present in the moment, and have some fun." Zoe may have been quieter than the rest of the Babes, but she knew how to ease Josie out of her comfort zone.

"I'll try." Seven days wasn't a long time. She'd already started her vacation by doing something new. Josie just needed to use her list as her guide and keep the momentum going.

"If you're ever unsure, ask yourself: WWRD?" Reina suggested.

"WWRD?" Keisha asked. She was the newest in the group and was still learning the Babes' lingo.

"It means: *What Would Reina Do?*" Zoe and Trixie answered at the same time.

"Oh." Keisha's eyes narrowed. "That sounds intense. Maybe take it down a notch?"

Everyone cracked up, even Reina. She was the most impulsive of the Boss Babes. Basically the opposite of Josie.

When they finally hung up, Josie's sides ached from all the laughter. Her friends always made her feel better. Even though she was starting the day late, she now had a list of places off the beaten track to explore.

At the bottom of her Adventures in New Orleans list, she added *Be more spontaneous.*

CHAPTER 9

W hat happened to your head?" Spencer's grandmother asked in Vietnamese from across the table.

"Bà Bà, I'm fine," Spencer replied in Vietnamese.

Her eyes narrowed from behind her mug of jasmine tea. She didn't believe him, but she didn't push.

Spencer swallowed a yawn. It had been late by the time Jimmy dropped him off. Wired from the café au lait and ideas for his film, he snuck past Nina asleep on the couch and into his childhood bedroom. He'd scribbled down ideas until he'd fallen asleep with his notebook in his hand.

But he still woke up early to heat up breakfast for Bà Bà. She was his most favorite person in the world, and he'd promised his parents he'd take care of her during the two weeks they were out of town.

"Would you like more rice or tea?" he asked.

"Maybe later. Did you get into a fight?" She set down her mug and reached for his hand.

Oh, she was really worried about him.

"No, just an accident with a tourist yesterday." Spencer switched to English because he'd forgotten the Vietnamese word for *tour-ist*. "But Jimmy brought me home last night. He said I was fine."

That seemed to placate her. She gestured for him to help her into the living room, where she watched her favorite Viet-dubbed dramas.

"I'm glad we have a young doctor in our neighborhood, since we don't have one in the family."

"Bà Bà, not this again."

"Everyone wants to marry a doctor. I want great-grandchildren before I die. So it's up to you and your sisters."

"Bà Bà, don't say that. You're not dying anytime soon," he protested. This time *he* was the one who was worried about *her*. The last time he'd come home for vacation she'd been much lighter on her feet. Now that he was living with her, the changes were even more noticeable.

Her skin had gotten paler. Her hair seemed even whiter than he remembered, though any hint of gray had disappeared from her hair before he moved again ten years ago. Her clothes hung off her shoulders. Bà had grown so much older and smaller while he was away. Her one hundredth birthday was only a few weeks away, and he wanted to spend as much time as he could with her.

One thing that hadn't changed, though, was her favorite recliner, which was placed in the prime spot for TV viewing. The ratty chair was literally falling apart. Before he'd moved away, the arms had been rubbed so thin the stuffing was falling out of them. She'd sewn covers for them instead of getting rid of the chair. But there wasn't much she could do to fix the thinning cushions or sagging seat.

Every Christmas he offered to replace it. She turned him down every time, citing it as a connection to his grandfather. He'd gifted it to her when his family saved enough money for their own apartment, instead of relying on the church's charity. He found the chair at a garage sale for five bucks and repaired it in secret. Eventually, Spencer's offer and his grandmother's rejection became a tradition. An inside joke of sorts.

After helping her into her recliner, he spread a blanket over her lap and tucked a pillow behind her head. She often dozed in her chair but refused to admit she'd fallen asleep. It took him a few days to learn to give her the blanket and pillow beforehand.

"You haven't eaten. Go, I have my shows." She waved him away.

Spencer chuckled as he made his way back to the kitchen. Some days he wasn't sure who was taking care of whom. Most days they ate breakfast together, but he'd scrambled to reheat the thịt kho trứng before she woke. She must've cooked it with Nina yesterday.

One good thing about moving home was the food. He'd ordered takeout from many Vietnamese restaurants in DC, but none of them made caramelized pork belly like his grandmother and mom. Assuming they even had it on their menu. The humble dish was considered home cooking and not something normally sold at restaurants.

He dished up a large bowl of rice with the pork belly. He opened his notebook and attempted to decipher his frenzied notes from the previous night. If Jimmy thought he'd flaked out on his other film ideas, then his family's opinion would be harsher.

He wouldn't give them a chance to criticize him about his

Krewe of Saigon film. Bà Bà would support him. She was the one who gave him the idea in the first place.

"Anh hai!" Nina's cheery voice interrupted his brainstorming session.

Maybe if he squeezed his eyes shut, he could pretend she wasn't there.

"Yo, big bro." Crap. Rose was here, too? That could only mean—

"Spence, it's time for an intervention."

Yup, that was Cynthia. All of his sisters were here. He opened one eye. He was surrounded.

"Why do I need an intervention?"

All three women exchanged looks. His sisters were close in age and had learned to communicate with one another without using words. Especially in front of him.

"You need a job," blurted Cynthia, the second youngest of his sisters. He could count on her to cut to the chase.

"My job for the rest of the week is taking care of Bà Bà." And working on his film.

"Obviously not this week," said Rose. "But you can start applying now and start when our parents get back."

"I've worked at the same job for ten years. I deserve a break."

"You've been here a month now—that's a long enough break. You're just being a bum." Cynthia swiped at his hair. "You need a haircut. Who do you think you are? Keanu Reeves?"

"Stop that! I like my hair." Spencer brushed his hair out of his eyes, but it only flopped back down again. So, maybe he did need a haircut, but he wasn't admitting that to his sisters.

"Anh hai." Nina used *that* voice. The one that had him

wrapped around her little finger. "We're worried. You left Bà Bà alone all day to wander around the French Quarter. Then you missed dinner."

"I'm sorry you had to cancel your date, Nina. I owe you one."

"Nah, it's fine. Mẹ set me up with one of her friend's sons or something like that. Thank God I had a good excuse to cancel."

Cynthia turned to Nina. "You didn't tell us that!" Spencer was also surprised that Nina hadn't told them about their mother's matchmaking attempts. The three sisters lived together, so there was very little they didn't share with one another.

"Focus. We're here for Spencer," said Rose. She turned back to him. "You need to stop moping around and do something, anything, to get out of this house."

"That's where you're wrong." Spencer held up his notebook. "I'm working on a present for Bà Bà's birthday."

"Not another film idea." Cynthia groaned. "How many have you abandoned?"

"They're on the back burner, simmering." He'd lost interest in them, but that didn't mean he couldn't revisit those projects.

"Our parents are also worried about you, but they're trying to give you space," said Rose. "Don't make Ba Mẹ worry more than normal."

"You're wandering around like a lost puppy, and a job could help. You could do anything. It doesn't have to be a career," suggested Nina.

"I *am* doing something. I've been researching the history of Krewe of Saigon." He flipped to his notes to prove his point. "Let me do this for Bà Bà's birthday party."

Another round of glances was exchanged among his sisters. Finally, they all nodded in agreement.

"We figured you'd have a reason to avoid getting a job. So, here's the deal," said Rose. "Promise you'll start applying for jobs now so you can have interviews lined up after Bà Bà's party."

He nodded. That didn't sound so bad.

"And you have to take over the rest of our shifts at the farming co-op until our parents get back," Cynthia added.

"All of them?" He'd killed every houseplant he'd owned. Working on a farm sounded harder than watering a tiny succulent. "And if I don't?"

"If you don't follow through, we're going to tell Mẹ you're ready to settle down and get married," Cynthia said, and smirked.

"She'll activate the Viet Auntie Network and have dates lined up for months!" Rose had to rub salt into the ultimatum.

He gasped. "You wouldn't! That's really low. I would never do that to you."

"Desperate times call for deperate measures," said Rose.

Spencer never won when they joined forces against him.

"Fine. I'll take your co-op shifts." Spencer sighed. "I'd say text me the details, but I need to buy a new phone first."

"Good, now that that's settled, what the hell happened to your head?" demanded Cynthia.

CHAPTER 10

Look for the unusual but capture the everyday.

Josie repeated her mentor's mantra whenever she took a photo walk. Her rental apartment was smack-dab in the middle of the colorful Marigny neighborhood. Her cabdriver yesterday had gently corrected her pronunciation to "MARE-uh-nee."

The houses and buildings were painted in bright blues, yellows, greens, pinks—all fun, energizing colors. There were murals on the sides of buildings, fences, and the walls in between stores and bars. She nodded her head and tapped her feet to the jazz coming out of bustling bars on Frenchmen Street. She wished she could photograph the sound of music, but she had to settle for capturing the musicians' energy and the mood they created.

With each block she photographed, her heart grew lighter. The fresh air had cleared her head. It was better to ease into her surroundings instead of diving into the deep end of Mardi Gras with hardly any planning. Perhaps she could avoid inflicting bodily harm on anyone today.

Had Spencer woken up with a splitting headache this morning? She hoped not. Josie shook her head. She had to forget about him and focus on her portfolio. Getting into the gallery would open up a completely different world for her work and push her to grow as an artist. She had more important things to do than pine over a guy she barely knew.

While she normally wandered on her photo walks, today she made her way to Baldwin & Co. per her mother's request. The bookstore was named after her mother's favorite author, James Baldwin. Not only did her mom want souvenirs, but Josie was instructed to text photos of the store. Outside *and* inside.

"Why couldn't she just google pictures?" Josie muttered to herself. Still, she pulled out her phone to photograph the two-story white brick building. The exterior was minimalist compared to the houses she'd seen earlier. Wait, the signage indicated that they sold coffee *and* books.

"I could do with an iced coffee and a pastry." Her skin was sticky from the unseasonably warm and humid January, and she'd worked up an appetite during her walk. A blast of cold air soothed her bare arms and face as soon as she stepped inside.

Josie made a beeline for the wooden counter with urns of brew coffee. Her mouth watered as she caught a whiff of the buttery pastries.

"Is this your first time here?" the barista asked from behind the espresso machine. She wore her hair in long fuchsia braids and had a small nose piercing. Her forearm sported a tattoo of an open book with roses emerging from it. Wow, she really liked books.

"Is it that obvious?"

"Yes, but we ask everyone that."

Josie laughed.

"I'm Gemma. I love your hair."

"Oh, thanks. I'm Josie." She was pretty sure her fro had doubled in size, no thanks to the humidity.

"Josie, what can I get for a lovely woman like yourself?"

"A large iced coffee and maybe one of those praline croissants. And these, too." Josie grabbed some store-branded T-shirts and mugs for her mom.

"Shopping for yourself or a girlfriend?" Gemma asked pointedly.

"Uh, for my mom and sister," Josie stammered. She didn't expect the barista to flirt so openly with her.

"Good to know." Gemma winked as she rung up Josie's purchases. "Do you want your croissant toasted? I recommend it."

"Oh, in that case, please." Josie appreciated how Gemma didn't rush her even though there were customers in line behind her. She supposed this was the Southern hospitality Trixie often talked about.

Josie tucked her purchases into her large tote bag and walked to the other end of the counter to wait for her coffee. The barista's bright hair contrasted with the store's exposed brick wall and wood counter.

Her mentor's voice echoed in her head. *Look for the unusual but capture the everyday.*

"Excuse me, Gemma?"

"Need something else?" The barista looked up from the prep counter.

"Sort of. Do you mind if I photograph you while you work?" Josie held up her camera. "I'm a professional photographer."

"Girl, you can take as many pictures as you want," Gemma crooned. "You want me to pose?"

"No, no. Do what you usually do. I want you in your element." Josie peered through the viewfinder and focused her lens.

Gemma flicked her braids behind her shoulder and playfully stuck her tongue out at Josie before returning to her drink order. She tried her best to capture the barista's energy as she danced between pulling shots at the espresso machine to sliding pastries into the oven. The woman clearly loved her job and enjoyed chatting with her customers.

"Can I see them?" Gemma asked when there was a lull at the coffee bar.

"Of course." Josie scrolled through the photos on the camera's display. Her favorite was when the barista did a little dance after handing a customer their drink. After taking boudoir photos for so long, she'd almost forgotten how much she enjoyed taking candid photos. Getting memorable shots that depended on a mixture of the subjects, timing, and pure luck.

"That's how I look when I make a latte? Damn, you make me look good!" Gemma said, as if she didn't believe Josie's earlier claim of being a professional.

"I'm putting together a portfolio for an art gallery, and I might use some of these photos."

"Look at you!" Gemma shimmied her shoulders. "Jake, I'm gonna be in an art gallery!"

A tall man at the front register gave her a thumbs-up.

"Maybe." Josie didn't want to get her hopes up. "But I'll need you to sign a waiver first."

"Gimme your phone." Gemma stuck out her hand. "I'll add myself in your contacts and text myself."

What was it with people in New Orleans demanding her phone? It was quicker than writing down someone's information, but Josie liked the feel of pen on paper. She wrote all her lists down on paper first.

"You'll send me copies?" Gemma asked. "When you're famous, I can brag to all my friends about you."

"I will mail you prints." Josie silently thanked her mother for sending her to the bookstore. She'd been able to capture a little bit of New Orleans magic in Gemma. She didn't care that her croissant was cold and the ice in her coffee had melted. If she got this lucky every day for the rest of her trip, she'd have more than enough material for her portfolio.

And thanks to Gemma, she could cross off *Hold a photoshoot in a bookstore* on her 30 by 30 list.

"You're not hiding any giant beads in your bag, are you?"

She recognized that voice. Her lips tingled, and heat flooded her body. Josie looked up from her camera.

"Spencer?" Her heart hammered in her chest. It *was* him. He sported what must be his signature jeans and T-shirt look. Light stubble covered his jaw. She couldn't remember if that stubble had scratched her face when they kissed. Somehow, he was even more attractive in daylight.

"How did you know I was here?" Josie had been so focused on the barista that the rest of the world had faded into the background. Zoe called it a flow state, when creativity became effortless and everything else disappeared. How else could she have missed him walking into the store? Not that she'd expected to run into him again in a city this big.

"I didn't. I came here to check out the community board and pick up my sisters' orders." Spencer held up a brown paper shopping bag almost bursting with books. "Looks like you got some sun today. You look great."

"Only if you consider humidity-induced sweat attractive." Josie cringed. *Humidity-induced sweat, really?* She didn't feel particularly attractive right now. Before she entered the store, her loose V-neck purple shirt had been glued to her back and her black leggings had given up on their air-wicking capabilities. Even though the air-conditioning had resolved all of that, she looked forward to a shower once she returned to the apartment.

"I consider anything to do with you attractive." His eyes bored into hers.

Heat flooded her cheeks—and farther down—as she recalled how eagerly their tongues tangled only twelve hours ago. This morning Josie had been tempted to ask his sister Nina for his number, but then she remembered that she'd made him lose his phone. The idea of asking his sister to be their messenger felt awkward and perhaps a little desperate. Last night was a fun diversion, but her plan for the rest of the week was to stay focused on her photography.

"Did you get any good photos today?" He pointed at her camera resting on her chest, its strap hanging around her neck.

"Yeah, Gemma—that's the barista—let me take photos of her as she worked. I hope I captured her vibe well."

"I have no doubt you did."

"You haven't even seen the pictures yet." Josie picked up her camera to show him, but he held out his hand to stop her.

"I don't have to. You're glowing and exuding this very sexy artist energy." He gestured up and down next to her side as if to illustrate waves of energy.

Josie wondered if he sensed how her body reacted when he was near her. Nope, that would only be a distraction. She cleared her throat, hoping it'd clear the lust building in her.

"How's your head?" She gestured at his temple.

"Better. Jimmy gave me the all clear."

"You trust him?"

"Of course. We've been friends since we were kids. He really is a doctor." Spencer chuckled. "He enjoys giving me a hard time."

"My friends teased me about last night, too." She licked her lips and added, "Hitting you, I mean."

Spencer's eyes widened at the quick swipe of her tongue. Josie looked away. She'd done it unconsciously, but obviously he was thinking about more than the beads incident. So much for trying to keep their conversation casual.

He cleared his throat.

"You're dressed for adventure." He pointed to her sneakers. "What's on your list for today?"

"Actually"—she laughed nervously—"my girlfriends convinced me to take it one day at a time. And today was exploring the Marigny district."

"And?"

"I love the murals depicting Black people who are happy and joyful. There's an unspoken language of community here." She waved at the books and people around them. "Is it weird to say it feels homey?"

"I get it. That's how I felt the first time I went to Eden Center. I was so homesick for my mom's and grandmother's cooking. A coworker took me there for lunch. I even stocked up on the 'buy five get one free' bánh mì deal from a deli there."

"Ah, the cheap bánh mìs. I'm very familiar with those." Those weren't as tasty as the ones from Zoe's parents' restaurant, which was also located in Eden Center. "But it wasn't as good as your family's food, right?"

"It never is. But eventually I found some restaurants closer to my apartment to satisfy my cravings between my visits home."

"I still go to my parents' for dinner at least twice a month. Mom makes a mean crab mac and cheese." She closed her eyes and rubbed her stomach. "She always puts her whole foot in it."

"She what?" Spencer asked. He mimed his foot stepping into something squishy.

"Oh!" She laughed. "It means her cooking is amazing."

"Crab mac and cheese sounds pretty good right now. Though the women in my family have plied me with food ever since I got back."

"That sounds delicious!" Her craving for Vietnamese intensified. Josie had a couple of Vietnamese restaurants on her New Orleans Eats list. Maybe she should try one out for dinner.

Spencer's phone buzzed. "Sorry, my sisters added me to a group chat and they won't shut up."

"Hey, you got a new phone! Let me send you some money for it." She pulled out hers and opened an app to transfer the funds.

"You don't have to do that. But give me your digits and I'll text you. That way we have each other's info."

Josie recited her number, secretly elated to receive his without going through his sister. This way felt less contrived. She told herself she was only exchanging information in case she needed to ask a local something about the city, not because she wanted to go out with him again.

"Do you have meddling siblings? I have three younger sisters who are highly skilled at pushing my buttons." He flashed his group chat screen before closing it.

"Well, I have a younger sister and four best friends who do the same!" Her laughter seemed to ease his stress about his sisters.

"My sisters threatened to tell my mother I was ready to settle down if I didn't start looking for a job. Meaning the Viet Auntie Network's matchmakers will set me up on dates with every eligible woman in the area."

"That sounds . . . intense."

"It's like Tinder, but I'm obligated to swipe right or risk disappointing every auntie within a ten-mile radius. And my mom."

"That's a lot of blind dates!" Josie was shocked that an edge of jealousy had crept into her voice, and she hoped he hadn't noticed.

"I figured I might as well check out the community board for job listings while I was here." He stepped toward the large corkboard. Flyers, brochures, business cards, even handwritten notes covered the entirety of the board. Half of the postings were covered by another piece of paper.

"I don't know what Vietnamese matchmaking entails, but it doesn't sound fun. I wouldn't want anyone to choose my partner for me," Josie said as she joined him at the community board. "Anything good?"

"Maybe." He yanked a flyer with a blue border out from under its thumbtack. "It's a competition for a multimedia exhibition in DC—the Fifty States Exhibition. They're looking for work from artists to represent each state. And the finalists will be invited to show their work in DC and be eligible for a grant to continue their work."

"Are you going to submit your film about your grandfather's krewe?"

"If I can finish it in time. But I'm not sure I qualify. Each proposal must have at least two types of audio or visual media."

"How about spoken word or singing?"

"Only when I'm drunk. And it's not pretty."

"Same." She laughed.

"Wait, what if we submitted an application together?" Spencer exclaimed.

"What? No way—I'm focused on getting my work into Stevens," she said, even though part of her wanted to say yes, if only to spend more time with him.

"You're already photographing New Orleans. We can find a way to make our work cohesive."

"I don't know." Josie chewed her bottom lip as she mentally started a pros and cons list.

"My offer from last night still stands. I'll give you the insider's tour and take you to all my favorite places!"

"It's tempting." She took the flyer from his hand. "It doesn't say that we both have to be New Orleans residents."

"And finalists are guaranteed a spot in the exhibition. Here's your chance to impress that art gallery of yours."

Pro: she'd get to spend more time with a very sexy guy. That was also a con, because he'd distract her from photography—even if he didn't mean to. But the biggest pro was that this competition could give her work extra exposure and clout for when she submitted her portfolio to Stevens. She couldn't pass up an opportunity like that.

"I'll do it," Josie declared before she talked herself out of it.

"*Yes!*" He reached up for a high five, but she didn't reciprocate. Josie held up a finger.

"*If* we can come up with a proposal that can combine our interests," she continued. She didn't want to waste most of her vacation if they couldn't create a winning proposal together. She'd give him a day—two at the most—to see if they meshed creatively.

"We will." Spencer grinned, extremely sure of himself.

"I'll feel better after we brainstorm some ideas." Josie reached into her bag and pulled out a notebook. "Why don't we start now?"

"Right now?" Spencer shifted his weight nervously. "I need to drop these books back at home first. How about I take you to one more touristy spot that's great for people watching, then we can grab some food and work on our proposal?"

"Spencer Pham, are you asking me out on *another* date?" She put a hand on her cocked hip and side-eyed him, but she was secretly pleased. If they were to come up with a proposal quickly, a working date was not a bad idea.

"It's a bar designed like a carousel. It even spins like one. Slowly so you can enjoy your cocktails." His eyes shined as he nodded eagerly.

"Fine." A smile slipped out. "Pick me up at six. I'll text you my address."

"I won't be late." He beamed as if he'd won the lottery.

Josie's body tingled with excitement at the possibility of another kiss. It was a working date, but that didn't mean she couldn't enjoy herself.

CHAPTER 11

Josie had no idea what to wear to a carousel bar, and Spencer was due to arrive in thirty minutes. She rifled through her suitcase and grabbed the jar of her favorite body butter. The scent of cocoa butter soothed her nerves as she rubbed it into her skin. Her jar contained a handmade formula with all-natural ingredients, but it had the same scent as the drugstore-brand lotion her mother had used to massage her and her sister after giving them baths.

Time was running out, so she tossed on something comfortable yet dressy enough for a bar. She unplugged her camera from its charger and packed it in her oversized bag along with her notebook and favorite fountain pens.

She'd agreed on the date because the bar intrigued her. And because she wanted to work on their proposal. Becoming a finalist would certainly put her work on the radar of Stevens Gallery.

That was the real reason she was meeting with Spencer tonight. Not because she was attracted to him. Not because he was handsome and sexy and a very good kisser.

Zoe's words echoed in her head. Josie didn't have to plan anything out. It was okay to chill and take things day by day. She could have fun and think only about the next few days without feeling twitchy.

Last night she'd been able to focus on the present at Cafe du Monde. Normally she wouldn't have thrown sugar at a guy like they were in a school cafeteria food fight. She'd had the urge and followed through. And was rewarded with a kiss. One that seared her lips and sent heat radiating through her body.

Her phone dinged with a text from Spencer.

Be there in five minutes.

She took a deep breath. Time to channel spontaneous Josie. Or slightly more spontaneous. If she could truly channel Reina's philosophy, she'd tell him to come to the door. Open it before he could knock. Pull him inside and kiss him until they could barely breathe. Then make their way to the king-sized bed in her room and—

"Carousel Bar first," Josie said aloud, as if it would strengthen her resolve not to get naked with a man she'd known for only twenty-four hours. The farther away she was from the apartment when he arrived, the better. She grabbed her jacket and headed out to meet Spencer.

The houses in the neighborhood glowed as the sun began to dip below the horizon. A twinkle of music tickled her ears. The New Orleans humidity was more bearable in the evening. Hopefully she wouldn't sweat too much on their walk to the bar.

A minute later, she spotted Spencer's now familiar form coming toward her. He was holding up his phone and was either recording video or taking photos but quickly tucked it away when he spotted her. He hurried over, his eyes bright.

"I'm not late, am I?"

"No, I wanted to take in the atmosphere before you arrived," she said. And keep temptation at bay.

"You picked a chill neighborhood to stay in. Ready for something a bit more lively?"

Josie patted her tote bag that held her camera and notebooks. "Ready."

Even though the French Quarter was less than a mile away, they took a cab. Josie was relieved to escape the humidity, even for a few minutes. Spencer asked the driver to drop them off at the edge of the French Quarter where it wasn't so full of people.

"We can walk from here. It'll take the cab too long to navigate through the crowds and get us closer to the bar," Spencer said. He exited first and held open the cab door for her.

Even on the outskirts of the Quarter, the energy was completely different from the area around her rental apartment. The air vibrated with music and laughter. A smattering of tourists passed by, taking full advantage of the city's open container law. It would take some getting used to, seeing people on the streets carrying booze.

"Six is a little early to party in New Orleans," Spencer said as he guided her to a quieter spot on the sidewalk, "but I want to make sure we get a seat at the bar. And hopefully it won't be too dark for photos."

"This is perfect, Spencer. I love sunsets." She touched his elbow. "Look, it's purple and gold. Perfect for Mardi Gras."

Josie tried to ignore how her hand tingled after touching him. They hadn't touched in the back of the cab, but she'd been acutely aware of the heat of his body next to her. Her hand itched to grab his now that the distance between them had increased, but she lifted her camera to her face instead. She clicked the shutter rapidly in succession to push aside the heat growing inside her. Her art needed to come first.

As if he recognized her flow state, Spencer remained quiet as she spent several minutes capturing the sunset from at least twenty different angles. She was doing her best to capture how the fading light landed on the ironwork on the upper floors of the surrounding buildings.

"The French Quarter is practically glowing," Josie said, and finally rested her camera against her chest, hoping she'd gotten a few good shots. Her cheeks hurt. Had she been smiling the entire time? She turned to find Spencer's eyes on her, his expression a mix of adoration and desire.

"So beautiful." He wasn't talking about sunsets.

"Are you trying to get into my pants?" She couldn't help teasing—no, flirting with him again.

He took a couple of steps to close the distance between them. Josie froze, her shoulders tense with anticipation. Would he kiss her in the twilight?

Spencer lowered his voice and spoke into her ear. "Would it be too forward if I said yes?"

"Not at all." Her voice was husky. She cleared her throat and swallowed. It wasn't that she didn't want to kiss him right there on the sidewalk. Part of her did, and the other part— "But you promised me a carousel bar and I'd like to see it."

Spencer took a step back, but the corners of his eyes crinkled in quiet laughter as if he'd heard the battle in her head. "Well, we should pick up the pace. The bar will fill up with tourists faster than you think."

"Lead the way," Josie said, and grabbed his hand.

She almost dropped it when Spencer inhaled sharply. He slipped his fingers between hers and squeezed. She thought he'd comment on their hand-holding, but instead he launched into a list of facts about Hotel Monteleone, where the bar was located. She quickly learned that as a kid he'd been into haunted houses and the hotel's fourteenth floor was haunted. He'd never stayed at the hotel or gone up in the elevators, but the bar was open to anyone old enough to drink. Josie knew she should listen to Spencer's facts, but honestly, she couldn't concentrate on his words. She had no idea why she'd grabbed his hand except that she'd wanted to. Shivers had shot through her body the minute her palm touched his.

Perhaps the hotel's history was interesting, but all she could focus on was Spencer's body so close to hers. He'd changed into a dark green button-down shirt but left it open to reveal the white T-shirt under it. She caught a whiff of fresh soap. He must have showered recently. No, she would *not* picture him standing naked as hot water beat down on his chest and—

"Almost there!" Spencer squeezed her hand and pulled her closer so they couldn't be separated by the crowd. The French Quarter was filling up by the second.

"Is it always this busy?" She spoke directly into his ear so her words wouldn't be lost in the jumble of conversations around them.

"Only during Mardi Gras. Oh, and spring break. If there's a college bowl game in town. Sometimes New Year's." He laughed. "So I guess most of the time? Locals don't really come out here in the evenings."

After two days down here, she could see why. The hordes of tourists, some who'd already had too much to drink, moved as giant masses on the city street. Josie didn't mind tight spaces—she'd squeezed herself into some interesting spaces to get the best wedding shots—but the crowd here seemed to move as one large wave, dragging them along.

Now she understood what Spencer had meant yesterday about getting caught in the crowd. Josie tripped on her own feet as she struggled to keep up. Spencer pulled her tighter against him and wrapped his arm around her waist.

"I got you," he whispered into her ear.

She nodded and leaned into him. His strong shoulder steadied her as they were jostled by the people surrounding them. It wasn't the cool winter breeze that caused her nipples to harden.

Pushing the thought aside, Josie squeezed his hand to let him know she was all right. He held her tight and found pockets among the throngs of people so that they had a bit of breathing room. He moved with the ease of someone who'd done this many times before.

When they arrived at the hotel lobby, it was packed and loud. There was a line of people standing outside the doors waiting to get in. She peeked into the dark room. The lounge was completely packed, too, but she couldn't miss the bright lights of the bar. Above it was the classic carousel umbrella decked out with exposed lightbulbs, mirrors with ornate frames, and chairs whose backs were adorned with paintings of wild animals.

Josie had envisioned something more playful, more childlike. Honestly, she was disappointed. Even the bar rotated extremely slowly. A full rotation every fifteen minutes, if she'd heard Spencer right. This felt more like a tourist trap than a historical site. A local historian may disagree, but this place didn't exude what she wanted for her photos for the gallery. The carousel bar was unusual, but there was too much chaos for her.

"Dammit." Spencer peeked around her. He looked as disappointed as she felt. "I was hoping we'd beat the nighttime crowd."

"What makes this place so special to you?" After his tirade against tourists last night, she was surprised he'd taken her here.

"Jimmy took me here to celebrate my move to DC ten years ago. We'd gotten lucky and snagged a spot at the bar." He pointed. "Sitting there, sipping our overpriced cocktails—I felt like I was on the cusp of something big. I was finally going to be on my own."

"You think we're on the verge of something tonight?"

"I think so. I've been feeling this way since I met you." He squeezed her hand. "That was one hell of a kiss."

"I've been thinking about it all day." Her words floated out so quietly, she could barely hear herself.

"I wanted to kiss you again the moment I saw you tonight."

"Me, too." Her heart pounded so hard that blood rushed into her ears.

Their heads were so close together, she could feel his breath on her cheek. His eyes fell to her lips. She licked them as a reflex. His eyes widened, and he leaned even closer. Her eyelids fluttered as the distance between their lips grew smaller.

Before she could kiss him, a loud, nasal voice interrupted their moment.

"Why is the line so long, honey? You promised to get me a seat at the bar. Not waiting in line forever."

"Fucking tourists," Spencer whispered.

Josie barked with laughter and the blonde with the nasal voice threw her a death glare.

"Fucking tourists," she echoed, and giggled.

"Let's get out of here." He wrapped his arm around her waist and once again guided her.

"The nerve of that woman!" Josie exclaimed after they stepped out into the cool air.

Spencer raised his eyebrows and mouthed what was now becoming a favorite expression: *Fucking tourists.*

"Stop it!" She bit back laughter. "You'll get us in trouble. We're surrounded by tourists."

"Says the tourist," he teased.

"Hey, you're supposed to show me how to be a good tourist." She swatted his arm playfully. He laughed. She enjoyed the sound of his happiness. He looked so carefree with his head tossed back. That had to be why she was so attracted to him. His confident yet chill manner made it easy for her to channel chill Josie.

"That's my bad. At least we're saving money on cocktails." He shuddered. "Prices have definitely gone up since my last visit."

"So now what?"

He dropped his smile. "To be honest, I have no idea where to go in the Quarter. We didn't really hang out here much when I was a kid, because of the tourists and everything being so expensive."

"What did you do for fun, then?"

"Mostly hung out at each other's houses and played video games." He stuffed his hands into his jean pockets. "My family lives out in Versailles, the suburbs where our Vietnamese friends and family are."

"That sounds better than that bar." Josie wanted to know how growing up in Versailles had shaped him and what he hid underneath his easygoing attitude.

"If you want, I can take you there tomorrow."

"Excuse me, sir and miss," an older Black doorman called to them. "I'm sorry to interrupt, but can you please take your conversation away from the entrance?"

"Yes, sir!" Spencer mock saluted, then pulled her away. He slipped his arm around her waist as they walked. She relaxed into his side.

"Why did you salute the doorman? And where are we going now?" This night wasn't going as planned, but Josie didn't care. She was having fun being silly with Spencer.

"I have no idea and"—he tilted his head—"and I still have no idea. Food?"

"Yes, but I need a break from crowds. Can we pick up some food nearby and go back to my place?" She wasn't looking forward to navigating another mass of bodies to end up at another crowded bar. "The host stocked it with all the booze a ten-person bachelorette party would want."

"Do you like sandwiches?"

"I could go for something hearty after all the walking I've done today."

"Then I know just the place." He dropped his arm from her waist and slipped his fingers between hers. "You're gonna love it."

CHAPTER 12

"T his place has the best muffulettas!" Spencer declared once they arrived at the unassuming sandwich shop. "They're good anytime of the day but especially late at night after a few drinks."

"I've never had one, but it smells so good in here." She closed her eyes and inhaled deeply.

"I'll order a couple of things for you to try. Are you allergic to anything?"

"Nope, but I'm not a fan of mushrooms." Josie pulled out her camera and waved him to the counter. "This place has so much personality."

While they waited for their sandwiches, Josie snapped photos of the small sandwich shop. Her expression was intense. He adored the way she bit her lip as she studied the restaurant through the viewfinder, trying to find the perfect shot. Spencer was surprised by what she focused her attention on. Other tourists were taking selfies of the signs hanging by the door. But Josie had her camera pointed toward the cashier, whose pale skin rocked a colorful tattoo sleeve, and the kitchen. She crouched down and pointed her lens up at an angle. At one point, she snapped photos of the napkin dispenser. When he asked about that, she showed him the shot on the small screen of the camera. She'd captured the blurred reflection of someone grinning as they picked up their order.

"Wow, I never would have thought of that. You have a great eye."

"*Look for the unusual but capture the everyday.* That's what my mentor used to tell me. She taught me to see things from a different perspective."

Once their order was ready, he grabbed the plastic bag and reached for her hand. She intertwined her fingers with his and pulled him closer. Their bodies fit together, and they found an easy rhythm as they walked back to her place.

Spencer was relieved that Josie wanted to chill at her apartment. He didn't care for the frantic energy of the French Quarter, especially during Mardi Gras. The farther they walked, the less crowded the streets became. They could stroll at their own pace instead of darting around packs of tourists.

"Listen." Spencer pulled her to a stop. "What do you hear?"

"Live music. Jazz?"

"That means we're headed in the right direction. The Marigny is known for its jazz. You've probably heard it as you walked around." He almost suggested they find a place and enjoy the live music. But he was done sharing Josie with the city. He didn't care that he was being selfish. He wanted her all to himself, where no one could interrupt them.

"I'll have to check out the bars another night when I'm not all peopled out. Present company excluded of course."

"Of course." He beamed.

Josie made a beeline for the kitchen as soon as she unlocked the door. "I think I saw some beers in the back of the fridge."

He kicked off his shoes by the front door and then followed her.

"Unless you prefer wine or a cocktail? You should be okay to drink, since your head is fine." Josie rummaged through the cabinets to inventory the booze selection. She set some liquor bottles on the kitchen counter. "My friend Trixie's boyfriend taught me how to make a mean appletini."

"Tempting, but these sandwiches are hearty, so let's go with beer."

"Oh, so now you're a beer expert," she teased. She grabbed two bottles of Abita Purple Haze. "Will these pair well with the food?"

"I don't care, because that's one of my favorite beers. It pairs well with everything!" He pulled the sandwiches out of the bag and set them on the kitchen counter. In hindsight, he might've gone overboard. Five sandwiches was a lot for two people.

"Let's eat."

Josie gave him a smile so wide, so bright that Spencer could barely breathe. Would he have found her so mesmerizing if they'd met in DC? Spencer wasn't sure. His life there felt so distant.

The past didn't matter anymore. Not at this very moment, when she was giving him all her attention. This woman had barreled her way into his life and changed its trajectory. His sisters had been right—he had been lost since he moved home a month ago. At least he had been until he met Josie yesterday. Because of her, he'd found a purpose and newfound inspiration for his budding film career.

He had to find a way to keep her in his life as long as possible.

"WHEN YOU SAID sandwiches, I thought they were going to be hoagies or subs." Josie held up the muffuletta. The big, round loaf was sliced like a hamburger bun. Instead of a meat patty, it was stuffed with olives, salami, ham, lots of cheeses, and more deli meats that she didn't know the names of.

Tonight had not gone as planned at all, but Spencer had seemed to roll with it. If she spent more time with him, she could learn how to go with the flow instead of worrying about the next thing to check off her list.

"Don't forget about the shrimp and oyster po' boys. They may look like a hoagie, but taste a hundred times better." He dug into the bag and pulled out yet another wax-wrapped oblong lump.

"You should have told me you bought po' boys, too. I would've paced myself. Everything I've eaten in New Orleans is so good," she said.

"That's one of the things I missed the most while living in DC," Spencer said. "The food isn't the same."

"You're being too harsh. Have you ever been to Hazel's Kitchen out in Northeast?" she asked him in between bites. "My friends own it. It's fusion soul food inspired by their late mom's recipes. She was from New Orleans."

"I never had a chance to visit. Maybe I would've met you sooner."

"Says the man who thinks the universe planned whatever the heck you want to call yesterday."

"I call it perfection." He winked.

"The food and cocktails at Hazel's will blow your mind," she said, ignoring his compliment. "When are you coming back to DC?"

"I don't know. Maybe when I finish this film project." He looked away from her. Suddenly he found his food very interesting. "I'm not ready to make any long-term commitments right now."

"Oh." Disappointment fell over her. Part of her mind had played out scenarios where they were back in DC and dating. "This exhibition will be a long-term commitment."

"That's different. I don't have to stay in one place indefinitely for it."

"What will you do after?"

"Josie, I'm finally free after being stuck in the same place for ten years. I'm not ready to jump back into some soulless job," he said, voice rising.

"Did you hate it that much?" she asked softly. Obviously, she'd hit upon a sensitive issue. She didn't want to ruin their fun night by unintentionally triggering him.

"Since high school, my life has been planned out for me. Make good grades, get a college scholarship, and find a good job. All the perfect ingredients to be a good son." He took a swig of beer. "I never wanted to be a data analyst."

"I never wanted to be a photographer." That was the first time Josie had told anyone that except for Zoe. "I got into it because my old boss was a wedding photographer and she started teaching me little things here and there. I fell into it."

"I don't believe it. Your work is so breathtaking. And not because they're boudoir photos."

"How would you know? I haven't shown you any of my work."

"There's this thing called Google," he teased, tapping his phone. "I searched for your name, DC, and boudoir photography."

"Well, look who knows how to use keywords." Josie bit back a smile. He'd looked up her business and liked her work.

"Hey, that's me. The data guy."

"Which you hate."

"Can't help how my brain is wired. But we're talking about how you got into photography, not my dislike of staring at a computer all day."

"In high school I had no idea what I wanted to be when I grew up," Josie said. "All I knew was I liked taking a bunch of random craft supplies and turning them into something new. So why not go to art school and figure out what I was really good at? But a girl like me coming from a barely middle-class family in DC—we don't do frivolous things like that."

"Why do you say that? You're smart. You could've gotten scholarships."

Josie scoffed. "Not with my grades. My parents barely made ends meet, especially after my sister got hurt in a hit-and-run. I couldn't afford to go to college just to try something new."

"I get that. Creative careers are a luxury for other people, not for families like ours."

"Exactly. My mom wanted me to be a teacher." Josie rolled her eyes. "I'd make a terrible teacher! I have no patience."

"Maybe you're not a schoolteacher, but you coach your photography clients. That's like teaching."

"How's that?"

"Don't you help them find poses that make them even more beautiful on camera? You're teaching them confidence and how to be comfortable with their bodies."

"You're quoting my website back at me." She narrowed her eyes even though she was impressed he'd taken the time to read it.

"I refuse to think that you"—he held his hand out toward her—"who has been so kind, patient, and generous with me, could be a bad teacher."

"I know what you're doing and I'm not falling for it. You're trying to convince me to be your partner for the exhibition."

"Yes and no." Spencer took a big bite of his sandwich and shrugged. He pointed at his mouth to indicate that he couldn't talk.

"I don't see how our work is related enough to work together."

He chewed faster, eager to reply to her objection.

"Part of it is because I want to spend as much time with you as possible. I like you, Josie." His eyes bore into hers. "But becoming a finalist in this competition will prove to my family that I have what it takes to be a filmmaker. At the very least, I want to have a short version to show at my grandmother's one hundredth birthday party."

"I see." Josie couldn't miss the earnest tone in his voice. This competition meant as much to him as it did to her.

"I don't know anyone else I'd rather collaborate with. Plus, we can make out during our breaks." And just as quickly, he'd gone back to being breezy and flirtatious.

Even behind his easygoing tone, she could tell he adored his grandmother. How many people did she know who would go through all this just for their grandmother's birthday? It was really sweet.

"Okay, how about this? You take me somewhere meaningful to you tomorrow," Josie began. "Somewhere that's not a tourist trap. You have to take this seriously if we want to become finalists in the competition."

"Is that a yes?"

"It depends on where we go tomorrow and what photos I can take while I'm there." Josie was hopeful. She'd give him one more try. If he didn't come through, she had her own agenda to complete.

"Yes!" He dropped his food and pumped his fist in the air. "I know exactly where to go, but I'm keeping it a surprise."

She cringed. Not surprises. Well, she had challenged him to impress her. She'd put the ball in his court, so now she would play along.

"Is the offer to use your camera still open? Can you teach me how to use it?"

"You're not touching Ruby until you wash the grease off your hands."

"Yes, ma'am!" He jumped up and saluted.

"It's just a camera. Not like you're going to Disney World."
Josie couldn't help but laugh. How was it that she simultaneously loved his easygoing nature and wished he could be a little
bit more serious?

"It's the first step in my new adventure. This *is* my Disney
World."

"Go!"

"I miss this food so much." He stuffed the last of his sandwich
into his mouth and moaned. "I'm going."

She was envious of how carefree Spencer was. Josie could deal
when life threw her curveballs, but this work trip turned vacation was completely off the rails. Usually, she'd go back to her
list and rework it. She was skilled at pivoting as long as she knew
what the end goal was supposed to be. Somehow, she'd managed
to keep up with Spencer the last couple of days without referring
to her list.

Spencer kept her on her toes. He embraced change and followed his mood, which felt chaotic to her. Yet it worked for him.
She'd had her list, but it was fun to experience the city with
someone else.

She liked the person she was around him. More relaxed. Excited about photography again. There was no point in fooling
herself that this was a bad idea. She was dying to kiss him again.
Maybe do more than that.

CHAPTER 13

"Wow, this apartment is bigger than I thought," Spencer exclaimed as he helped Josie unpack her camera equipment in the living room. He'd been so focused on Josie when they passed through the living room toward the kitchen earlier that he missed the hallway leading to even more rooms.

"That's why my client and I chose it. For the spacious rooms, neutral decor, and lots of natural lighting." She pointed at the large windows with soft, billowy curtains, then to the wall behind him. Josie sighed and added, "The exposed brick would've made a great backdrop, too. The couch is not comfortable, but at least it looks good in photos."

"Thanks for teaching me how to use your camera. I've only taken footage on my phone." He'd lost the parade footage from yesterday when he'd lost his phone. But all the previous film projects were safely uploaded to the cloud. He hoped they could be repurposed for a future project.

"Don't tell Ruby," Josie whispered, "but she's past her prime. She's the first fancy camera I bought on my own. Your new phone's camera is probably better than Ruby."

"So I don't need to shell out for a fancy camera right now," he said. Replacing his phone put a huge dent in his savings, and he wasn't sure if he could swing any other equipment.

"I know it's supposed to be a surprise, but will we be indoors or outdoors tomorrow? That way I can show you the essentials."

"Oh, indoors. I want to interview my grandmother first."

"Hmm, in that case, let's set the camera on the tripod." Josie tapped her chin. "Lighting can make or break an image, too. Since we'll be inside, let's do this."

She assembled umbrella lights and attached them to their stands. She directed him to different areas of the living room with the lights until she was satisfied.

"It's not perfect, but good enough for our lesson."

"I hate to ask, but I have no budget for this film." He bit his lip. Maybe his sisters were right. He needed a job to fund his film. "Can I borrow your lighting equipment tomorrow?"

"I've already offered my camera, so adding lighting is no big deal. But you'll have to help carry it."

"I can do that. Thank you for taking a chance on me." Spencer placed a hand on her arm. Her confidence mesmerized him, drew him in.

"So what else do you have planned for tomorrow?" Josie asked. She turned away, but her cheeks were flushed. She felt the energy between them.

"I'll figure it out as I go. Ask my grandmother some questions and record her responses." That was as far as he'd gotten with his plans. Bà Bà had agreed to an interview, but they hadn't decided when that would happen. Hopefully she'd agree to do it tomorrow.

"Oh." Josie sucked on her bottom lip, which him made wish he were the one sucking it. She pulled her notebook out of her bag and uncapped her pen. "Maybe prepare some questions in advance?"

"Good idea. And I can figure out where exactly I want to record the interview." Spencer kicked himself. He'd taken that one film class in DC where they went over stuff like that. The class was years ago, and he couldn't remember much from it.

"It feels overwhelming now, but we'll break it down into smaller steps," Josie said. "It'll feel easy then. Trust me. I do this for my girlfriends whenever they have a new idea."

She looked him in the eyes and gave a reassuring smile. He stared back into her amber eyes and realized that he did trust her. She'd stayed with him yesterday after hitting him with the beads. Someone else might have taken his "fine" at face value and left him on his own.

He admired how she had everything planned out, confident that she'd accomplish whatever she set out to do. She'd already created a thriving business in DC. She knew what it took to succeed.

Spencer wanted his idea to come to life. This film was how he could make a difference in the world without sitting in some cubicle. It would honor the sacrifices his parents and grandparents had made for him.

Whatever doubts he'd had before disappeared when she looked at him that way. She believed in him even though she had no idea what he was or wasn't capable of doing. This must be what her clients feel like during their photoshoots.

"I trust you." He hoped his declaration wouldn't scare her away.

"I'm flattered." She blushed. "And thank you."

"No, thank you for making me think I can actually make this film. I used to sit with my grandfather and listen to his stories about life in Vietnam and coming here to New Orleans." Spencer's chest tightened with emotion. He missed his grandfather so much. "People need to know."

"That's beautiful, Spencer." Her eyes shined and her pen flew across the page as she made notes.

"Let me show you something," he said, and grabbed his notebook from his messenger bag and sat on the plush rug.

"Your grandparents sound like trailblazers." Josie grabbed a pillow off the couch and sat next to him.

"When I moved back home, I found this shoebox I'd stuck in the back of the closet. Inside was this." He carefully slid out a photo from the back pocket of his notebook. "It's my favorite photo of me and Ông ngoại. That's Vietnamese for *grandfather*."

"Oh, look how cute you two are in almost-matching outfits! How old are you in this picture?"

"Eight. Don't let that cute face fool you. My mom said I was a handful at that age. But Ông ngoại"—he tapped the man's chest—"I'm pretty sure I was his favorite grandkid because I didn't mind dressing up in the clothes for Tết—Lunar New Year—pictures."

Spencer loved his family's loud Tết gatherings. Since everyone worked during the week, they celebrated on the weekend that fell closest to the New Year. He stuffed his face with bánh chưng, collected red envelopes, and spent his newfound money playing the dice game bầu cua.

"Oh, I see all the food behind you two! I've been to my friend's for Lunar New Year. So much good food and laughter." She gingerly took the photo from him. "Whoever took this has a great eye for composition. They offset you and your grandfather just enough to highlight the food and decorations on the wall."

"I don't know who took it. My parents, maybe?"

"See? Creativity is in your DNA," Josie said. "I bet you have a good eye for composition, too." She returned the photo, and he tucked it back into his notebook.

"God, I hope you're right." The only person he'd shown his footage to was Jimmy, but what did a doctor know about film-making?

"Sounds like you two were really close. I didn't know my grandparents very well. They died when I was just a baby."

"I'm sorry. We were close, but I won't talk about him anymore if it'll make you sad."

"I want to hear how your grandfather and your dream of film-making come together." She gave him an encouraging smile.

"Did you know he didn't speak any English when he arrived? Yet, somehow, he was able to support my grandmother and their children—my mom and her siblings—through fishing." Spencer opened to the pages in his notebook where he'd scribbled things he remembered and what his grandmother had told him. "He fell in love with this city, especially Mardi Gras, because it was the closest big holiday to the Tết. Mardi Gras season here is basically one big party that starts in early January and lasts for almost two months."

"As I've witnessed in the last couple of days. Tourists, right?" she teased.

"I want to do this because my grandparents each worked multiple jobs in order to survive in a brand-new country. They loved New Orleans so much that they founded the first ever Vietnamese krewe." Spencer's chest tightened with emotion. "People need to know."

"That's beautiful, Spencer. Your grandparents sound amazing. Your family will love it." Josie nodded encouragingly.

"I hope so. I think they're proud of me, but they don't talk about those things." Spencer had never talked about this with anyone except jokingly with his sisters and Jimmy. Maybe it was too American to want his parents to say *We're proud of you.* But he was American as well as Vietnamese. This desire for spoken family approval had become a sort of joke among his Asian friends because there was so much truth in it.

"Why would you think they're not?" She capped her pen and set her hand on top of his.

Her touch electrified his skin. As if she were passing on her empathy and confidence to him. His heart began to beat faster. Still, Spencer hesitated. Was he sharing too much too soon? Technically, this was their second date, but whatever this was, it was different from his other romantic relationships. The universe was giving him a sign by allowing them this time together.

"It's okay if you don't want to talk about it. I want to help you make this film. And not just for the competition." She squeezed his hand.

Already Spencer found himself telling her things he hadn't told anyone. She cared about what he wanted and how he felt. He wasn't used to that. No one in his family had ever asked him what he wanted to do with his life. They offered him a set path disguised as suggestions and filial responsibility.

When he lived in DC, he took care of only himself. Because he contributed financially from afar, the weight of everyday duty wasn't on his shoulders. Now that he'd moved back home, he was once again tasked with taking care of his family. Of course he loved his grandmother and wanted to care for her. But it hadn't been presented as a choice. As the only one of his siblings without a job, the role fell to him automatically.

Here, in this large apartment, in this moment, he could do what he wanted. Like follow a career that may or may not be financially lucrative. Josie gave him the space to take action in the hopes of fulfilling his dream.

"Are you sure you want to hear my entire life story? You can opt out right now." He took a swig from his bottle. The cold beer shocked his body, as if to remind him that he, too, could opt out of telling Josie his past.

"There's nowhere I'd rather be right now, Spencer." Her voice was soft and soothing, and her eyes were bright. Encouraging, even. She picked up his hand and intertwined her fingers with his.

"I'll give you the short version," he said. "I worked my ass off to be the best son for my parents. As the oldest, they expected

excellence from me, even if they never said the words. I felt it."
Spencer's gut twisted as if he were betraying his parents. They'd
taught him that whatever problems their family had stayed in
the family.

"I never asked for anything," he continued. "I studied, applied
for scholarships, and helped out at home as much as I could. I
didn't want me and my sisters to be a burden on them. They had
so much to worry about already."

"Spencer, I don't know your parents, but they have to be kind,
loving people to raise someone like you," she insisted. "They
couldn't have seen you as a burden."

With her other hand, Josie ran her fingers up his arm. He
shivered at her touch.

"Maybe they didn't, but I felt like a burden. My father woke
up before dawn in order to take his boat out fishing. My mom
worked at a dry cleaner's, mostly altering people's clothes. Every
day they came home bone-tired. I didn't want to make their life
even harder."

The way Josie nodded, he knew she understood the struggle.

"After the Deepwater Horizon oil spill, the ocean was literally
sludge. My dad couldn't fish or even sell his boat. We didn't have
much savings to begin with." Spencer clenched his fist. That was
over twelve years ago, but the memories still caused a visceral
reaction. "And there was so much bureaucracy involved to apply
for compensation. At least they had me to help fill out the paperwork. We waited and waited, but there was always an excuse
why the checks weren't arriving as promised."

"How did you end up in DC?"

"I applied to jobs all over out of desperation. Even accounting for the cost of living in DC, the data analyst job was the best offer. So I took it."

"You left to take care of your family."

He rubbed his face. "I had no choice."

"Oh, Spencer." Josie's soft whisper emanated sympathy for him. She reached out for his hand and squeezed it. Spencer's view had gone blurry, but he quickly blinked away the tears.

"I know it's been tough, but it's time to follow your dreams instead of theirs," Josie said gently.

"That's easier said than done." He dropped her hand. "I can't flip a switch and—*voila!*—put myself first over my family."

"You're not the only kid whose family worked two and three jobs to put food on the table." She tapped her chest. "I'm the oldest kid in my family, too. Yes, we've been through a lot, but we are in charge of our futures."

He opened his mouth, but nothing came out. Heat flooded his face, and he seesawed between anger that she didn't truly understand him and shock at being called out. He wasn't ready to admit that the best way to follow his dream was to disappoint his parents.

"If you want your family to see you as someone with his own hopes and dreams, then you need to show them." Josie pressed her hand to her chest. "Hell, I should be following the same advice."

"How am I supposed to do that when I'm living back at home and my savings are dwindling faster and faster?" His jaw clenched as he tried to brace himself against the truth.

"We're both scared to do new things. We have to stop thinking about what we want, and actually do it."

"How do you propose we do that?" Spencer challenged.

"Like this," she whispered, before pulling his chin until he faced her and setting her soft lips onto his.

CHAPTER 14

Spencer froze. How dare she kiss him after telling him that he was too scared to pursue his dream! But deep down, he knew she spoke the truth. Maybe her words hit him harder because she wasn't his family. Or maybe it was because her opinion mattered to him.

His anger dissipated as Josie's soft touch warmed his lips. Her words had been hard to hear, but he felt she wrapped him in empathy and encouragement. He relaxed into her embrace and returned her kiss, opening his mouth to taste her.

Their first kiss had been slow and exploratory, but this one was anything but that. Spencer wanted to claim her. To kiss and suck her lips until they were swollen, and then do it all again. He didn't want his lust to take the lead, though. He also wanted to know which types of kisses made her sigh and which ones elicited moans. Now that they were finally alone without any distractions, he'd take the time to learn every single touch that brought her pleasure.

Josie must have sensed his initial hesitation. She ran one hand through his hair and deepened their kiss. He groaned, letting her tongue take the lead. He relished the way she claimed his mouth. Her tongue dove in to caress him. Each touch teased him and begged him to take what he needed from her.

"Time to take action, Spencer. Kiss me the way you really want to," she whispered, before plunging her tongue back into his mouth. She climbed onto his lap and ran her hands over his chest. His heart pounded against her palm. With the other hand, she found his nipple hard underneath his T-shirt and rubbed her thumb over it. He groaned.

"I want you, Spencer. Do you want me?"

"Fuck yes. Can't you feel how much?" he growled into her ear. He pressed his erection against her thigh.

She answered by biting his neck. He gasped. He wrapped his arms around her body and pulled her to him. Her lips and tongue grew more insistent. Her soft breasts were hot against his chest. Suddenly his shirt felt confining. He wanted her soft, bare skin against his.

As if reading his mind, she grabbed the bottom of her top and pulled it over her head to reveal a purple lace bra that barely contained her gorgeousness.

"You're fucking beautiful." He wanted to thank her not just for the gift of herself, but for her compassion. She'd treated his deepest thoughts and feelings with empathy. "I have a weird request."

"I'm scared to ask," she said.

"Will you wear *the* beads?"

She laughed. Without leaving his lap, she leaned over and reached into her bag. He took the beads from her and slid them over her head. They were stunning against her bare skin. He kissed the swell of her breasts, which rose with her sharp inhales.

She closed her eyes and let her head fall back as he continued to caress her body. His mouth teased the dark outline of her nipples through the lace.

He pressed his lips against her neck. He kissed and nibbled his way to her earlobe, relishing every sigh and moan each action elicited.

Without breaking their kiss, he leaned her back onto the cushions. Of course he wanted her. He'd wanted her from the moment she apologized for hitting him. She protested when he pulled away and looked into her eyes. How could he not want to pleasure this woman until the sun rose? Then turn around and do it again?

"I want to pleasure every part of your body." He pressed the length of his body against hers, letting each soft curve of her body stoke the fire burning inside him. She released a throaty sigh.

"Will you let me?" He ran a hand down her hip and back up to her waist as a promise of how he wanted to pleasure her. She groaned, grinding her hips against his cock.

"Yes," she hissed. "But I want to make you feel good, too."

"You already are." He rolled the beads against the nape of her neck, then placed a soft kiss where the beads had been. Spencer tugged down the straps of her bra. He showered her bare shoulders with delicate bites in between kisses.

Her body hummed as he explored her. The beads vibrated in time with her sighs and moans. He'd won the lottery when she hit him with those beads.

"You're fucking beautiful, Josie Parks." He dipped his head and caressed the curve of her breasts with his lips. "You deserve everything you want."

He would give this woman anything and everything to make her happy. Make her feel good. He traced her dark brown areolas over the lace and watched goose bumps spread across her chest.

Josie's eyes closed as his mouth teased her breast out of the lace. His tongue swirled around her nipple until it tightened. She moaned, arching to offer more of her breasts to him. He complied, lavishing the same attention on her other breast.

"Spencer, I need more." She grabbed for his shirt, trying to pull it over his head.

"A little impatient, aren't we?" he teased, even though his eyes betrayed the same impatience as hers. "What the lady wants, the lady gets."

"Take off your clothes," she demanded.

He pulled off his shirt and jeans, tossing them behind him. Josie removed her leggings and bra, leaving only her lace panties on. The woman actually took the time to set her bra on the coffee table! But it didn't matter how she took off her clothes, only that she did.

"Stunning," he said, his breath catching in his throat.

"I had no idea data analysts were so buff."

She licked her lips appreciatively. He'd removed everything

except for his boxers, but the thin fabric did nothing to hide his hard cock tenting it. He wasn't ripped like a bodybuilder, but he hadn't been just sitting on the couch the past few months. He'd made time to stay in shape.

He inhaled sharply as she ran the flats of her palms up his abdomen. By the time she reached his chest and rolled his nipples between her fingers, his eyes were closed and his breath was ragged. She took his nipple in her mouth and sucked. She huffed against his chest as if she were pleased at the gasps and moans she'd elicited from him. Her fingers skimmed the elastic on his boxer shorts.

"My turn." Spencer grabbed her wrist. It had been a while since he'd been with a woman. He wasn't sure how long he'd last if she touched him now. He had to make sure Josie came first.

He pushed her back down onto the cushions. Now that her breasts were free, he took his time exploring their sensitive undersides as well as giving plenty of attention to her rock-hard nipples. By the time he began kissing his way down to her navel, Josie's body was limp with pleasure.

"Spencer, I need to come. Touch me here." She grabbed his hand and placed it between her legs. Fire blazed through him and his cock twitched. A woman who knew what she wanted was fucking hot.

"Like this?" He cupped her labia and squeezed gently. Her hips rose to meet his hand. Her pussy pulsed against him as if inviting him to push aside the lace and slip his fingers inside her. "These are soaked, Josie. Is all this because of me?"

"Yes," she hissed. Her body was tense, as if ready for him to touch her most sensitive parts. She was offering herself to him and showing him how she wanted to be touched. He wouldn't let her down.

"Take these off," Spencer growled, and tugged at the sides of her panties. She lifted her hips to help him pull them off. As soon as one leg was free, he pushed her legs apart. Her wetness shimmered on her thighs. He licked his lips.

She wasn't ready for that yet. He wanted her to beg for him before tasting her. He squeezed her swollen lips and ran a finger down her slit. A slow, deep moan escaped from her mouth. She bucked, offering more of herself to him. The scent of her arousal beckoned him.

Spencer accepted her offering. He bent his head down and licked the same path his finger had just traced. The muscles in her thighs tensed, and she grabbed his hair.

"So sweet," he whispered.

He wanted to plunge his tongue deep inside, but he forced himself to slow down. This was about what Josie wanted. Not him. He explored every inch of her, relishing how her thighs pressed against his head. By the time he sucked her clit into his mouth, she was gasping loudly, back arched.

"So close." She threaded her fingers through his thick black hair and pulled him even deeper between her folds. He complied by tracing circles around her clit before taking it into his mouth again. Her moans became more frantic as he brought her closer to the edge. She needed more.

Without removing his mouth from her, Spencer adjusted his body. Then hers. Enough to slip his hand between them. He eased his fingers into her tight muscles. She was so fucking wet and needy.

"Yes, please," she begged.

He curled his fingers, adjusting the position until her legs shot up in the air. There. Her G-spot. He curled and uncurled his fingers inside her while his lips and tongue worshipped her clit.

Josie pushed herself harder against his mouth and hand. Her hold on his hair tightened. Her entire body tensed as if frozen in time before a guttural groan emerged from her.

Spencer ignored the rush of blood in his ears and focused on Josie's moans. All that mattered right now was her. He didn't care that his cock was painfully hard. He was laser focused on her pleasure and her gift of allowing him to be the one who gave it to her.

Her muscles began to ripple around his fingers. He increased his pace to match her hips' rhythm. Her body arched as she pushed herself harder against him. He greedily took as much of her as he could.

Josie cried out as her orgasm rocked her body. Her grasp on his head tightened as her muscles clenched his fingers. Spencer gave himself to her as she rode his hand and mouth until a second orgasm encompassed her body.

After her breathing slowed and her body relaxed, Spencer extricated himself from Josie. He pulled himself up next to her.

"You're absolutely amazing," he whispered as he traced circles around her navel. She shivered and smiled at him with closed eyes. It didn't take long for her breathing to turn slow and steady as sleep overtook her.

This woman had turned his view on life upside down in a mere twenty-four hours. Their time together might be short, but he vowed to live each day of her vacation to the fullest. He'd show her how they were meant to be together.

CHAPTER 15

Josie woke up next to Spencer's warm body. His eyes were partially hidden by his hair. Seeing him so calm and peaceful made her realize how much turmoil he hid behind his confidence. Last night he'd opened up even more deeply about himself and his family.

She didn't regret telling him to get off his ass and do something. She understood how important it was to take care of those closest to her. Losing his job and moving home were big changes, but his pity party would've been harder to shut down the longer it went.

She had no regrets about last night. Both giving him the hard truth he needed to hear and kissing him. Again.

Still asleep, Spencer shifted closer to her, as if seeking her warmth. He draped an arm across her abdomen. That small, possessive movement made her smile and even sent a tingle up her spine as she recalled how he'd pleasured her last night.

She hadn't shared a bed with anyone in a while. Not to say she didn't have her share of hookups and friends-with-benefits. But she hadn't met anyone she wanted to wake up to the next morning. That's what she'd been telling herself instead of admitting that her high standards for a partner were a shield. She wasn't perfect, so why did she expect that from another person?

She didn't remember making their way into the bedroom, yet here she was, with Spencer sleeping next to her. Apparently, she'd had the forethought to grab her satin bonnet off the nightstand and cover her hair. Thank goodness for that.

"Hey, you're awake." Spencer's sleepy voice cut through her racing thoughts. "You were perfection last night."

"Is that so?" She drew light circles on his arm. "If I were perfect, I would've returned the favor instead of falling asleep after one of the best orgasms of my life."

"Only one of the best? I'm happy to work my way to the top spot if you're willing."

She laughed at his assurance that there would be a next time. Which, of course, there would be. She wanted to explore his body the same way he'd mapped out hers.

"I hope I wasn't too harsh last night. Telling you to put on your big girl panties—sorry, big boy pants—and all that," she said, brushing his hair out of his eyes. Josie turned her head to meet his and kissed him. Their kiss was soft and sleepy. Comforting yet still new. Right now that was enough.

"You were right. I hate to admit it, but even my sisters are right. I've been feeling sorry for myself for too long." He reached for her hand and laced his fingers through hers. "I have to get serious if I really want to be a filmmaker."

"Did you just vow to be more serious?" She heard more conviction in his voice this time. Last night, he'd been more in love with the *idea* of making the film.

"Only when it matters." He kissed her bare shoulders, sending goose bumps across her neck. "Like last night."

"Mmm." She leaned into him, relishing the heat spreading across her body.

"Turnabout is fair play. It's my turn to give you advice: you should go to art school."

"What? No!" Josie pulled away. "Definitely not on my thirty by thirty list."

"But you said—"

She bit her lip and thought about the high school version of herself. That Josie had big aspirations and wanted to change the world somehow. Now she had different goals.

"I still think a lot about art school. But now I don't know if I want to go to a place where people tell me what to do. I've been doing things my way for too long."

Josie's words shocked herself. All this time she'd hung on to the anger of being denied art school, yet it might not have made her happy.

"I know your parents wouldn't have liked it if you'd chosen art school, but you're so goal oriented. Why did you give up the idea?"

Josie took a deep breath.

"I was a senior and my sister was a sophomore in high school. Tasha was crossing the street when a car barreled through the intersection and hit her. The driver didn't even stop."

"Holy crap." Spencer's hand tightened around hers. "She's okay now, right?"

"She is. And there's not one day I don't send thanks to the universe for that. None of her injuries were life-threatening, but her leg had been broken in multiple places. There were several surgeries and then lots of physical therapy. It took years for her to recover." Josie's chest tightened as she was reminded how hard it had been for Tasha. "I kept thinking, if I'd been there with her, I could have pulled her out of the way. But I'd stayed late that day to work on a painting for the school art show."

"There's no way you could have known." Spencer dropped soft kisses on her shoulder and arm.

"I know that now. Back then I beat myself up. I'm her big sister. I'm supposed to protect her."

"You were a kid yourself, but I get it. I have younger sisters and did everything I could to take care of them while my parents were at work."

She nodded, surprised at her relief that he understood.

"My parents worked a lot, too. They used up their sick leave and vacation time taking care of Tasha. So they took turns taking unpaid leave. Then bills were piling up. I overheard them one night as they went over the numbers. So I did what I had to do. I gave them all my savings from my part-time job."

"The money you were saving for college?"

"It wasn't a lot, but it was enough for my parents to figure out a way to catch up on the bills." Josie inhaled and blew out a long breath. "I figured my art got Tasha into the mess, so I didn't deserve it. Sounds so stupid, doesn't it?"

"It's *not* stupid," he said emphatically. "You were brave."

She'd pushed the experience into a corner of her brain for so long that she'd never taken the time to truly work through her feelings. Yet here she was naked in bed with a fine man, spilling her fears and regrets. He'd helped her realize that she'd given up art school not just because she wanted to help her parents, but out of misplaced guilt.

She sniffed and blinked rapidly. "I'd never thought of young Josie as being brave. I just did what was necessary."

"You're a strong woman, but you don't have to be strong all the time. I can be strong for you when you need me."

Spencer rolled onto his side and wiped away her tears. Josie pulled him down for a deep kiss. For the strength he was giving her at this very moment and the promise of it later. She wasn't sure what the future would bring. But she knew she wanted him to be part of it.

"From now on, I need my coffee before I discuss the reasons behind my life choices," she joked weakly.

"I have something that could wake you up." His eyes darted to the sheet covering his hips.

"A triple espresso with cream and a shot of mocha?"

"Not exactly, but it'll get your blood pumping." He nibbled her ear. "Want a taste?"

Josie replied with a deep kiss. Her heart was already racing as her body remembered how he'd touched her last night.

A buzzing interrupted them.

"Don't answer it." Josie snaked her arm under the sheet and wrapped her hand around his cock. He was rock hard.

Spencer groaned. "It's my alarm. I'm supposed to take you somewhere meaningful today, remember?"

"You could show me something else right now." She tightened her hold around him.

"Fuck." His eyes rolled back in his head. He gritted his teeth. "Rain check?"

"You better keep that promise," she said, and pulled her arm out from under the covers.

"I will move the ends of the earth to keep that promise." He kissed her. "But if we want to interview my grandmother, we have to do it before lunch."

After their deep conversations, she wanted to meet the woman who inspired him to make his film. Josie had a feeling that she'd find the unusual for her photos.

CHAPTER 16

Are you ready to meet my grandmother and sister Nina?" His words came out too loud and overly excited. If it had been an email, there would have been at least three exclamation points at the end of the sentence. He was nervous. This was the first time he'd brought a woman home. As in, ever. There hadn't been anyone he'd felt serious enough to introduce to them.

"Ready. I trust you not to throw me in the deep end." Josie's eyes glittered with excitement. He was relieved that she didn't pick up on his nervousness.

"Thanks for letting me use your stuff for this." Spencer adjusted Josie's heavy equipment bag that he'd slung onto his shoulder after the taxi dropped them off.

"I'm glad it's getting used. I only packed bare bones for this trip. You should see my studio. I've got all sorts of fun gadgets."

"If this is bare bones, I don't want to lug around what you'd pack for a regular shoot." The bag was easily forty or fifty pounds.

"Wuss." She grinned and elbowed him. "Give it to me."

"Hell, no. I'm invested now." He nodded down the short pathway to the front door. "I don't have that far to go."

The bright yellow front door of his house was flung open. Nina waved and called out, "Are you going to stand there and make eyes at each other all day?"

Spencer opened his mouth to yell a response but thought better of it. He looked at Josie. "That's my baby sister Nina. She's very annoying."

"But you love her," Josie said with a laugh, waving at Nina before starting toward the door. "How many sisters do you have again?"

"Three. Before you ask, Nina is my favorite sister," Spencer admitted.

Josie, carrying only her camera and her purse, practically skipped to the door to introduce herself to his sister. After a brief exchange, she stepped inside.

"Need some help?" Nina called out when he was only a few feet from the front door.

"Now you offer to help. I'm already inside," he said as he entered. Spencer kicked his shoes off just inside the doorway.

"You didn't ask." His sister flipped her hair and winked, knowing how much her tone annoyed him. "Oooh, is she why you didn't come home last night?"

"Shut up." Spencer's cheeks grew warm.

"Oooh!" She clapped her hand over her mouth to keep quiet. "Look at you!"

"Can we not talk about that? You're my little sister." He lowered his voice. "Please don't embarrass me in front of her. Or Bà Bà."

"I'll try, but you know how wily Bà Bà gets."

He was counting on that for their interview.

"I prepped her like you told me to. She's excited that you're going to make her famous," Nina said, then snorted.

"I'm glad she has a lot of faith in me. Where did you send Josie?"

"I didn't send her anywhere. She's introducing herself to Bà Bà." Nina nodded in the direction of the living room.

"Dammit." Spencer pushed past her and set the bag down gently in the hallway. He'd wanted to be the one to introduce Josie to his grandmother. They were already chatting away. His grandmother was sitting in her beloved recliner, and Josie sat on the side of the couch nearest her.

"Bà Ngoại, you've met Josie."

"Your girlfriend is very nice," Bà Bà said in Vietnamese. "And very pretty."

"She's just a friend. Who's a girl," he stammered in Vietnamese, heat flushing his cheeks. Yes, they'd gotten to know each other extremely well last night, but that didn't mean they were dating. He explained in English, "She's helping me out with the filming."

"Come give your bà a kiss," she said in English, ignoring his protest. "Be a good grandson."

He did as instructed. Josie chuckled from behind him.

"Your Bà Bà is funny."

His eyes widened in surprise. Bà Bà was what they called her because when Spencer was little he couldn't pronounce *ngoại* properly. Everyone thought it was cute and the shortened version stuck.

"She told me to call her that instead of Mrs. Nguyen."

"There are so many Mrs. Nguyens, but I'm the only Bà Bà around here," his grandmother said.

"I bet you're the best Bà Bà in the neighborhood," Josie replied.

Oh, Josie was good. Either his grandmother was completely charmed by her, or Bà Bà had an ulterior motive. He wouldn't be surprised if it were both. His grandmother was always up to something.

"It's true," he said, and sat on the couch next to Josie. "Bà Bà was the unofficial candy shop in the neighborhood. She set Costco-sized bowls of candy in the window and sold huge candy bars for a buck each. Her most popular product was red Kool-Aid frozen in paper Dixie cups. Kids knocked on the door all day long during the summer for them."

"You were quite the entrepreneur," Josie said. "I have my own business, too." She uncrossed her legs and relaxed into the couch. The movement caused Spencer to slide closer to her. How was it that her nearness always intoxicated him? Even after spending forty minutes in the taxi together.

"You should always have your own way to make money. Never rely on a man," his grandmother said matter-of-factly.

"Hey!" Spencer protested. He deserved credit for contributing to his family.

"Okay, except for our family, especially Spencer, who took care of us after the oil spill. That's why he's been gone for so long." Bà Bà gave him a stern look, making him feel like a little boy again. "But I'm glad he's home."

Josie must have sensed the mood shift between them, because she said, "Are you excited that he's making a film about the krewe? Spencer asked me to help, since I have experience taking pictures of people." He was grateful she'd steered the conversation away from his return to New Orleans.

"Why didn't you tell me about this yesterday?" Bà Bà asked him. "I could have cleaned the house."

"It's already clean," Spencer said. The living room was as spotless as it had been the day before. In fact, it looked even cleaner. "You didn't vacuum, did you?"

"Nina did. What's the point of having grandkids if they don't do things for you?"

"You took care of us, and now we're taking care of you, Bà Bà," said Nina in a sweet voice. "We love you."

"Where are we going to film?" Bà Bà asked him. Before Spencer could answer, his grandmother turned to Josie. "Do you know how to do makeup? My friend says you need good makeup for the camera because it adds fifty pounds. My friend said I shouldn't be shiny. Help an old lady out of this chair so we can go to my room."

"Anything for you, Bà Bà," Josie quickly replied. She jumped up and gave Bà Bà her arm to pull herself out of the recliner. The two of them walked out, leaving him with his mouth hanging open. What the hell? Josie was just as smitten with his grandmother as Bà Bà was with Josie. He had no idea how it had even happened so quickly.

"Bà Bà criticizes all my friends," Nina said. "I can't believe she won Bà Bà over in less than five minutes." Nina carried the equipment bag as if it were a tiny purse and placed it next to Spencer's feet. When had she started working out?

"Me neither," he said. It had to be a record. Growing up, their grandmother was critical of all their friends. She'd constantly reminded them that the people they spent time with reflected well or badly on them.

"You like her. Josie."

"No shit, Sherlock." There was no reason to lie to his sister about it. It was probably all over his face. "But she's only here for a few more days before she goes back to DC."

"You can always search for another job there."

"I'm working on this film for Bà Bà. For me." Spencer looked his sister in the eye. "I don't want to find a job, because documenting our family history is important."

After his talk with Josie last night, Spencer was done trying to be what his family expected him to be. He'd turned a new leaf. This week he would do what he wanted. Not what someone expected of him.

"Anh hai finally stands up for what he really wants." Nina smacked his shoulder. "About time, Spencer!"

"Ow!" He rubbed his arm. "That really hurt."

Nina wrapped him in a big bear hug. After his shock wore off, he hugged her in return.

"I'm glad you finally got your head out of your ass. I miss my favorite brother," Nina said after she finally let him go.

"Very funny. I'm your only brother." But Spencer smiled anyway. Knowing Nina supported him lifted some weight off his shoulders.

"You're still working my shifts at the co-op, right? You promised."

"Actually, I bet Josie would like to go there." He'd only been a couple of times. It was still strange to think of his parents as full-time farmers. They'd always had a small garden in the backyard to grow Vietnamese vegetables. It was more out of necessity, since they couldn't run to the corner grocery store to pick up bitter melon or fresh culantro.

"Good, I'm supposed go tomorrow so Bà Bà can rest."

He couldn't believe he was making plans in advance. Josie was already changing him. He just had to nail this interview with his grandmother to prove to Josie she'd made the right decision by collaborating with him.

CHAPTER 17

"That was nice of you to help her with her makeup," Spencer said softly as Josie helped him set up her camera and tripod. "She likes you a lot. She hardly ever invites anyone into her room. Not even us."

"Your grandmother is adorable," Josie whispered.

Bà Bà had used makeup as a ruse to grill her, even asking for her exact birth date down to the hour. Josie was surprised she hadn't asked for her Social Security number. They did manage to borrow some powder from Nina. Josie wasn't an expert, but she'd picked up a few makeup tips from her boudoir sessions. After applying some powder and a little blush, she'd left his grandmother in her room to change.

"Thanks again for letting me use your equipment," Spencer said, running his hand through his hair as his lips turned up into a grin.

"As long as I can take some photos of your grandmother after you interview her." Josie patted her back pocket. "I'll also take some shots on my phone while you two are talking."

"She won't mind. That's part of our plan, right?"

Our plan. Josie liked the sound of having shared plans with him.

When she'd challenged him to show her something meaningful, she thought maybe a childhood hangout. She hadn't expected it to be a some*one*, and definitely not his grandmother.

"It's my turn to help out at my parents' co-op farm tomorrow. I thought you'd want to join me?" he said.

Josie hesitated. Today was supposed to be a trial run. He'd brought her to his home, but she still didn't know what their exhibition proposal would look like. If they couldn't figure that out by the end of today, she'd rather focus purely on her list and her portfolio.

His grandmother's door opened, saving her from responding. Everyone turned their attention to the hallway.

"Bà Bà, you look beautiful!" Josie exclaimed.

Both Pham siblings echoed Josie's sentiment. His grandmother was dressed in a dark blue áo dài, a long traditional dress with high side slits worn with loose pants. It looked similar to the ones Josie had seen Zoe and her family wear during Lunar New Year celebrations.

"If you're making a movie about your grandfather, I have to look my best." Bà Bà beamed. "Now let's get started before my naptime."

Everyone laughed and moved to their positions. His grandmother settled on her recliner while Spencer sat on the couch next to her. He and Nina had moved it so that they could fit both their grandmother and Spencer in the frame. To their left was a large sliding glass door that let in the afternoon sunlight.

Josie had set up a studio light to knock out some shadows on the right side. It was the best she could do with the equipment she'd brought with her.

"Whenever you're ready, I'll press record. Bà Bà, try to look at the camera like we talked about," Josie said. She hadn't planned to play director. It came naturally after years at her studio.

"Bà Bà." Spencer turned to his grandmother and spoke to her in Vietnamese. She reached for his hand and replied to him. It sounded like a mix between instructions and a pep talk, though Josie wasn't sure who was giving whom the pep talk.

That moment between them was so tender and sweet. Josie hit the record button so as not to miss it. She pulled her phone from her jeans back pocket and tried to be as unobtrusive as possible. The contrast between his grandmother's pale, thin, delicate hands on top of Spencer's thick, sturdy fingers—the same ones that had pleasured her so well last night—and tanned hand was too striking not to photograph.

"You can start now," Spencer called out after they finished their conversation. Josie nodded and mimed starting her camera.

"Bà Bà, tell me why you and Ông ngoại loved Mardi Gras so much." Spencer squeezed her hand. "I know this story, but I want you to tell it in your own words."

Bà Bà looked at the camera. A smile settled on her face, as if she were reliving the moment.

"When we first came here, we had very little money. Everything went to rent, clothes, and food for your mother and uncle. Our first winter was so cold." She shivered. "We have no winters in our village back in Vietnam, you know. We didn't have the right clothes. Thank goodness the church that sponsored us gave us sweaters and coats. Your mom hated wearing other people's old clothes, but at least they kept us warm."

"That's why she always insisted on buying me new clothes instead of wearing hand-me-downs from the church," said Spencer.

"People had been talking about Mardi Gras for weeks. Someone from the church gave us a king cake." Bà Bà made a disgusted face. "Too sweet—blech. But they kept talking about these parades where strangers threw prizes at you. Some of them even threw food! Can you imagine having so much money you throw food at people on the street?"

They all chuckled. It did seem strange if you didn't know anything about Mardi Gras.

"Your ông and I took your mom and uncle to a parade. It was very loud, but I liked watching the different, uh"—his grandmother paused and looked at Spencer—"I can't remember the English word. The moving cars in the parade."

"Floats," Spencer supplied.

"Yes, the floats. They were all decorated in funny ways, and the people on them were wearing these flashy clothes. I'd never seen people so happy to give away brand-new necklaces and cups—even food!" She threw her hands in the air. "Who in the world throws chips and Moon Pies off a moving car?"

Spencer's chest shook as he held in a chuckle. "Did you catch anything?"

"We caught everything! I made your ông hold out his shirt

like this." She held out the front of her áo dài to create a big pocket. "When people saw him trying to catch the food, they gave him some of theirs, too. Your mom and uncle caught beads and cups. They ate so many Moon Pies that they had stomachaches later."

"What was it about that parade that made Ông ngoại want to start a krewe?" Spencer asked.

It was obvious to Josie that Spencer and his grandmother were close. He was able to guide their conversation smoothly without making it feel overly rehearsed. Both of them were naturals on camera. Josie had a feeling his grandmother was always this lively during conversations whether the camera was on her or not.

"The next day, Ông woke up and said he wanted to be rich enough to give away things that made people happy. But not just Moon Pies and chips. He wanted to celebrate all things Vietnamese *and* American, because he was an American now. At least in his heart." Bà Bà sniffled. "Con, I miss him every day."

"I know, Bà Bà. I miss him, too." Spencer patted her hand.

Josie spotted a box of tissues on the coffee table. Making sure she was out of frame, she pushed it closer to Spencer. He immediately caught on and offered his grandmother a tissue. Bà Bà grabbed one and dabbed her eyes with it.

"He asked around, but everyone said that you needed to know someone and pay a lot of money to join. Many of them didn't want our people to be in their krewe." She wrinkled her face in disgust. "But that didn't stop him. That made him want it even more."

"You've never told me about that before. Did he actually ask to join any of the other ones?" Spencer asked.

"I don't remember. If he did, he didn't tell me. But our people never give up. We work hard. So he asked people at church to help. So many people said yes and donated bags of shrimp chips." Bà Bà threw her hands in the air and laughed.

For the next half hour, they relived her early days as an immigrant in a brand-new world. Spencer and his sister were captivated by their grandmother. Spencer was truly in his element. His body language was relaxed, and his face radiated love for his grandmother. He asked questions that were encouraging nudges, digging out the nuances of her experiences.

A red flash caught Josie's eye. Her camera was almost out of juice. She was sad to stop them, but she signaled Spencer so he could wrap up the conversation.

"We got lots of great footage! Bà Bà, you looked great on camera," Josie said, and quickly showed her the camera while it still had power. Bà Bà nodded with approval.

Seeing Spencer with his grandmother, Josie felt a pang in her chest. She suddenly missed her family. Back in DC, she texted her mom every day. Tasha worked at her studio, so they often had lunch together. It was so easy to forget about her daily routine when she was around Spencer. His go-with-the-flow energy was exhilarating once she allowed herself to trust in his process. This was exactly the energy she needed to get into Stevens.

"Spencer, I'm officially in. I'll do the collab with you for the exhibition."

"You are? Yes!" He picked her up in a hug and spun her around the room. "We're going to have so much fun together."

Josie couldn't help but laugh. Whatever happened this week, she vowed to live in the moment and enjoy herself.

CHAPTER 18

"Spencer, if you're doing this movie," his grandmother said after he'd finished celebrating Josie's decision, "then why are you getting a job?"

"I, uh, the girls, they told me I needed to find one." Spencer tried to find Nina so she could explain how they'd threatened him—but his sister had disappeared. In fact, he hadn't seen her in the last hour. Where had she gone?

"Just because I'm old doesn't mean I don't hear everything that happens in this house." His grandmother pursed her lips and stared him down.

"You're not that old—"

"You let those girls bully you too much. You spoil them."

He knew better than to keep secrets from Bà Bà. She saw through his lies and omissions every time. He felt like he was ten years old again, morphing into the quiet kid who never wanted to disappoint his grandmother.

"Do not listen to them. I want you to make this movie." She patted his hand. "If you need money for it, come to me. I'll give it to you."

Spencer's jaw dropped. Where did she even— How much? His brain short-circuited.

"You don't need to do that," he finally said. "I still have some savings."

"You will run out of money fast, because you sent most of it home." Bà Bà spoke in rapid-fire Vietnamese. As worried as she was, he knew she didn't want to air all their family drama in front of a stranger. Even if she had taken to Josie. "You take care of everyone, but not yourself. That's why you ate so much yesterday morning. You did not eat enough the night before. How are you supposed to find a girlfriend if you are so skinny?"

"Are you mad at me?" he asked. He spoke in Vietnamese, hoping she'd go easier on him if he used his mother tongue. He almost added that Josie liked him, but didn't think it was the right time to tell her.

"How can I be mad at my grandson?" she said. She had switched to English, and he let out a quick breath. That meant she wasn't very angry with him. "You should tell your parents about this film when they get back. They will be proud of you."

He wasn't too sure about his parents, but he nodded.

"This is for you," Bà Bà said. She pulled out a red envelope from her pants pocket. They were the same ones she would tuck crisp twenties into and hand out every Tết.

"Bà Bà, I can't take your money. You're not even working."

She clicked her tongue in disapproval before opening his hand and placing the envelope into his palm. "You've missed many family gatherings while you were away, including Tết. I've been saving these lì xì for you."

"Cảm ơn, Bà Bà." Spencer thanked her, knowing better than to argue more. Even though he had come home to visit as often as possible, he'd missed many Lunar New Year celebrations.

Maybe it was his red envelope money or maybe she needed an excuse to give him money without embarrassing him in front of Josie. He tucked the envelope into his pocket, relieved to have some cash.

"Now, who's ready for lunch?" Bà Bà said, and clapped her hands. "Josie, do you like Vietnamese po' boys?"

"Is that like a bánh mì?" Josie asked. "If so, I love Vietnamese food!"

"You know what bánh mì is? Now I know why Spencer likes you!" His grandmother winked at him. "She even says it the right way."

"I'm very familiar with Vietnamese food back in DC." Josie laughed and grabbed Bà Bà's arm as they walked to the kitchen together. He wasn't sure how his not-girlfriend and his grandmother became best friends, but seeing them side by side made his heart do a little somersault.

He found Nina in the kitchen with them. She immediately gave him the job of assembling the sandwiches while Bà Bà and Josie sat at the table. Nina served them each a steaming mug of jasmine tea.

"Where were you?" he hissed at his sister. "Bà Bà knows y'all are making me find a job."

"After Bà Bà met your Josie, she stuffed some cash in my hand and made me go to Dong Phuong to pick up bánh mì fixings," she whispered before sliding the baguettes into their old toaster oven. "Only the best for your girlfriend."

"She's not my—" Spencer threw his hands up in the air. "I give up."

"For a not-girlfriend, you sure are giving her some puppy dog eyes," Nina teased.

"Shut up!" Spencer grabbed the packages from Nina and unwrapped the pickled vegetables. She chuckled, pleased at how easily she got him riled up.

He and Nina fell into an easy rhythm as they assembled lunch. She spread mayo on one side and chicken liver pâté on the other side of the baguette before passing it down to him. He layered the pâté side with sliced chả quế, a cinnamon-infused steamed ham, then topped it with cucumbers, cilantro, and pickled carrots and daikon.

Standing at the kitchen counter elbow to elbow with his sister brought back memories of Tết prep. Their mom covered the dining table with newspaper and gave each Pham kid a task. His sisters had the easiest job: pulling the rice paper wrappers apart and stacking them onto a separate plate. He'd graduated from that tedious job to rolling the egg rolls themselves. He'd never quite figured out the right amount of the pork-and-shrimp filling for his rolls. They weren't as pretty as the ones his mother rolled, but they tasted damned good.

"Ai-ya, don't forget the Maggi!" Nina elbowed him.

"How could I forget?" He bypassed the small plastic cup the bakery had prepared and grabbed their huge bottle from the cabinet. No bánh mì was complete without the sauce's umami flavor.

After he added the finishing touches to the sandwiches, Spencer inched closer to the small table so he could eavesdrop on the two women. He wanted to make sure Bà Bà wasn't saying anything that could embarrass him. Like some long-forgotten story from his childhood. Their conversation surprised him.

"Bà Bà, did you and your husband ever ask the Black krewes about joining?" Josie asked. "I don't know a lot about them, but I did see there were some during my research."

"We didn't know there were any until much later. We only saw white people in that first parade. Ông and I didn't speak a lot of English, so we only socialized with the people at our Vietnamese church. We didn't meet a lot of people like you until later." Bà Bà touched Josie's arm to indicate her skin color.

"Oh." Josie leaned back in her chair.

"No one has asked me that before, but I'm glad you did." His grandmother sighed. "When we came here, we wanted to prove that we deserved to be here. So we worked hard, tried to be like Americans."

"You mean the white ones."

"Yes. Anyone could see that mỹ trắng treated people with your skin color very differently. We didn't want to be treated differently. I don't know the right English words." She turned to Spencer. "Can you explain?"

His grandmother spoke in Vietnamese so quickly, he barely caught all of it. What he did grasp explained some things he'd seen as a kid. Behind him, he heard Nina's sharp inhale, mirroring Spencer's surprise.

"We've never talked about this before, Bà Bà," Spencer said. He was caught off guard. When he was younger, he'd hear other Viet folks say racist things about Black people. But never his grandparents or parents. They actually tried to change people's minds.

"Spencer, can you translate, please?" Josie asked, eyebrows furrowed. She looked back and forth between them.

"She said that after she and my grandfather became friends with some of the Black fishermen, they realized how wrong they'd been. No matter how hard they tried to be what was expected of them, the white folks would never consider Vietnamese people as equals.

"Their new friends treated them as equals, even when they barely spoke English. Black fishermen helped them grow their business and vice versa. Bà Bà and Ông raised our parents to treat everyone with respect. Even though there're still Viet people here who don't believe the same thing she—we—do." Spencer looked at his grandmother, who nodded at his attempt to explain her words.

"She's right about how they raised us. Those fishermen and their families are close friends of ours. They were at many of our Tết parties and crawfish boils," Spencer added.

The kitchen was quiet as they waited for Josie's response. Even his sister stopped rustling bags and waxed paper.

"That's a lot to take in," Josie finally said. "Bà Bà, thank you for telling me. You raised good people."

Bà Bà had tears in her eyes. She patted Josie's hand.

"Can I meet these fishermen friends of yours?" Josie looked at his grandmother and then at Spencer. "I'd love to photograph them and hear their stories, too."

"They are coming to my old lady birthday party," Bà Bà said. "It's also the church's Tết festival." She smiled. "You should come and meet them."

"That's three weeks away, and Josie is only in town for a few more days," Spencer put in, hating the reminder that their time together was so short. "This year the church pushed back the festival to coincide with Bà Bà's centennial."

"Maybe you can come back? For this old lady?"

"Um . . ." Panic crossed Josie's face. From their brief time together, Spencer knew she wouldn't be able to commit to a plan like that until she'd checked her calendar and lists. Time to change the subject.

"Hey, who's hungry?" Spencer slid past Nina with the platter of bánh mì she'd arranged. He set it on the table and sat next to Josie. "How about we let Josie think about the party. Okay, Bà Bà?"

"Wow, this is a lot of food," Josie said. "Not that I'm complaining." She grabbed a sandwich and placed it on her plate. She whispered a quick thanks to Spencer.

His observant grandmother didn't miss the exchange between Spencer and Josie, but she didn't bring it up again. The lunch conversation became much lighter when Bà Bà asked how the two of them met. Spencer volunteered to recount the story, laughing his way through it while Josie shook her head at his dramatic retelling.

"You continue to amaze me," Spencer told Josie after his grandmother had gone to her room for a nap. "Will you come on camera with me to interview everyone else?"

"What? No!" She shook her head. "I prefer to be behind the camera."

Josie was adorable when she was flustered.

"Josie, you charmed my grandmother in less than five minutes. Then you proceeded to get her to speak more candidly about race and our family friends than I've ever heard. You're asking questions that I wouldn't have dared to ask my elders. I don't know if she would have told me all of that. But she opened up to you." Great, now he was babbling.

She bit her lip, considering his proposal.

"Please?" Spencer begged as he put his hands together in prayer.

"I know I agreed to collaborate with you, but being on camera is different. I'll think about it."

"I knew you'd say yes!" He grabbed her hand. For Josie, thinking about something meant she was close to saying yes.

"I did not—"

Spencer sealed the deal with a kiss. Josie relaxed into his touch and deepened the kiss. Her lips and tongue were assertive, as if to remind him that she preferred to be in charge. He didn't mind if she took the lead as long as it got him where he wanted to go.

Nina cleared her throat. "Get a room!" she said. "I'm still here."

They broke apart and laughed. Spencer had almost forgotten that his sister was sitting across from them.

"Ha ha, very funny," Spencer said sarcastically. "I promised I'd show Josie around town and I'll be out pretty late. Is it okay if you stay with Bà Bà for the next few days?"

"Seeing as you two are freaking adorable and Bà Bà has approved of your film, I won't stand in your way." Nina didn't seem too upset. "But don't forget you're going out to the co-op tomorrow to check on our parents' share."

"I remember." He wouldn't go back on his promise, but it meant spending half a day away from Josie.

"And there'll be other great-aunties and great-uncles you can interview, too," Nina added. She turned to Josie. "I bet they'd love to show off their part of the garden and pose for photos."

"Your grandmother was such a great storyteller, I forgot to take photos. I bet the gardens will be a fantastic location for a shoot," said Josie.

"If you want to catch people to interview, you should get there at six A.M.," Nina said with a smirk.

Spencer groaned. He knew she was leaving out something important. But it was too late to take back his promise to help. He hadn't gotten up that early since he'd lost his job.

"It's a plan, then." He couldn't believe those words came out of his mouth.

Even though his future was unknown, in this moment everything felt right in the world. Nina and his grandmother fully supported his project, and Josie—well, with Josie by his side, he could accomplish anything.

CHAPTER 19

"Did you go into the city often?" Josie asked as they waited for their rideshare. Though she'd only spent a few hours with Spencer and his family, she'd gotten a deep look into his childhood here. It'd been so different from hers. "This area feels like its own bubble."

"I suppose Versailles is an enclave of sorts. Growing up, it had everything we needed. It was easier to stay close, since my grandparents didn't speak English when they arrived. They went to a Vietnamese church, shopped at Vietnamese markets, and didn't have to go far to spend time with their Vietnamese friends. As you learned, their jobs took them out of the neighborhood and they soon made friends from other races and cultures."

"Like the other fishermen." She thought about what his grandmother had told them.

"Josie, I'm not proud that so many Viet people here—or in the DMV, as you know—will judge you solely by the color of your skin. I wish that weren't true, but I hope the voices and actions like my family's are louder than the racist ones. I do my best to drown them out the same way when folks mock my 'slanted' eyes and 'yellow' skin." He used air quotes around the words *slanted* and *yellow*.

She didn't know why it mattered so much to her that Spencer's family accepted her for who she was. It wasn't as if this thing between them would be anything but a fling. He'd already said he had no plans to return to DC anytime soon. She'd built a thriving business there and couldn't imagine life without her sister or friends.

Spencer touched her cheek. "I'm not tied to the community the same way my grandparents were back then. If my people can't accept that we're friends, fuck 'em. My family raised me to judge people by their character, not the color of their skin. And it's obvious that Bà Bà thinks you're a wonderful person. She's a tough critic."

"Thank you for saying that." Josie nodded in appreciation.

Bà Bà exuded a lively energy Josie hadn't expected from someone who was almost a hundred years old. Spencer was right. His grandmother welcomed her the moment they laid eyes on each other.

Josie was surprised how important it was to know where his family stood about her community. This was supposed to be a vacation. She should be focusing on doing things that made her happy. Like spending the rest of her time here with him. She hoped some of it naked in bed.

"Do you mind if we make a stop at the French Quarter before we head back to your place?" Spencer asked as their rideshare pulled up.

"Where are we going?"

"It's a surprise." He gave her a mischievous grin. "I promise it's not a tourist trap. Jimmy told me about it."

"Fine. We can't stay out too late, though, because we promised your sister we'd be at the co-op at six in the morning." Despite the early wake-up time, she was looking forward to his surprise. He hadn't let her down so far. Well, except for the Carousel Bar, but that was because he'd been trying too hard to impress her.

"Ugh, don't remind me. However, I love that you're always planning ahead."

"It's my superpower. Which I'm glad you finally appreciate."

"I'm glad you said yes, because that's the address I put into the rideshare app." He grunted as he picked up her equipment bag.

"If you want to be a filmmaker, you better get used to hauling around heavy equipment," she teased.

"You didn't complain about my delicate touch last night," he whispered into her ear.

His breath and the memory sent shivers down her spine.

"I'll complain if you keep me out too late for me to take advantage of you tonight." She lowered her voice and added, "I've been thinking all day about you naked in my bed."

Spencer groaned. "Maybe we should scrap the surprise and go straight back to your place."

"Oh, no. I'm committed now." She took her bag from him and slung it over her shoulder. "Let's go."

THE CAR DROPPED them off on Royal Street. The post-lunch lull meant the streets weren't busy. The historic buildings with the classic wrought iron balconies were not dissimilar from the ones she'd seen in the French Quarter. She pulled out her camera and quickly took some shots to contrast the evening photos from the other night.

"Spencer, what are we doing here?" She spotted several bars around them. "I'm not sure I'm up for hanging out at a bar right now."

"Do you trust me?" His face was bursting with excitement, as if he were a kid waiting for Christmas morning.

Did she trust him? His tone had been light, but Josie took his question at more than face value. She wanted to trust him. Her heart told her he was a good man. Her brain had a different story. It wanted to make a list of pros and cons and fact-check all the things she knew and had yet to learn about him. The practical side of Josie didn't want to believe someone could earn her trust when she had the barest of information.

"Let's say I'm optimistic." She kept her tone airy, just as his was. "Your track record has been acceptable."

"Ouch, that sounds like an Asian F." Spencer placed his hands on his heart dramatically.

Josie bit back a laugh. "Any day now, Spencer."

"We're already here." He spread his arms out to present a store on the corner they'd been standing on. "I present to you Papier Plume."

When she didn't respond, he pointed to a wooden sign hanging above the shop door. Underneath the engraved name were a feather quill and an inkpot. Her mouth dropped open.

"A stationery store! That's very thoughtful of you."

"Not just any stationery store." Spencer grabbed her hand and pulled her to the display window.

"Are those fountain pens? And inks? You get an A plus." Josie's cheeks ached from smiling, she was so excited. She didn't care if he'd planned it all along or thought of it at the last minute. He'd done this just for her.

"Yes! They make their own New Orleans–themed inks here." He winked. "I'm glad I did my homework. Oh, and there's a bunch of art galleries on this block and the next. We can check out some local artists if you'd like. As a thank-you for going all the way out to Versailles to interview my grandmother."

Josie held his face with both hands and planted a big kiss on his lips. He pulled her tight against him and deepened their kiss. Yes, she did trust him. He'd been listening to everything she said since that unlucky parade.

She'd been on the verge of burnout when she arrived in New Orleans. Maybe he didn't know exactly what she needed to find her creativity again, but he was trying so hard to help someone who was basically a stranger to him.

"Okay, first I need a new notebook," she said, and clapped her hands. A brand-new notebook offered so many possibilities. Fresh pages for her lists! Blank pages waiting patiently for her to outline and plan her goals.

"You're so cute with your analog ways."

"Have you ever written with a fountain pen so smooth it glides across the page like Surya Bonaly across the ice?"

"I'm sorry, who?"

"Only the greatest Black figure skater of all time!" Josie put her hands on her hips. "My mom introduced me to her. She's a French Olympian, who was so powerful yet graceful on the ice."

"You know, you're adorable when you're talking about sports. I learn something new about you every hour. But the only sport I care about is football. Specifically the Saints."

Josie opened her mouth to reply, but he shushed her with his finger.

"For your safety, do not spout anything bad about our city's beloved football team." He leaned in and mock whispered, "We all know that they don't have the best record, but this city likes to root for the underdogs."

"No argument here. I have no desire to discuss the merits of sports ball teams."

"Did you just say 'sports ball'?" he sputtered.

"Shhh, you don't want to upset the locals." She pushed the door open and dragged him inside. The store was bright and airy for such a small space. Every shelf was filled with notebooks, papers, art prints, wax seals, and, of course, fountain pens and inks. A small squeal escaped her lips. "Sorry. I'm so excited."

"Go, explore. I'll be fine." He squeezed her hand and nudged her toward the bottles of ink.

She didn't need any more encouragement to explore the shop. Josie skimmed shelves on her left and her right, unsure where to start until she spotted a display in the middle of the store. The small table held tiny ink bottles sealed with red wax. Apparently, these were the store's exclusive collection inspired by the city. *How charming!*

Spencer was thoughtful, if a little sneaky, to bring her here. How was it that he knew what surprises would bring her joy without overwhelming her? Maybe spending this week with him would offer her clarity on what she wanted to do next with her life.

The last few days with Spencer had proven that she needed to trust her intuition more often. He'd led her on adventures that had awoken the spark she'd been missing for so long. A fire she'd lost months ago but couldn't put into words until she set foot in that lonely apartment.

Whether they stayed in touch after this or not, Spencer had irrevocably changed her life. Even if he hadn't meant to. He'd shown her that there were more possibilities if she'd look past her lists. That going down a previously unseen path could lead to something new and exciting. Like meeting his grandmother and now being here.

Josie vowed to enjoy herself with Spencer for the rest of the week, both exploring the city and in bed.

CHAPTER 20

After Josie explored every inch of the stationery shop, they'd returned to the apartment to work on their application. Using her new pen, she written a *Win a Spot in the Exhibition* list of what had to be done in order for her and Spencer to work together.

At the top of the list was finding where her work and his project overlapped. Like a Josie-Spencer Venn diagram. In the past, she'd subconsciously created a theme for her photo walks. She'd taken hundreds of photos in the past three days. Hopefully a theme would reveal itself.

After downloading the photos off her memory card, she scrolled backward. Bà Bà had allowed her to take photos when they were in her room. Josie had captured her laying out different outfits and applying makeup. His grandmother had a quiet strength in her eyes. She'd lived through a war and several natural and man-made disasters, yet she still found so much joy in her life.

Josie had only one major hardship in her life—Tasha's accident and giving up art school. Her problems paled in comparison. How had Bà Bà managed to be so relaxed, so seemingly carefree, while Josie worried and planned for any possible disaster before taking action?

These pictures were trying to tell her something. What were the unusual in these photos? The everyday? How did Spencer's grandmother fit into the images from yesterday and the day before? Josie's stomach turned. What if there wasn't something connecting these photos? Putting a collection together for her boudoir clients was easy because there was only one subject. Maybe she didn't have what it took to get into a gallery.

A loud rustling distracted her. Across the breakfast counter from her, Spencer balled up the wrappers from the leftover bánh mì his grandmother sent back with them. He cringed when he caught her eye.

"Sorry. I didn't mean to disturb you."

She pushed her laptop away to grab a soda from the fridge. "I don't think our collaboration will work."

"No, don't say that." He rushed behind her and rubbed her arms. "We haven't taken the time to brainstorm properly."

She relaxed back onto his chest, letting his body surround her. He wrapped his arms around her. Why did he have to feel so good next to her? She already knew it would be hard to walk away from him at the end of the week.

"Are you happy with your photos so far?" His kneaded her shoulders and neck. Slowly the tension eased away along with her frustration.

"If you mean the composition and light, yes." Josie closed her eyes as he worked out a knot in her right shoulder. "But they're not cohesive. Because I don't know what I want from New Orleans."

"You're trying to force it. Relax and trust your intuition."

"I hate it when people tell me to relax." She pulled away and turned to face him. "I'm not like you. I can't go into something without some sort of plan, even if I have to change it later."

"I don't want you to be like me. Sometimes I don't want to be like me." His squared his shoulders. "My grandmother is expecting something great, so if I have to plan a little in order to give her that, I will."

Did she hear him correctly? He wanted to make plans.

"Your grandmother means a lot to you, doesn't she?"

"She's experienced a lot of hardship. I know she's spry, but who knows how many years she has left. I want to make them good for her."

"Bà Bà is very inspiring." She pulled up the photos from their conversation in his grandmother's bedroom. "She talked about you and your sisters the whole time. She and your parents worked hard so you could have more choices than they did."

She'd been overthinking her burnout since she landed in New Orleans, yet couldn't come up with an ideal fix. Maybe she was trying too hard. Bà Bà and her husband hadn't had the luxury to overthink their decisions. They went to work because they had people to take care of.

Josie had Tasha and the rest of her employees to take care of. She was the name and face of her business. The studio would suffer if she couldn't get over whatever this creative block was. If she made the wrong decision, it could affect her staff's livelihood.

But if Josie only made choices that were good for her family and employees, what kind of life was that? She didn't want to take boudoir photos for the rest of her life. The admission shocked her.

This trip had given her a reason to step back and allow all the noise of DC to fall away. She couldn't give up now. No matter how different she and Spencer were, she had to go all in on this collaboration.

It was time she chose her desires over what she thought her family and business needed. If she didn't put her all into this competition and her portfolio, she would regret it.

"I have a plan for our brainstorming. Bring your laptop over here," she told him. Her body tingled with anticipation.

He grabbed it and set a stool next to hers. For this to be a true collaboration, they had to study and understand each other's work.

"I'll look at your footage from today. You scroll through my photos. Let's see if we can make a connection."

They each bent over the other's laptop, going through the other's work. Spencer took notes in his black notebook. Jose drew a column and pulled out different colored pens. She marked similarities in their work, letting them simmer in the back of her mind.

After an hour, the kitchen grew too dark to take notes. Josie's back was stiff, but her body was wired from all the ideas jumping around in her head.

Spencer handed her a beer. "I got nothing."

"I think I have something." She shivered as the cold beer went down her throat.

He gestured with his bottle for her to continue.

"The unsung heroes of New Orleans." She waved her hands in the air as if it were a marquee.

He covered his mouth.

"You don't like it?" Her heart sank.

"No!" He scratched his head. "Yours is so much better than mine. The best I had was the real people of New Orleans. You know, like that Facebook page."

"Spencer, that's someone else's project. We can't copy it for a competition." She drummed her fingers on the counter.

"That's why I didn't say it out loud earlier. Wait! What about the lesser-known history of New Orleans?" he suggested. "Like my family or the people of Versailles."

"Oooh, I like that!" She grabbed her pen before they forgot. "I've been thinking about that doorman at Hotel Monteleone. He's gotta know some cool stuff that happened there."

When it came down to it, she still loved photographing people. She tapped her foot against her stool. This would be the opposite of her mentor's philosophy.

"We can seek the everyday and capture the unusual," Josie almost shouted.

"You're going too fast. The gears in your head are smoking," Spencer said. He must have sensed her frenetic energy, because he tapped his beer bottle against the side of the counter.

She explained her mentor's mantra. Then added, "What if we focused on the people who make this city run? The ones that everyone walks by without a thought. And find their unusual past."

"I get it! Like fishermen or the busker who serenaded us at Cafe du Monde."

"Exactly. The woman who's been making muffulettas and po' boys for thirty years. You record their story while I photograph them."

Finally, they had something. Josie felt it in her bones. They could make this work.

"What should we do next, now that we have a direction for our project?" He pointed at her notebook. "You already have a list, don't you?"

"I did, but now it's out of date." That one had been just for her, when she wasn't sure if they could do this. "But we can make a new one together."

"A new list? Wait!" he yelled as he ran out of the kitchen.

CHAPTER 21

Spencer dug in his backpack for a small package wrapped in brown paper and ran back into the kitchen. He sat next to her again and slid the package across the counter.

"When did you have time to buy me a gift without me noticing? We've been together all day."

"I have my ways." He waggled his eyebrows and grinned to hide his nervousness. "I wasn't going to give it to you until your last day here, but I think it's the right time. Open it."

Josie flipped the gift over and slid her finger under the tape. She carefully peeled the tape away and unfolded the paper, making sure not to rip it.

"Ah, so you're that kind of gift opener. Want some help?"

She swatted his hand away. "Shhh, I'm concentrating."

"You're sexy when you're so serious."

When she finished opening it, Josie gasped. "This notebook is gorgeous!"

He wasn't an expert on fancy notebooks, but this had felt luxurious in his hands. The dark gray linen cover was embossed with a stylized image resembling the lace ironwork that lined the balconies of the French Quarter. He hoped she'd think of New Orleans—and him—every time she wrote in it.

"The guy at the store assured me it's great with fountain pens."

"You've thought of everything."

She opened his gift and ran her fingers over the pages. Closing her eyes, she pulled the notebook to her nose and inhaled. Spencer tried to memorize her face at this moment. Happy, peaceful, and hopeful.

A woman as strong as Josie carried a lot on her shoulders. Her eyelids twitched. He swore he could see the thoughts zooming through her brain. What else was going on in that smart, beautiful head of hers?

Josie's eyes flew open. They sparkled. The energy around her had changed from somber to electric.

"What?" His body started to hum with excitement. Spencer hooked his ankle around the leg of his stool to keep steady. He couldn't believe that his on-the-fly suggestion about the lesser-known history of New Orleans had actually worked for Josie. "Did you figure something out?"

"It's time I did something different, too. I'm giving up my lists for the rest of the week."

His mouth dropped. "Are you sure? What about your thirty by thirty list?"

"Don't worry, it's still there as inspiration." She laughed and ran her fingers over the notebook pages again. "I plan on journaling my vacation, but I'm not going to let my lists dictate how I spend the rest of my time here."

"There's nothing wrong with your lists, Josie. I love how organized and prepared you are."

"Yes, there is. They make me focus on what's next. Instead of what's standing in front of me."

Josie's tongue darted out to lick her lips. Her fiery eyes bored into him.

"Or, rather, *who* is standing in front of me."

That damned pink tongue gave him an instant hard-on, as if he were still a teenager who couldn't control his hormones. This woman brought out alpha urges he didn't know he had. His fingers twitched, ready to throw her over his shoulder and take her to bed.

No, this moment was for Josie. She was exploring a new version of herself, at her own pace. He quelled the lust raging throughout his body as best he could. He would take things as slow or fast as she desired. They had the entire place to themselves.

"I'll be here all night. You only have to ask." Spencer opened his arms, offering more than his body to her. He'd give her his heart if she asked for it. The revelation rocked him, and he swayed on his stool.

Josie leaned into him, placing her hand on his chest. He allowed the heat of her palm to brand his heart as he silently vowed to do whatever it took to make her happy.

"Good. How about a private tour of that hot body of yours?" Josie's husky voice sent tingles down his neck.

CHAPTER 22

Josie was ready for a break from the project. They'd combined their pursuits into one exciting theme. Now she was ready for a different kind of excitement.

"Lucky for you, my schedule is wide open." He cringed. "I can't believe I said that."

"Then shut up and kiss me."

He kissed her deeply. Explored her mouth until the only thought in her head was getting naked. He reached down to grab the hem of his shirt, but Josie stopped him.

"Let me." Lust made her voice husky.

His hands froze at her command.

Josie reached for his shirt. The back of her hand grazed the front of his jeans. His hard cock twitched at her touch. He was turned on by the way she took charge.

She grabbed a fistful of his shirt and pulled him closer until he was on the edge of his stool. But she was the one who felt off-balance from the heady combination of taking charge and his masculine scent. His breathing was hot and heavy.

She closed her eyes as their lips met. Their kiss was slow and languid. As if neither of them wanted to go too fast. Because that meant whatever it was between them had to end. When they finally pulled away from each other, he had to grab the counter to keep from falling off his stool.

She slid off her stool to stand between his legs. His cock singed the outside of her thigh through their clothes. She tugged his shirt off and ran her hands over his bare chest. With one finger, she traced the lines of his muscles. She dropped light, feathery kisses across his pecs. He closed his eyes, and his head lolled back. A sigh escaped his lips.

Josie pulled his head down for another kiss. She couldn't get enough of his lips, his tongue—the carefree way he approached everything. She sighed, her nails digging into his back.

"Let me worship your body," he said before nipping at her neck.

"It's my turn." Josie pulled away, her chest heaving.

She raked her nails across his chest before surrounding his nipple with her hot mouth. Spencer grunted. Heat pooled between her legs.

"God, I want to bend you over this counter," he groaned.

"Mmm, that sounds fun. But not yet." Taking control electrified Josie. His pleasure was in her hands.

His eyes flew open. They were gleaming with a combination of surprise and lust. He gave himself over to her.

"I'm all yours."

He trusted her the same way she'd trusted him to give her pleasure last night.

Josie pulled off her V-neck top. She'd caught his not-so-covert glances at her breasts throughout the day. Now she rewarded him with a close-up of her breasts, this time accentuated by a pale pink lace bra.

"Stunning." He stood up, wrapped his arms around her waist, and pulled her against him. His skin was hot against hers. He dipped his head and kissed the exposed skin between her breasts.

She unhooked her bra and tossed it aside. They both watched it sail somewhere across the kitchen. Last night she'd been so careful with her undergarments. Tonight, all she cared about was that her hard nipples were rubbing against his chest.

"What do you want right now, Josie?" he growled, as he rubbed himself against her thigh. He peppered kisses down her chest until his lips found her nipples, taking them into his mouth.

"To get you naked," she gasped. She fumbled with his jeans. Together they made quick work of removing the rest of their clothes. "Finally, a view of your cock. It is as big as it felt this morning."

"Cheeky, aren't we?"

"Pick me up and take me to the table."

He reached around her knees and hoisted her up around his hips. She gasped. He wasn't wasting time. She nipped at his neck as he walked to the small dining table in the breakfast nook.

As soon as he sat her on the smooth wood, she grabbed his cock. It surged in her hand. He groaned as she worked his length, her fingers wrapped tight around him.

"Josie, I don't know how much longer I can—" The rest of his words turned into a deep moan as she rubbed her thumb over the head of his cock.

"Do you have a condom?" she asked.

"Yes," he gasped. She let go long enough to find his jeans and pull it out. He held his hand out for it, but she shook her head, eyes gleaming.

"Stand with your back to the table."

He did as he was told. She fell to her knees and reached for him again. She caressed the underside of his cock with her tongue. From root to tip and back down again. His knees started to buckle. He grabbed the edge of the table to keep himself upright.

"Josie, if you don't stop right now, you're not going to get what you want." His words came out in between gasps.

"Party pooper." She swiped her tongue across the tip of his cock before taking it into her mouth.

He hissed, pulling her away before their evening ended prematurely.

"Ooh, I'm in trouble now." She batted her eyelashes, not even a tiny bit contrite over how she was torturing him.

"Give it to me," he said, chuckling at her unexpected playfulness.

"Your wish is my command." She grabbed the base of his shaft and captured his hard-on with her lips.

"Fuck, Josie."

She gave him no choice but to take her mouth. She swirled her tongue around his shaft as she slid up and down. He set a hand on her shoulder but didn't stop her.

Finally, he hissed and pulled her up. He turned her body to

face the table. Grabbing the condom out of her hand, he opened it and slipped it on.

"Bend over and hold on. I'm going to make you come until you beg me to stop."

Josie shivered. Her pussy pulsed. Her thighs were damp with her arousal. She needed him as much as he wanted her.

"Challenge accepted," Josie panted. Her breasts and forehead pressed against the cool wooden table only made her body burn hotter.

"You're so beautiful right now. Your gorgeous round ass in the air is a precious gift."

She flinched at first when his hand landed on her butt. His caressed the curve of her bottom, muttering accolades of her body. Each swipe of his hand sent shivers through her. She closed her eyes and bathed herself in his adoration and touch.

All the thoughts about the future that had clouded her mind previously dissipated. Instead, she focused on the way her body shivered when he slipped his fingers between her lips. The sigh that escaped her mouth when he circled her clit. Her moans as he slipped a finger inside her throbbing pussy.

She clutched the edge of the table as he slipped in a second finger. Then a third. Her hips bucked when he pulled them out and slowly slid his fingers back into her. When his thumb landed on her clit, her inner muscles spasmed and she cried out as her body exploded in pleasure.

"Spencer, don't make me wait," she whispered after coming down from her orgasm. "I need you."

She meant more than physically. More than sex. She needed him by her side to remind her how exciting it was to follow your gut. To live in the moment. She wanted to be free from the structures she'd put up around herself. They were barriers she'd constructed to feel in control. With Spencer in her life, she didn't need a plan to feel safe. Only him.

He grabbed her hips and slid himself into her heat.

"So soft," he panted as her muscles twitched around him. "And tight. I want to fuck you hard. And watch you come again and again."

"Yes," she hissed.

Heat flooded her chest as he moved inside her. Pleasure built up in her body. Her skin grew tight and hot as her pleasure began to peak. He increased his pace until she could no longer contain herself. Josie cried out as her body exploded. His fingers dug into her hips as he thrust deep and hard. His body tensed as he too cried out. He was so beautiful when he came.

Her life had been all routine and duty until she met him. Spencer was meant to be in her life. Those beads brought them together on this path. They didn't always agree on how to do things, but it worked somehow. They complemented each other in so many ways. Both in how he fit inside her and how they were exploring their passions together.

Maybe he could be more than a vacation fling.

CHAPTER 23

Look who's here!" called a familiar voice from the entrance of Crescent City Co-op.

"Jimmy, not so loud," Spencer whispered. "It's too early to be so perky."

Jimmy lowered his voice to an acceptable level. "I didn't think you'd make it here so early."

"I promised Nina, so here I am. With fucking bells on," Spencer grumbled. "What are you doing here?"

"I'm helping out my parents at the co-op today. No thanks to you, I owe Nina twenty bucks." Jimmy didn't seem heartbroken about it.

"You bet on me?" Spencer said

"Good morning, I'm Josie." She handed Jimmy a to-go cup of coffee. "We made extra. Hope you like cream and sugar."

"Josie? From Cafe du Monde?" Jimmy's head swiveled as he looked from Spencer to Josie. Realization dawned on him, and he pushed past Spencer and escorted Josie through the metal gates. "Have you ever been to Crescent City Co-op?"

Josie shook her head, her camera swaying from its strap

around her neck. She uncapped the lens and started clicking. Jimmy turned around and waved at Spencer to catch up.

He glared at his friend as he strode over to join them. After last night, Spencer was irrationally possessive of Josie. He wanted to be the one to give her a tour, even if he wasn't as familiar with the farm as Jimmy.

"Hey, your grandmother is here! Bà Bà!" Josie waved. His grandmother gestured for Josie to join her. "If you don't mind, I want to take some more pictures of her."

Both men nodded, and she ran off into the field.

"How's your head?" Jimmy tilted Spencer's chin to check his injury.

"Barely notice it till I look in the mirror. At least my hair covers most of it." He hoped the bruises healed quickly so he could get his hair cut.

"I see things worked out after Cafe du Monde," Jimmy said, slapping Spencer on the shoulder. "You hook up with her already? Three days is impressive, man."

"Don't make it gross." Spencer gave him a friendly punch in the arm. "We're just having fun together."

A small smile quirked Spencer's lips. Last night had changed him completely. Not only were they creating art together, but they were making magic in bed, too.

"Oooh." Jimmy whistled. "You've got it bad."

"It's not that serious," Spencer lied. He was trying to keep his heart out of whatever this arrangement was, but his feelings for her had snuck up on him.

"Keep telling yourself that."

"Did Nina send you here to check on me?" Spencer asked.

"Yeah," Jimmy confessed. "Then your grandmother heard you were bringing Josie, so insisted on coming, too."

"My family is so nosy."

"They care about you."

Spencer scowled.

"And are nosy, too," Jimmy said, and laughed.

"Let's catch up with them before Bà Bà tells her any embarrassing childhood stories," Spencer said. He spotted the pair ahead. Their arms were intertwined and heads close together as if they'd known each other for years.

"Spencer, Nina told me about your project. I want to help."

"Nah, I'm good. Josie's helping me." Spencer didn't want to share his time with Josie. He wanted this to be their project. It was selfish, but he didn't care. Someone like Josie doesn't hit him with beads every day.

"Dude, chill and let me help you. Nina says you need a camera. You can borrow mine. It's in my car."

"No way! That's really nice of you, Jimmy," Spencer said. Then he narrowed his eyes. "You seem awful chummy with Nina these days."

"Nah, she hates my guts. Let me grab the camera for you. I even charged it!" His friend jogged to a row of cars in the gravel parking lot.

Spencer shielded his eyes from the morning sun and scanned the garden. Where had they gone? There were at least twelve people, Black and Asian, working in different areas. Most of them looked to be around his parents' age, though there were a few around his grandmother's age. He'd already lost sight of Josie and his grandmother, who must've walked behind the big trellis to the left.

"Here. It's old, but you can use it till you buy a better one," Jimmy said, and held out a black nylon bag.

Spencer accepted the bag. His stomach ached. His friends and family wanted him to succeed. What if the film sucked? He'd have wasted their time and money.

"You've only been here a couple of times, right?" Jimmy continued, oblivious to Spencer's growing doubt. "Why don't you practice filming by interviewing the people here today?"

"I don't know anyone here. When I came with my parents, they put me right to work."

"I can introduce you. It's not only us Viet who have survived and thrived here. I've learned a lot since I started volunteering. Come on, I'll show you around."

Winters in New Orleans were mild compared to the snowmageddons that hit DC. But they had their share of cold and dreary days in January. Maybe that's why Mardi Gras season started so early, after the first of the year. Residents needed revelry to keep their spirits up. While the grass and trees outside the cooperative's gate were mostly green with patches of brown, walking through the threshold felt like passing through a magical portal.

To either side of the dirt pathway were rows of raised beds of various greens and vegetables. Many of them he recognized from accompanying his mother and grandmother to weekend markets. There were also empty sections where the earth had been turned, awaiting warmer weather.

Spencer was surprised to see a mix of people working on the farm. Jimmy pointed out each person by name and gave him a brief background. He'd assumed they'd all be Vietnamese, but there were Black and Cambodian farmers, too.

"The co-op has a little over two acres of land, with twenty shares. Most shares are run by a family unit, like yours. Your parents and sisters help out. Each farmer has their own plot that they work on. Things are quiet right now since it's winter, but there're still herbs and some lettuce. We're hoping to build a greenhouse over there soon." Jimmy pointed to an empty area a few hundred yards from them.

"I had no idea you knew so much about farming." Spencer had only thought of his parents as a fisherman and a seamstress. The farmers around them had various tools and machines to help them till the soil. For some reason he'd expected everyone to be on their knees working the crops by hand.

"If you think back, our families knew tons about it. Remember how everyone in our neighborhood had backyard gardens because they couldn't find bitter melon or bean sprouts at the Piggly Wiggly?"

"We had one. And we ate well from it, too," Spencer said. He inhaled deeply. The earthy scents of the soil and bright fragrance of herbs transported him to late evenings with his grandparents. How they sent him out to the backyard to pick mint or cilantro to make the plate of fresh herbs that often accompanied their dinners. There was also that time he and his sisters "helped" their grandfather harvest his tomatoes. He was so angry when he discovered they'd picked the ripe *and* the green tomatoes.

"Let me introduce you to the other farmers."

"What about Josie and Bà Bà?" Spencer had completely lost track of the two women.

"Your woman can hold her own."

"She's not—"

"Yeah, I know. She's not your woman," Jimmy said in a sing-song tone.

Spencer threw his hands in the air in exasperation. Even if he did like the sound of Josie being his woman.

"You like her a lot," Jimmy said, then tilted his head. "Oh, you love her."

"Shhh!" Spencer spun around to reassure himself that no one had heard his friend. "I wouldn't call it love yet. She's really spectacular, Jimmy. Sharing the air with her inspires me to do something important with my life. I might have given up on this film without her."

"Really? I'm so happy for you, Spence." Jimmy broke out in a wide smile and clapped his hand on Spencer's shoulder. "I admire you for following your heart."

"You what?" Spencer blinked several times. "Come on, man, you're a freaking doctor and have time to give back to the community. You're like the number one Viet son around here."

"That's what I want everyone to see. It's easier that way." His friend shrugged and dug the toe of his sneaker into the dirt.

"You're brave to break away from what your parents wanted you to do."

"It doesn't feel that way. So what do you really want?" Spencer asked. He shouldn't be surprised, but Jimmy had always come off so confident about his life choices.

"Let's talk about it later. You're here to interview people." Jimmy stopped and pointed. "Hey, there's Josie and your grandmother!"

"We better catch up before Bà Bà proposes to Josie or something."

CHAPTER 24

O h, wow, what is all of this?" Surrounded by the lush green crops and trellises, Josie couldn't believe this was still New Orleans. The farm was a far cry from the historic French Quarter or her rental in the Marigny.

"Bà Bà, is it okay if I take pictures of you and the farm?" Josie held up her camera.

"Yes, take lots of pictures. Maybe you can make me famous?" Bà Bà laughed. "Or you can make my herbs famous? They're the best in New Orleans."

Josie followed her to a raised bed. One side had a profusion of tall bushes. The other half contained tall, slightly wispy stems with leaves she recognized as cilantro.

She crouched down to take some close-ups of the plants. Beyond them, she spotted Spencer's orange shirt next to Jimmy, who was in blue. A twist of her lens and the figures blurred as the camera focused on the rough, pebbly texture of the herbs.

The sun felt brighter today. The fragrance of the different herbs combined was intoxicating. Either that or she was still on a high from sex with Spencer last night. Probably all of the above.

She also felt a little off-balance as she'd left her regular leather notebook with all her lists at home. In its place was the new notebook Spencer had gifted her.

Bà Bà crouched down slowly next to her and picked some leaves that were not cilantro and handed them to her. She lifted a hand for Josie to help her back up.

"Rub between your fingers. Then smell."

Josie copied Bà Bà's movements. Almost immediately a bright and intense aroma made her nose tingle. She'd been right.

"Mint! Is there a lot of mint in Vietnamese foods?" She usually ordered the same dishes at Zoe's parents' restaurant and couldn't recall any mint being in them.

"Oh, yes. Salads, and you can put it in phở and other soups right before eating."

"Like a garnish?"

"Garnish is a strange idea. The kids who work here say people don't eat garnish. It's decoration only." Bà Bà scrunched up her face. "What a waste of perfectly good food!"

"You have a point there," Josie said with a laugh. "Bà Bà, you are very wise."

"Yes, because I am older and know more than you." She tapped a finger to her temple and nodded. "We farm mint because it grows like weeds and the local chefs buy a lot."

"So most of the crops are sold to restaurants?"

"Yes, and also farmers' markets. Okay, you take my picture

here." Bà Bà posed at the end of the row. She held a small bouquet of mint and cilantro. She wore very practical loose black pants, a floral tunic, and red slip-on sneakers. A cone-shaped straw hat that kept the sun off her face completed her ensemble.

Josie peered through her viewfinder. If she hadn't known better, Bà Bà and the backdrop of the garden could easily be in Vietnam and not in the Versailles community. It made the composition even more dynamic. She skimmed the horizon for something that screamed New Orleans. There! A water tower.

"How do I look?"

"Beautiful as always," Josie replied as she tilted Bà Bà's hat to see more of her face. "Can I scoot you over this way a little bit?"

She directed Spencer's grandmother a few steps to the left until the water tower peeked into the frame.

"Now, Bà Bà, I'm going to take several photos all at once. It's okay if you move your body but try to stay in that spot for now. Do what feels good."

Spencer's grandmother beamed. Josie had already witnessed Bà Bà's camera presence during the interview yesterday. Today was all her. Without her grandson prompting her, it took a few minutes for Bà Bà to warm up. At first, she stood very still and smiled timidly. Once she realized Josie wouldn't stop, Bà Bà made full use of her bouquet by raising it in the air, hiding her face behind it, and even posing with one leg kicked back in the air like a dancer.

"Bà Bà, you are a natural. Are you sure you don't have modeling experience?"

"No, no. Not model. But we took lots of pictures when we had the Mardi Gras krewe. Some were serious, but we took fun ones, too." She tossed the herb bouquet in the air.

Josie kept her finger on the shutter as the plants cascaded down around Bà Bà.

"Are you and Spencer dating?"

"What?" The camera slipped out of Josie's hands, and she sighed with relief when she touched the dark red strap keeping the camera around her neck.

"Are you dating my grandson? Or what do you kids call it now—banging?"

Josie's cheeks grew warm. She bit her lip. Did Spencer's grandmother just ask if they were *banging*? Josie opened her mouth to respond but nothing came out.

"Maybe both so I can have great-grandchildren?" Bà Bà winked.

Now her cheeks burned.

"We're seeing each other but only while I'm here," Josie said. "So don't get any ideas about babies, okay?" She didn't want to say the wrong thing and get his grandmother's hopes up. She and Spencer had barely discussed their plans for today, much less kids. She shuddered. She wasn't even sure she wanted any.

"He's a good man, but he works too much. I haven't seen him this happy in a very long time," Bà Bà continued, not deterred by Josie's response. "You two are well matched. I asked the fortune teller."

"Is that why you asked for my birth date?" Josie didn't put much stock in fortune tellers, but her heart leapt at the assessment. That could explain why they had clicked—and kissed—so quickly.

"Auspicious matches are good on paper, but it's important that there are fireworks. You need both. Do you like Spencer?"

"I do. He's funny and a good listener." *And a good kisser who is amazing in bed.* Not that she'd admit anything that intimate to Spencer's grandmother.

"Good listener means good husband. You don't want a man who doesn't listen to you," Bà Bà said. She scoffed then grabbed Josie's wrist. "My grandson makes you happy?"

"Yes, but I'm going back to DC on Saturday," Josie protested weakly.

"Is Spencer going back with you to DC?" Bà Bà asked. She scowled. "He will miss my birthday party."

"You should ask him." *And tell me what he says.*

Josie didn't have the right to ask Spencer to give DC another try. He'd found himself, and the film had given him purpose again. She couldn't ask him to give that up and leave his family.

She didn't want to ruin the good time they were having by asking about the future. How ironic, since it was the opposite of how she dealt with everything else in her life. She, a planner, was avoiding making future plans with Spencer.

"It's good having him home again," Bà Bà said. She had removed her hat and fanned herself with it. The breeze relieved some of the heat that had rushed to Josie's cheeks.

Josie followed Bà Bà as she pointed to Spencer and Jimmy still chatting near the farm entrance. Based on Spencer's rigid back, the conversation must have been very serious. Then Jimmy slapped Spencer on the back and the two men laughed.

"Spencer is happy again." Bà Bà's entire face lit up. "Of all my grandchildren, I worry about him the most. But he has good friends. Jimmy and now you."

Josie forced a smile. Her insides twisted. Would this proposal work out and they could remain friends? Or more than friends? She'd forced herself to live in the present, but the future would catch up with her. What would she do at the end of the week?

She peered through the viewfinder to take more pictures and keep her hands busy. As much fun as she'd been having, Josie missed her girlfriends. She'd gone almost two full days without talking to any of the Babes. She'd never done that before. Even though Spencer had found a place in her heart, Josie needed her family, too.

CHAPTER 25

W ait a minute." Spencer stopped and tried to catch his breath. Bà Bà was fast for her age, and he and Jimmy had practically sprinted across the farm to catch up with the two women.

"Whoa, you're out of shape. Good thing you no longer have a desk job," Jimmy said. Unlike Spencer, Jimmy had no difficulty with their pace. "Do you want me to come up with a doctor-approved exercise plan for you?"

"Not funny." He forced himself to slow down and breathe deeply, without losing sight of his grandmother.

They'd stopped by a crop of lemongrass. The woodsy and citrus scent made Spencer's mouth water for his mom's bò kho, a stew with beef, taro, and carrots seasoned with crushed lemongrass and star anise and simmered in broth with some coconut water. If touring the farm reminded him of a different Vietnamese dish at every crop, he wasn't sure he could make it without gnawing his arm off from hunger.

His grandmother stopped to talk to some other farmers, which gave him and Jimmy a chance to finally catch up to her and Josie. Bà Bà was very friendly with a tanned Southeast Asian couple and a tall, light-skinned Black man with a full head of salt-and-pepper hair and a beard. They were all around his parents' age. Their conversation seemed lively, though he couldn't catch any of it. Josie stood next to Bà Bà, nodding and adding to whatever they were discussing.

"Spencer, what took you so long?" Bà Bà chastised once they were close enough. "I want you to meet my friends."

He was still out of breath, so he shrugged and stood next to Josie.

"Everything good?" he whispered to her.

She slipped her hand into his hand and nodded. Spencer's heart did a little somersault. What *had* the two women talked about before they caught up with them?

"Hey, you got a camera!" Josie exclaimed.

"Jimmy's letting me borrow it." He held it up. "Is it a good one?"

"You could do worse. That's a very, very nice one. Almost brand new, looks like," she whispered.

Oh, his friend Jimmy, he was being sneaky because he knew Spencer wouldn't accept such an extravagant present. That's why he pretended it was an extra. But who was Spencer to look a gift horse in the mouth or whatever that saying was? He'd use it until he could buy his own.

"Is it okay if I take photos of you while you catch up?" Josie asked the farmers. She held up her camera with her free hand. "I promise my camera will be out of the way."

Everyone nodded. Spencer squeezed her hand before letting

her go. She took a few steps back and began walking around them while looking through her viewfinder. He turned his attention back to Bà Bà's friends.

"We would've been here sooner, but Spencer was sniffing the lemongrass and getting hungry," Jimmy said, jerking his thumb in the direction of the tall stalks.

Their elders laughed.

"Seriously, now I'm craving bò kho and some crusty French bread." Spencer rubbed his stomach. "Or noodles. I'm not picky."

"What's that?" asked the Black man.

"This is Mr. Williams," Jimmy said, making the introductions. "Spencer is my high school buddy who finally returned home."

"And, Mr. and Mrs. Seng, meet Spencer," Jimmy continued.

"We're old friends," Bà Bà added. "They knew your grandfather. They also had shrimp boats before the spill."

Spencer greeted everyone before describing the Vietnamese beef stew to Mr. Williams. Apparently, the Sengs made a similar Cambodian dish. Which wasn't surprising, since Cambodia and Vietnam share a border.

"Funny how so many cultures have a beef soup with potatoes. Now you're making *me* hungry." Mr. Williams chuckled and turned to Bà Bà. "Will you serve it at your birthday party?"

"If you want to make a request, you better bring me a big birthday present!" Bà Bà teased. "I will ask my daughter. She's planning it."

"We can make our beef stew for your celebration," Mrs. Seng offered.

"All these years we've known each other, and you've never made it for me. Now you have to make it." Bà Bà beamed when Mrs. Seng agreed. Who could deny an almost one-hundred-year-old woman such a minor wish?

His grandmother was well loved and respected in Versailles even before he left for DC. Now it was obvious she'd also earned the friendship and respect of the other farmers at the co-op. The four of them continued to discuss her birthday party. It would be the biggest community gathering this year, since the church was combining it with Tết festivities. Everyone who had a connection to his family or the church would be there.

"Your grandmother tells us you're making a film about your grandfather and the Krewe of Saigon," said Mr. Seng.

"Yes, he will be a famous filmmaker!" Bà Bà said, hooking her arm through Spencer's and pulling him closer. "He interviewed me yesterday on camera, and he asked very good questions."

"Bà Bà, I'm still new at this," Spencer protested, shifting his weight from side to side. "The film could be terrible. I don't want to get anyone's hopes up."

"Ah, it is already wonderful because I'm in it." Bà Bà laughed. "You should interview them, too."

"Actually." He cleared his throat. "I would love to interview all of you later this week. We can do it in your home or wherever you feel comfortable."

"We're already here, so why not now?" said Mrs. Seng. "The trellis would make a pretty background." She pointed to a wooden structure that was covered with vines not dissimilar to the bitter melon his grandmother had in her backyard.

"I'd be honored," replied Spencer. He'd do his best to find the unusual that Josie had talked about. She could photograph everyone after he interviewed them.

"Well, I've never been in a movie before. I'm in!" Mr. Williams declared. "We can say we knew you before you became famous."

Spencer wasn't sure about being famous, but he was bolstered by their confidence in him. Bà Bà always saw the best in him and now she was recruiting her friends to join his hype team.

He couldn't believe it was this easy to find people willing to go on camera. Though, taping the interviews would be easy. He still had to figure out how to edit the footage to tell a story. Spencer still didn't know how he'd tie together all these stories, but he'd figure it out later.

He wasn't doing this alone anymore. Josie was his partner. In more ways than one, it seemed. Spencer couldn't imagine living without her. He only hoped that she felt the same about him.

CHAPTER 26

Keeping her eyes on her camera display, Josie walked backward away from the group to find the perfect composition. None of her usual tricks seemed to be working. She'd held the camera high for a downward perspective, tilted for a slightly off-center vibe, and even plain straight on.

But nothing seemed to capture this momentous gathering of farmers. In front of her were three generations of people from three diverse backgrounds standing on a farm they co-owned with other people of color. How was it still a secret outside of New Orleans? She doubted many people in the city even knew the farm existed. The occasional car sputtering by on the highway reminded her that they were still in a metropolitan city. There couldn't be that many urban farms in the United States.

Hoping that she'd find her rhythm, she tried different angles, never removing her finger from the shutter. Yet nothing felt right. What if she got closer and focused on one or two people at a time instead of wide-angle shots? She tiptoed back over toward the group to grab more candid shots.

The first face she zoomed in on was Spencer's. His face was lit up in conversation, and his arms gestured with excitement. He was so animated, just like the first night at Cafe du Monde when he spoke of his vision for this film.

"Spencer's got a good eye. And people open up to him."

"Hey." She had been so focused on Spencer that she hadn't noticed that Jimmy had walked away from the group.

"You can see it, too." He pointed at her camera display showing Spencer's animated face and one arm in the air. "I'm glad he's got you to keep him motivated. Since he's been home, he couldn't stick to one film idea. He's more focused today than he's been with his other, unfinished projects."

"Sometimes art works that way," she said. "You can't choose your inspiration." Every artist needed a push. She just happened to be the one who gave it when he most needed it. She didn't need credit for a little nudge.

Josie turned the camera on Jimmy. She wasn't sure what he was trying to tell her, but keeping the camera between them felt safer.

"I came here to escape the limelight." He started to put his hand up but shrugged. "Why not?"

He stuck his hands into the front pockets of his jeans and mugged for the camera. Like Spencer, Jimmy's natural confidence presented in his relaxed shoulders and mischievous smile. She also found sadness in his eyes, as if he were searching for something.

"So what's *your* badass vision?" she asked him. She stepped back to get a wider angle. While the elders looked frail at first glance, Jimmy looked like he worked on a farm. A very hand-some farm boy in a dirty shirt that accentuated his muscular arms, stained jeans, and utilitarian black rubber boots. Maybe he could pose with his family for a few pictures.

Now, that was an idea to explore. Find out how many of the farmers' younger family members helped tend the fields and create a series with them. She wondered how many of them had had professional family photos taken recently. That was something her family had skipped when finances were tight. Maybe she could offer her services in exchange for including their photos in her portfolio.

Josie filed the idea away for later. She'd already invested so much time on this project with Spencer. Switching to a new project meant it would take longer to complete her portfolio for Stevens Gallery.

"Being a medical doctor's not enough?" Jimmy said, and shrugged. "You know, even in high school Spencer was a dreamer. Even if he ignored it to make his parents happy. He's meant to do big things, and I want to help him."

"That's great. He needs all the support he can get." Especially after she left.

"I've never seen him this happy. He's finally doing something he enjoys and owning it instead of trying to make everyone else happy." Jimmy's eyes turned dark. "He may seem confident and strong, but my man Spence has a soft heart. I hope your intentions are good."

"My intentions?" Josie scoffed and dropped her camera. "This is not some period romance movie. Both Spencer and I are consenting adults. We know this isn't permanent." Was Josie trying to convince herself as well as Jimmy?

Jimmy held up both hands to defend himself from her onslaught.

"Sorry," she said. "I got carried away."

"I had to be sure you won't break his heart."

"There are no hearts involved, so that's not a problem," Josie lied.

Her heart pounded in her chest. She'd told herself over and over that this was just a fling. A little vacation fun. But deep down she'd known that they were in too deep. He'd shared so many of his fears and dreams with her the past few days. Now she and Spencer had begun to produce a brilliant project together.

Josie took a deep breath. She had to get out of her head.

"Let's go see what Spencer is doing." She started back down the path without waiting for Jimmy.

The main group stepped back as Mr. and Mrs. Seng led them over to the vine-covered trellis. Josie followed them, staying back far enough to press the shutter as they navigated the rows of crops. The couple stood tall and proud next to their crops as they pointed to various parts of the trellis.

Spencer was a natural. He'd convinced them to do an interview on camera within minutes of meeting them. He directed them out of a shaded spot to a position with just the right amount of sunlight. And it wasn't in their eyes, so they could look at the camera.

He'd remembered her tips and applied them to an outdoor space. Her chest swelled with pride. She couldn't hear the conversation, but there was no doubt the couple was comfortable sharing their stories with him.

"Josie, wait." Jimmy caught up with her. "Whatever is going on between you two, I hope you'll be honest with him."

"Of course. Why wouldn't I?" Josie forced a smile to hide her tangle of emotions.

"Good. Thanks for listening," Jimmy said. He left her standing alone between rows of basil. If Josie were to take a self-portrait right now, it would be titled *Turmoil*. She hadn't planned to fall for a complete stranger halfway through her vacation.

CHAPTER 27

Oh my God, the cold air feels so good," Josie moaned from the back seat of the car. Their rideshare driver blasted the air-conditioning for them but cracked open his window a couple of inches. Probably because they stank from touring a farm for the last six hours.

As tired and achy as she was, those six hours were some of the best of her vacation so far. She'd learned more than she ever needed to know about farming and Asian vegetables. The best part was the stories. The community elders were so thrilled that the "younger folks"—as they called her, Spencer, and Jimmy— were genuinely interested in their past experiences. Her storage card ran out of space before they ran out of stories.

"If you keep moaning like that, I'll have my way with you as soon as we step into the apartment," Spencer whispered.

"Really? Have your way with me?" Josie giggled. Still, desire flashed through her as she imagined his hands on her body again. "You're so cute when you talk like that."

"I can't tell if that's a compliment or an insult. Aren't those guys usually domineering jerks?" Spencer tapped her arms lightly with his fingers. They were both too hot to hold hands.

"Not once you get to know them. That's the best part. They're all broody and commanding until they meet the woman who makes them lose their minds. Then they bang."

"The banging part sounds good to me." He tossed her his best attempt at a smolder, then laughed. "But maybe when we're not stinky and sweaty."

"You'll never believe what your grandmother said to me!" Josie sat up. "She asked if we were banging."

"I can't believe she even knows that word in English." Spencer's face contorted in horror and turned red. "I'm so sorry. What did you tell her?"

"Nothing! I couldn't think of an appropriate response. Though she did say something about great-grandchildren."

"Oh, no." Spencer covered his forehead and groaned. "I'm sorry. I've already told her several times you weren't my girl-friend."

"That won't work. I let her assume we're dating because I'd rather talk about that than how I'm banging her hot grandson. Besides, I adore your grandmother." Josie truly did. She'd miss Bà Bà after her vacation was over.

"So you think I'm hot?" Spencer leaned across the back seat and pursed his lips for a kiss.

"Stop it! As if your head wasn't big enough already."

"Well, thank you. I know it's big." His tossed her a smug grin.

The rideshare driver cleared his throat loudly before turning up the radio. Josie and Spencer exchanged looks before bursting into hushed laughter.

"Behave. You're going to get me a bad rating." Josie's attempt to chastise him failed as she broke out in giggles.

"Okay, change of subject," Spencer said, raising his eyebrows and looking pointedly at the back of the driver's head. "Did you get some good pics?"

"I'll have to pull them up on my laptop, but there are plenty of gems. My favorites are the ones of your grandmother before you and Jimmy showed up. She's really happy you're home."

The conversation between her and Jimmy popped back into her mind. After Jimmy's heart-to-heart with her, she'd packed her confused feelings into a little box and shoved it aside in order to finish touring the farm. Now, without the distraction of others, she couldn't stop thinking about her plans for the future.

"Yeah, me, too. I've missed her. Though I don't miss how nosy she is about my love life!" He kissed the back of her hand and set it down quickly before the driver noticed.

"Would you consider moving back to DC? For the right opportunity?" Josie blurted. Before Jimmy spoke to her, she hadn't considered continuing their relationship past Saturday. But now she had to know. There was no point in torturing herself.

"Honestly? It would have to be a really amazing opportunity. Like earning a spot in the exhibition." He spread his hands out. "Seeing the farm and meeting everyone today reminded me how rich in culture Versailles is. I didn't appreciate it enough when I was here."

"There is a ton of culture in DC."

"Of course there is! It's our country's capital."

"Won't you miss Ben's Chili Bowl?" she asked.

"Too crowded."

He had a point there.

"And all the adorable baby pandas at the zoo?"

"They have twenty-four/seven webcams. It's not the same as going to the zoo, but I can get my cuteness fix."

"What cultural things in DC *will* you miss?" Josie couldn't stop grilling him. If he gave up on her hometown so easily, would he let her walk away without a fight?

"Sometimes I took the Red Line and ate lunch at the indoor courtyard at the American Art Museum. My favorite is the Nam June Paik exhibit. I took trips to Eden Center to eat. It's not as good as the food here, though. Hey." He caressed her check. "What's going on? Why are you asking me all these questions about DC?"

She shrugged, unsure how to explain the uncertainty swirling inside her.

"I liked living in the DMV, but ten years is a long time to be tied to a place. There are so many other cities to explore. I want to play things by ear for a while."

Of course he did. She'd expected too much from Spencer. It wasn't fair for her to judge him for all the things that made her want him. She adored his playfulness and spontaneity and how he introduced her to places and foods in New Orleans that she might not have discovered on her own. He had the same energy in bed. Why would she expect him to act differently about his career?

"I'm glad you have time to figure it out." Josie forced a smile. He had plenty of time, but she only had a few more days before going back to her real-world responsibilities. "You're doing something you love, and everything will fall into place."

"You're right." He smiled and nodded. His posture relaxed; he was obviously relieved that she'd dropped the discussion. "You know you're the best thing that's happened to me in a long time. We're good together. Meant to be."

"We've only known each other for four days. How can you be so sure?"

"Because there has to be a reason we ran into each other twice in two days. I have to believe that." His voice cracked. "You pulled me out of a funk and challenged me to finish something for once. I hope I've given you something just as life-changing these last four days."

His face was so earnest. She envied how easily he dove into life without stressing if things would work out. What if the past four days had been a mistake? And she'd wasted time photographing a farm instead of pictures for her portfolio?

Suddenly the air was freezing and the space in the back seat started to shrink. Josie shivered. She started to roll down the window but stopped when she recognized where they were. The driver pulled in front of the apartment a minute later.

"Do you mind bringing our stuff? I need some space." Josie bolted out of the car.

WHAT THE HELL went wrong in the car?

Spencer had whiplash after his conversation with Josie. First they were flirting and the next moment she was attacking him about returning to DC. Something must have happened at the farm. He hoped it wasn't anything his grandmother had said.

"Um, thanks." He waved awkwardly at the driver and followed a few steps behind Josie. She needed space, but he couldn't let it go.

"Josie, you're upset, but I'm not sure why," he said once they were both inside the apartment. "I don't want us to fight. I only have you for a few more days."

"I don't want to fight, either."

He followed her to the bedroom that they'd shared last night. She didn't look at him but rummaged through her suitcase instead.

They'd left too early to make the bed. The sheets were twisted from their second round of lovemaking. She'd been so responsive, so fucking hot last night. He resisted the urge to pull her back into bed and—how had he worded it?—yes, have his way with her.

"Josie, stop." He grabbed her hands to still them. "Talk to me, please?"

"I wish we could make the magic of the past four days last forever. And we didn't have to worry about things like jobs and businesses. And taking care of people who depend on me." Josie sighed heavily and dropped the clothes she'd dug out. She sat on the end of the bed.

"What happened to enjoying the moment?" he said, and sat next to her. He was relieved that she didn't move away but leaned into him.

"I tried. But I'm not wired like you. Carefree and trusting that things will work out. I *need* to know how things will happen. Or at least plan for all possible contingencies."

"That's okay. I still lo—like you." Spencer caught himself. He'd almost slipped and declared his love for her. This wasn't the right time. He'd only scare her off. "Your lists are smart. That's why I was surprised you were giving them up for the rest of the week."

"I miss my lists!" She laughed dryly. "I didn't even make it a full day. I kept forgetting that I wanted to call Tasha because I didn't write it down. Not in my notebook or my phone."

"If you love your lists, don't stop. Hell, I'll even start making lists."

"You'll hate it."

"I'll do it if it makes you happy." He kissed her softly. "You can teach me all your tricks the same way you did with the lighting. I'm a good student."

"You picked up my tips super fast. I saw you guide the Sengs into better light."

"Do I get an A? I'm not used to getting an A minus."

"Stop being so Asian," she joked. Finally, her mouth curved into a smile. "But if you want that A plus, how about some extra credit?"

This time it was Josie who pulled him in for another kiss.

CHAPTER 28

Josie didn't care that her kiss was needy. She wanted reassurance that things could work out between them. Maybe not exactly how they wanted, but how it was meant to be. If only she knew how they'd make it work living in two different cities.

She bit his lip. When he gasped at the pain, she took over leading their kiss. He sucked her bottom lip as if to remind her that it was okay to let go and enjoy the moment. A throaty moan escaped her lips.

Their mouths became more urgent. Her chest heaved with ragged breaths in between each kiss. She was distracting him from their discussion because she was afraid to express her doubts about them. About her decision to get involved with him. He relaxed into her kiss as she pressed her breasts against him.

She parted her lips, parrying with him as he explored her mouth. A fire spread in her belly. She wanted to rip off her clothes and bury him deep inside her.

Josie pulled at his clothes as if whatever doubts she had before had taken second place to carnal pleasure. He obliged by pulling off his shirt. She reached for his waistband, then stopped.

"How about we take this into the shower? We can clean up and get dirty again." Josie saw herself in the mirror. Her eyes shined bright with lust. Her lips were puffy from his kisses. Never had she felt so out of control with need.

"Finally, I get to have my way with you."

She smacked him playfully. "Whatever your way is, I have my own plans."

"That's a promise!"

Josie slipped a shower cap over her hair and stepped into the hot shower, willing it to wash away all her doubts. With the multiple jets pounding water on her from different angles, forgetting them felt too easy. All she wanted to think about in this moment were her hands and mouth on Spencer's body. To remind herself that this was supposed to be a no-strings fling. She hadn't meant to get attached to someone who wasn't planning a life in DC.

The steam swirled around them as Spencer soaped her back. He reached around and circled her breasts and rolled her nipples between his fingers. She let her head fall back on his chest and allowed the heat radiating through her body to block out any thoughts about the future.

After he deemed her chest clean, he dipped his fingers between her legs. Josie shuddered. Finally.

"So wet," he murmured. His fingers twirled lazy circles around her clit.

She closed her eyes and let pleasure shoot up her torso. His relaxed meandering across her body was too little yet almost too much pleasure at the same time.

"Stop torturing me." Josie tilted her hips back until his cock was nestled against her ass. The soapy water gave her just enough slickness to push back and let him slide deliciously against her backside.

"Now who's torturing whom?" He groaned and grabbed her hips as she continued teasing him. She smiled as she felt him harden further.

"You like it." Josie turned around and walked him to the built-in bench in the shower. She tossed a washcloth onto the floor and kneeled on it. He grinned and opened his thighs wider for her.

She fisted his soapy cock. Slowly, she slid her hands up and down. Her fingers tightened around him each time she reached the base.

"Fuck, Josie." Spencer's eyes rolled up into his head. "If you keep doing that, I won't be any good after."

"Shhh." She pulled his head down for a wet kiss. "Lean back and enjoy."

He didn't need further convincing. Not after she pulled her fist up over the swollen head of his cock and back down again. He gasped as his hips bucked, pushing himself faster into her hands.

His breath was ragged, as if he could barely keep from letting himself go. Josie's pride swelled with the knowledge that his orgasm was in her hands. He was so beautiful with his eyes closed and his cheeks flushed. This man who effortlessly lived in the moment. So unlike herself.

"Josie, come here." He patted for her to sit on the bench next to him. "I need to touch you."

Without letting go of him, she pulled herself up next to him. Spencer reached for her knee and pulled it open, hooking his leg around hers. She gasped when his fingers parted her lips and pinched her clit. She adjusted her legs and hips to give him a better angle while still fucking his cock with her hand. The position was awkward, but she didn't care.

"Will you come with me?" he sputtered.

Josie half nodded. He slid his fingers into her pussy. She moaned as his fingers curled inside her and his thumb pressed on her clit. Pleasure and power clouded her head. She had one goal: to make him come before letting herself go.

Her hand tightened around his shaft and she increased her speed. He gasped and his fingers fucked her faster.

"Come for me, Spencer."

That was all it took to send him over the edge. His body tensed, but his fingers didn't stop pleasuring her. Josie closed her eyes as an orgasm overtook her. She rode his hand as he came apart in hers.

CHAPTER 29

Want to grab some food?" Spencer called from the living room into the bedroom, where Josie was getting dressed.

The tension between them had eased after their lovemaking. He and Josie finished showering for real after. He didn't know exactly why she'd been adamant that he declare his love for the DMV, but it had come from something deeper.

If only he knew what. She was right that he didn't really know her. Four days wasn't enough to truly know someone. Or even fall in love. Yet he had. It didn't make sense to him, either, but the thought of living without her made his chest hurt.

He'd spent most of his life doing what he thought his parents wanted. Without the tedium and stress of his old job, he could listen to his intuition more. It turned out his gut wanted him to express his creativity as a filmmaker.

Maybe she had strong feelings for him, too. But he didn't want to rush her. She was the type of person who needed time to think things through. Whatever her doubts about them, he had three more days to convince her that they could make this relationship work long past her vacation. Long past their collaboration.

"The Pythian Building has a food hall I've been meaning to check out. The building has a ton of history, and there's a park across the street," he added.

"As long as it's not sandwiches." The bedroom door opened. Josie had changed into a flowing pink and purple floral dress. She'd wrapped a fuchsia scarf around her hair. She finished attaching big gold hoops in her ears as she walked out. "We've eaten way too many the last few days."

"Wow." He suddenly felt like a slacker in yet another T-shirt and jeans.

"After getting dirty at the farm, I wanted to feel a bit more feminine." She flashed a smile and spun so the skirt of her dress puffed out. Her movements were lighter and more playful than earlier. "I always loved twirling in my dresses as a little girl."

"You should do it even more, then. Young Josie shouldn't have all the fun." He lifted her hand and spun her round and round. She was so joyful. He wished he could stop time right here and spin with her like nothing in the world mattered but each other.

"Spencer, I'm getting dizzy." Josie laughed as she lost her balance.

He wrapped his arms around her and caught her as they both fell onto the couch. She laid next to him with her eyes closed. He dropped kisses on her eyelids until the room stopped spinning around them. Why couldn't every moment between them be this carefree?

"I wish this didn't have to end." Josie spoke quietly.

"Why does it have to?" He caressed the soft skin of her arms.

"Because I have to return to real life. Home in DC."

"We don't have to think about that yet. We still have time to enjoy each other. Let's not ruin the next few days by worrying about the future. We can talk about it Friday?"

"Or right before my flight?" Josie asked with resignation in her voice. "What are we doing here?"

"We're having fun. And collaborating as artists. Not everything has to be planned out far in advance."

Josie sighed.

"Hey, let's get out of here." He sat up. Sitting here and discussing their lack of a future was a total mood killer. "I've been reading up on the Pythian Building and I think you should photograph it. If you want to, I mean."

"Okay. One more day and then we need to discuss what's next. Especially our application for the exhibition. There's no way we'll finish it in the next three days."

"Sounds like a plan. You know I'll work on it for as long as we need." He nodded, relieved. "But we can't work twenty-four/seven! We have to experience new things to feed our minds."

"You've got a point. I could use a break from taking pictures for my portfolio." This time she gave him a real smile. "You said something about a food hall?"

"Yes, it's set on the bottom floor of the historic Pythian Building. It was one of the first African American–owned high-rises when it was built in the early 1900s."

"How do you know all of that? Have you been planning ahead?" she teased.

"It's been on my radar for a while."

"Food halls are great. We can try dishes from every place without feeling guilty."

"I hope you're hungry because there's soul food, a chicken and waffle place, Vietnamese, even a Caribbean place."

"Is it bad if we order something from each one?"

"Hell no. I'll be honest. I've never been to the Pythian, so don't expect an insider's experience there."

She laughed. "Fine, we'll just be tourists."

He shuddered dramatically to make her laugh. And she did. Her laughter was now his most favorite sound in the world.

"I'm looking them up." Josie tapped on her phone. "Apparently they have something called a phở-rito."

"God, I hope it's not an abomination." Spencer loved phở and he liked burritos, but did they really need to be combined?

"There's only one way to find out."

"THE JERK SHRIMP was the best thing we ate." Josie licked the spicy sauce off her fingers. A shower and food in her belly always cheered her up. Her doubts about Spencer didn't feel as dire or as serious when her belly was full and she was laughing at his bad jokes.

Their small industrial-style table was littered with wrappers and empty trays. Between the two of them, they'd ordered at least one dish from every food vendor in the hall.

"I can't believe I'm saying this, but phở-ritos are damned good," Spencer declared.

"It was different, but I liked it, especially the dipping broth on the side. However, here's the true test." Josie leaned in. "Would you say that in front of your family?"

"Never. They'd take away my Viet card." He covered his face with a brown paper napkin.

"That's what I thought!" she said. It was always easy to laugh with Spencer.

She'd been more stressed than she'd thought about her portfolio and their collaboration. He must've known she needed to do something that wouldn't ultimately become her work.

Maybe that's what he'd meant earlier. How he knew they were meant to be because they complemented each other. She helped him plan and focus. He showed her that when they took things moment by moment, creativity flowed better.

She wanted to make them work. She owed it to herself and Spencer to see if their fling could grow into something, well, more collaborative.

"Spencer, about earlier," Josie said softly.

His smile dropped and he turned his full attention to her.

"We don't have to talk about it if you're not ready," he said.

"I want to. I need to know our plans for the fu—"

Josie's phone clattered on the table as it vibrated. She saw that she'd missed several calls from Tasha and Zoe. Then a text from Zoe came in.

Call me. 911!

She froze. Something bad had happened. She could feel it.

"Josie, what's wrong?" Spencer asked with wide eyes.

"I have to call home. Something's wrong."

CHAPTER 30

Josie ran outside. Her heart wanted to jump out of her chest, it was pounding so hard. The sun had slipped under the horizon. How long had they been in the food hall? She immediately called Tasha and paced the sidewalk as it rang. It went to voicemail. Zoe was next.

Zoe answered on the first ring. "Josie! We've been trying to reach you."

"What happened? Is someone hurt?"

"Your studio was broken into right after closing. They stole a bunch of equipment."

"I don't care about the equipment." All those things could be replaced. She had insurance. "What about Tasha?" Her sister sometimes stayed after closing to catch up on emails.

"I can hear you pacing." Zoe's voice hitched. "You're not at the apartment. Where are you? Can you sit down?"

"I'll be fine. Just tell me." Josie weaved around the tourists on the sidewalk. She forced herself to slow down so she didn't turn at such a dizzying pace or run into anyone.

"Tasha was working late when they broke in. She'll be fine—
she's just a little bruised."

Josie froze.

"Bruised how?" Blood rushed to Josie's ears. Once again she
hadn't been around to protect her sister. Now Tasha was hurt.

"Her wrist is sprained. But us Babes are taking good care of
her," Zoe said, trying to soothe Josie. "I didn't want to ruin your
vacation, but we wanted you to know. It's all under control."

"Zoe, tell me exactly what happened," Josie whispered. She
leaned against a bike stand and cradled the phone. As if the
phone were as fragile as she was at the moment.

"The guys smashed the glass on the door after dark. They saw
Tasha at the front desk and grabbed her. Obviously she was terrified and told them the studio had no cash."

"She's right. We do everything electronically."

"They made her unlock the equipment storage room. They
cleaned it out and locked her inside. Luckily she had her phone
in her back pocket and got ahold of me. She didn't want your
parents to worry."

"No! And she tried to call me, didn't she?" Josie looked at her
phone and finally read her sister's texts. Bile rose into her mouth.
Tasha needed her and she hadn't heard her phone ring. While
she was having fun, Tash had gotten hurt.

"Josie, listen. She's bruised and her wrist is sprained, but Tasha
will be okay."

"I should've been there," Josie said softly. "I should've come
home as soon as my client canceled."

"You're not a psychic, Josie. No one could have predicted a break-in. Don't blame yourself."

"Of course I blame myself. If I weren't on vacation, she wouldn't have been working late." Josie's thoughts swirled at a tornado's pace. "You called the police? Did Tasha tell them about the security cameras?"

"Yes, she called the cops first. They wrote up a report and checked for fingerprints. Your insurance company will want a report. And yes, they know about the security cameras." Zoe shot back the responses quickly as Josie went down her checklist of questions in her head.

"I'm taking the next flight home." Josie made a mental list of all she needed to do in order to check out of the apartment. Maybe the hostess could make an exception. Or she could pay extra for cleaning.

"No, you should stay. Eat more amazing food and hang out with Spencer."

"He's just a fling. Someone fun during vacation. He doesn't mean anything."

"Oh." Zoe paused as if debating whether to ask for details. She didn't. "You got lots of pics, right? After we take care of everything. I'll help you pick out the best ones for your portfolio."

"The last four days have been intense." Josie's voice broke. "I'll tell you when I get back."

She hung up the phone. Spontaneous Josie was finished. It was time to stop indulging her fantasies of being a famous photographer. She had people back in DC who loved her and needed her.

"Hey, is everything okay?"

Spencer! She spun around. Had he heard what she'd said about him? His expression didn't reveal anything.

"No, Tasha is hurt. I have to go home." Josie's mind was on overload. "I shouldn't have left her to run the studio alone."

Spencer wrapped his arms around her and pulled her close to his chest. He smelled of soap and phở.

"Breathe with me."

The steady up and down of his chest soothed the anxiety in her belly. She followed his deep inhale and exhale. After a few minutes of deep breathing, he let go.

"Let's go back to the apartment and we'll figure out what needs to happen next. We'll talk about us later."

She nodded and let Spencer take care of her.

CHAPTER 31

Josie barely remembered returning to the apartment. All she could focus on was Tasha. Images of her sister in a hospital bed after the hit-and-run flashed in Josie's head. *She's okay, she's okay,* Josie repeated to herself. This was different from what happened in high school.

Spencer helped her out of the cab and into the apartment. He pressed a glass of water into her hand and made her drink.

"Josie, I talked to Zoe on the ride back. I hope it's okay that I grabbed her number from your phone so we could put together a plan." He rubbed her back. "She's changing your flight for you while I take care of things here. We're getting you back to DC, okay?"

Josie nodded. "I'll go pack."

"No, I'll take care of it for you." He cupped her cheek and she burrowed into his hand. She needed this touch. "Are you ready to talk to Tasha? She's home from the emergency room."

He dialed Tasha's number and handed her the phone.

"Just call out if you need something." He left her in the living room but kept her bedroom door open to keep an eye on her.

Her sister answered on the second ring. "JoJo, I guess you heard?"

Josie exhaled in relief. Tasha's bright voice had warmed her. Her sister sounded fine. Thank goodness.

"Tash, I'm so sorry I wasn't there," Josie blurted. "I'll be home soon to take care of you."

"Everyone is taking care of me. I mean *everyone*. Mom, Dad, the Babes. Don't cut your vacation short for me."

Josie wouldn't be able to relax knowing her sister was recovering from a sprained wrist. And she'd already ruined things with Spencer.

"I need to be with you, silly." Josie's laugh sounded hollow. "And take care of you like a big sister should."

Her sister yawned. "The pain meds are kicking in. I should go lie down."

"I love you, Tash. I'll be home soon."

"Love you, JoJo."

Nothing was going the way Josie had planned. She'd spent four days all over New Orleans and had no idea if she had good photos to show for it. To make everything worse, she might have hurt Spencer's feelings by saying he didn't mean anything to her. She didn't want to ask if he'd overheard her in case he hadn't.

Because it wasn't really true. Even if they never talked again, she'd treasure the time they had spent together.

He walked into the living room with a towel in his hands. His shirt was wet.

"I drew you a bath." His forehead creased in thought. "My sisters usually take long baths when they need a lift."

"A bath does sound nice." Talking to her sister had helped the fog around her disappear.

"Did you know this place has three full baths and one of them has a clawfoot tub?" He pointed down the hall. "I thought you might like that one."

She'd never been in one of those. Josie followed Spencer to find the deep tub filled with bubbles. Flickering candles were set around the bathroom. How had he managed all of this?

He pointed to a half-empty bottle on the sink. "I saw some in the cabinet. It's supposed to be rose-scented. I might have added too much."

She sniffed.

"Smells good." If the circumstances had been different, this would've been very romantic. "Thank you for this, for taking care of me."

"I care about you, Josie." A flash of hurt crossed his face and disappeared just as quickly. "We can talk after your bath."

He helped her out of her dress and made sure her fro was covered with a shower cap. He held her hand as she stepped into the warm water, bubbles popping against her skin. Spencer was gentle with her, as if she might break.

"Josie, no matter what happens after this, I want you to know that I care about you. I want you to do what's best for you. Even if it means that I'm not a part of your life."

He slipped out the door and shut it behind him, leaving her with only her thoughts.

She missed his playfulness. She'd gotten used to him by her side for the past four days. The room felt empty without him.

Had she judged him too quickly and assumed there was no future for them?

"How DID YOU even find this?" Josie padded into the kitchen wrapped in an oversized white terrycloth robe. The zombie look in her eyes was gone. Spencer was thrilled to see color in her cheeks again.

"In the linen closet. I figured you needed as much comfort as I could give you." He continued loading the dishwasher. "Zoe texted. She got you a flight out tomorrow morning."

"Thank you, Spencer." She placed a hand on his back.

He shrugged. "I did what had to be done."

His heart had twisted when she'd gotten news about her sister. Seeing Josie shut down had been a shock. Even though he'd only known her for a few days, she was always calm and confident. She always had a plan. Except this time.

Spencer couldn't stand there and let her flounder. She'd do the same if something happened to his family.

"Once I'm done in the kitchen, I'll head back to Versailles. You can get some sleep before your flight tomorrow."

"Spencer, stop." She tugged his sleeve. "I tried to talk to you about us, but you didn't want to."

"I thought we had more time to be together." He turned to face her. "How can I mean nothing to you after the past four days together? I told you about my dreams. You met my family. I thought we had a connection."

Josie froze. "So you did hear me."

"I didn't think it was the best time to talk about it. You needed comfort and I didn't need to add to the stress you were already under."

"I'm sorry—I didn't mean for it to come out that way. I'm grateful that you shared so much with me. Your grandmother is a blessing to the world."

"We have chemistry. Doesn't that mean anything to you? Isn't it worth pursuing?" Spencer's chest tightened. He wasn't ready to let her go.

"Oh, boy, do we have chemistry. But is it enough? We're so different. You're exploring your options and learning to be a film-maker in New Orleans. I run a business in DC, one where a lot of people depend on me for their livelihood."

"You're giving up on us, aren't you?"

"I had a really long bath to think about us. About what I—and you—want next."

He knew it was coming. She would officially end things between them. Without even giving them a real shot.

"I believe in your vision for your film. It's better if we keep our relationship professional. I can't uproot my life, my plans for someone I've only know for a few days."

"Just like that? We're done?" He huffed. He was beginning to hate those words. *Only a few days.* A lot could change in just a few days. His family's fortune changed in less than a week after the oil spill. The decision to move home after losing his job took only a few days.

He wanted to be angry, but he was tired. Tired of being pulled in so many directions. And when he'd found something he enjoyed and a woman who shared a passion for telling stories—she'd given up on him.

"We're not done," she continued. "I believe in your film and your vision. We'll finish our application. But I'll have to do it from DC. Which means you'll have to do most of the heavy lifting."

Spencer's heart skipped a beat.

"I'd like that." Things weren't over. She still wanted him in her life even if it was professionally. This meant he had time to convince her that he was truly boyfriend material. Long-distance was better than nothing.

Josie let out a long breath. "I wasn't sure if you'd still want to see me again. We're going to kick ass on this application."

She traced his lips with her fingers before tiptoeing up for a kiss. He held her to his chest. His lips were hungry for her, but he held back until she opened her mouth for him. He closed his arms around her body and held her tighter as he poured all the love he had into her.

They were both gasping for air when they broke apart. To her it was a last kiss. But that kiss gave him hope that they had a future together.

"Thanks for making my vacation so fun." She ran a thumb over his cheek. "I've done so many firsts and checked things off my list. I'm glad I smacked you in the head with beads."

Spencer nodded and broke out in a big smile. This time he'd prepare. He would formulate a plan to get her back.

CHAPTER 32

"Thanks for dropping me off, Jimmy. I owe you another one." Spencer waved at his friend.

"You going to be all right?" Jimmy's lips were pursed in concern. "Sorry things didn't work out for you two. But if you need anything, I'm a text away."

"I'll win her back." While it wasn't that late, Spencer was grateful that Jimmy had picked him up from the Quarter after Josie broke up with him. Jimmy made good time to Versailles despite the tourists clogging up the streets.

Josie's flight was early in the morning. He made sure she'd set her alarm to leave for the airport in time. He even asked Zoe to check up on her. He was worried about Josie, but he couldn't stay with her another night. Not after being dumped.

Now he was home. Again. He wouldn't waste any more time. The past few days with Josie had taught him that art wasn't only about finding inspiration, but also about follow-through, even when things got hard.

All he wanted to do was slide into bed and sleep. Hopefully Bà

Bà was in bed and Nina had gone home for the evening. Once he was settled, he could text his sisters and beg off his shift at the co-op tomorrow.

Except he walked into the house to see that his sisters and Bà Bà were watching a Vietnamese-dubbed Chinese drama in the living room. His grandmother was up past her usual bedtime of seven o'clock.

"Spence! What are you doing here?" Nina held a bowl of steamed rice with a fried egg topped with soy sauce.

They were all eating breakfast for dinner in front of the television! Something his grandmother never let him do with her.

"It's a long story." After a night of staying strong for Josie, exhaustion hit him hard.

His sisters and Bà Bà exchanged glances. Rose rushed to grab his bags.

"I'll make some tea. Sit," commanded Cynthia.

Spencer plopped onto the couch. When the tea arrived, he cupped his hands around the mug and inhaled. It was his grandmother's favorite fragrant jasmine tea. He associated the tea with his childhood memories of her.

"Con, tell me what happened," Bà Bà said in Vietnamese, in that nurturing voice she'd used so often when he was younger.

Spencer told them about Josie's sister and the break-in at her studio.

"Josie doesn't think she knows me well enough for us to be serious. But my heart says she's the one."

"Ah, the fortune teller told me this would happen." Bà Bà

rubbed his head as if he were still a little boy. "She said you were compatible but there were many obstacles in your way."

"Bà Bà," Cynthia interjected. "That could mean anything. Don't give him false hope."

She shushed his middle sister. "She was right about you. That you wouldn't return home until your thirties."

Cynthia opened her mouth but thought better than to argue with her. She returned to eating her dinner.

"If I was wrong about us that means I could be wrong about everything else," Spencer said, ignoring the interchange between them. "Taking the severance package. Moving home. Making a film about Krewe of Saigon."

He'd been so sure about all those decisions. Yet it took one woman to make him doubt himself. But Josie wasn't any woman. He loved her.

"Ai-ya." His grandmother tsked. "You were lost and now you've found your way home. Bà Bà is here for you."

"I just want Ba Mẹ to be proud of me." Spencer turned to his grandmother. "How can they be proud of an unemployed son who has no idea what he wants to do with his life?"

"They are proud of you. We all are," Bà Bà said, as Spencer's eyes widened in disbelief.

"Why have they never told me?"

"Because it's not our way," said his grandmother. "We show pride by bragging about you to our friends. You should hear them talk about you when they're at the farm."

"So basically tell everyone but the person they're proud of," Nina said, rolling her eyes. "That's messed up."

Spencer wanted to roll his eyes, too, but the front door swung open.

"We're home early!" His parents dragged their suitcases inside. His mom was dressed in a tracksuit while his dad wore baggy cargo pants and a polo. "Did you miss us?"

They weren't supposed to be back until next week. Great. Everyone was here. Once his breakup and fuckups became public knowledge, there would be nonstop advice given, especially from his mom.

"The whole family is here!" his mom yelled in English. Though she'd immigrated here when she was ten, she'd never quite lost her Vietnamese accent. "Spencer, have you been eating? You are too skinny!"

"You haven't been gone two weeks, Mom. I couldn't have gotten skinnier that fast." Spencer had no idea why he needed to defend his weight to his mother.

Cynthia whistled loudly. Everyone froze.

"Hey, everyone chill," Cynthia said in English. "Spencer is having a rough night. His girlfriend dumped him."

Everyone started talking at once again. Spencer caught his name several times, but the rest was too jumbled, and he was too tired to make out the different conversations. Even the actors on the television were arguing.

Bà Bà turned off her show and stomped her feet. When that didn't work, she made Cynthia whistle through her teeth again. They quieted down.

"Listen, Spencer has something important to say," Bà Bà announced.

No one dared disobey their matriarch. His parents sat on the couch next to him while his sisters sat on throw pillows on the floor.

"I do?" Spencer tried to catch his sisters' attention, but they studied their nails instead.

"Tell them what's in your heart," his grandmother encouraged.

Spencer shook his head, but she smiled and nodded at him.

"I don't want to find a job. I want to make movies," Spencer blurted.

For once his mom was speechless.

"You do?" asked his father. His typically stern face softened. "I thought you wanted to move to DC."

"I took the DC job because it paid well. I wanted to send money home after the oil spill."

"Spencer, we didn't want you to move away, but you insisted," said his mom. "You were so sure it was the right thing to do. I couldn't change your mind. You've been like that since you were little."

"We thought you'd miss us after a short while and come home," his dad added. "Every time you came home for vacation and complained about your job, we thought you might quit."

"You—I—what?" So they'd wanted him home sooner?

"Your mom and I wanted you to be on your own. All your life you've been surrounded by us." His dad nodded at his sisters, who were whispering to each other. "It gets a little noisy around here. Hard to think."

"Why didn't you tell me you missed me?"

His mom and dad exchanged bewildered looks.

"Of course we missed you," his mom finally said. "Why do you think I called you every week?"

"I thought you were making sure I ate."

Rose smacked his head. "Oh my God, Spencer. What do you think that means?"

"Ow! You know I have a head injury." He rubbed the back of his head.

"Ăn cơm chưa is how they ask if we're okay," Nina said. "Food is our family's love language." At least Nina didn't smack him, too.

"I'm sorry, I've been an idiot." All those times he'd talked himself out of quitting and moving back to New Orleans. He'd been stuck in a box that he'd created for himself.

"You're not," his mom replied.

Cynthia snorted, but their mom gave her the death glare.

"I'm glad we're finally talking about this," his grandmother said in Vietnamese.

"But what about money? They said I'd be a burden on you if I didn't get a job soon." He pointed at his sisters. They feigned innocence.

"If you really want to, you can help out at the co-op. The farm's doing very well. And I don't smell like fish anymore." His dad laughed at himself. "We don't need your money, Spencer."

"Ba!" All three of his sisters chastised him. His dad ducked as if they had thrown something at him.

"Don't say it that way. It's insulting," Cynthia explained to their father. She turned to Spencer. "The co-op is doing gang-busters, big bro. All the big celebrity chefs are fighting over our local, organic, farm-to-table produce. They're literally eating it up."

"Cha-ching," Rose said, rubbing her thumb over her fingers in the sign for money. "White men are finally paying us the big bucks."

"They're right. I volunteer at the co-op and help with the bookkeeping," added Nina, the baby of the family. "So you don't have to work a job you hate ever again. At least don't blame it on the family."

Spencer laughed quietly. As annoying as his little sisters were, he missed their bluntness. They bickered constantly, but they were one another's best friends, because they'd shared a room for most of their childhood.

"So you want to make movies? Like Jackie Chan?" asked his mom.

"Not like Jackie Chan." Spencer chuckled. "I want to make films about real people, like recording the history of New Orleans, especially our people here."

"He's been working on a really cool project this week. Tell 'em, Spence," Nina said encouragingly.

Spencer explained his original idea—which his dad was in favor of—and how it evolved into a collaborative project with Josie to enter the competition.

"I've interviewed Bà Bà, the Sengs, and Mr. Williams at the farm," he added.

His parents beamed. That would be the closest they'd come to telling him they were proud. For now it was enough for Spencer.

"What competition?" asked his father.

"We're submitting our work to the Fifty States Exhibition. Josie—that's the woman I'm working with for the competition—had the idea for a series of interviews and photos. But she had to go back to DC, so we're going to finish our application virtually."

"How can we help?" Rose asked.

"I need editing software and some equipment to record a few more interviews. But my savings is almost gone."

"You've been stressing out about money all this time?" Rose shook her head. "You can ask for help, you know. Even if you're the older brother."

Spencer's brow knitted as he tried to understand what Rose meant.

"Ba Mẹ, tell him," Nina said.

"You have funds for the film if you want it," his dad admitted. "The farm was profitable pretty early on, so we saved almost everything you sent home."

"Almost?" Not that it mattered how they'd spent the money. Spencer would've never put any restrictions on it.

"You helped pay for my accounting degree, Spencer! After the farm took off, Ba Mẹ had me set up a savings account for you." Nina pulled out her phone and tapped it a few times before showing him the screen. "That's the balance."

"Holy shit!" Spencer hollered. He almost fell off the couch. "That's a lot of digits!"

"Spencer," his mom warned. "Language."

"Sorry, Mẹ."

His mom rubbed his hair. "You need a haircut."

All of his sisters agreed.

"Everyone is happy! That means I'm happy," Bà Bà declared. She pointed at his parents. "You two better not scare away any more of my grandchildren. This family needs to talk about their feelings more."

Spencer's exhaustion had dissipated. He could really do this, but not alone. His family wanted him to be happy and to follow his passion. It only took him ten years to figure it out. He was glad he'd come home.

Spencer's chest wanted to burst with happiness and his family's love. But there was still that Josie-sized hole in his heart. He still had to win her back.

CHAPTER 33

"Sit," Josie commanded her sister. She pointed at the chaise lounge her staff had dragged in from one of the photography studios. For the last two days, since her return from New Orleans, she'd struggled to keep her sister at rest.

"Why am I here if I'm not allowed to work?" Tasha pouted but sat down anyway. She waved her arm, which was in a splint. "It's only a sprained wrist."

Josie saved the edits on her client's photo before answering. "That's exactly why you're here. I don't trust you to take it easy unless Zoe or I am with you."

"You're one to talk. Didn't even finish your vacation." Tasha crossed her arms and cringed. She gingerly rested her sprained wrist on the back of the chaise.

"We're not having this conversation again, Tash. There's no way I could enjoy myself knowing you were hurt."

"You're not enjoying yourself now."

"I've had a lot to do since I got back." Josie had dived back into work. Because of the burglary, there had been even more things to check off her Fix the Studio list. It was a very reasonable way to avoid her feelings about breaking up with Spencer. It was better to keep things professional between them.

Because of the stolen equipment, they'd had to reschedule most of their shoots. There were stacks of paperwork for the insurance company. The cops had shared the surveillance footage with local news outlets but didn't think they could recover the cameras and lights. Equipment that size and with such high value was too easy to resell. In between all of that, she booked follow-up appointments with Tasha's doctor to make sure her wrist was healing properly.

"I could've helped reschedule our clients for you. I only need one hand and a headset for that. Come on, JoJo." Tasha groaned loudly. "I'm so bored. And you haven't worked on your portfolio since you got back. You only have six more days to submit your work to Stevens Art Gallery. Otherwise you'll have to wait until next year when they reopen for submissions."

When Josie didn't respond, Tasha tossed a crumbled granola bar wrapper onto her desk.

"Please let me finish touching up these photos before Zoe gets here to take us to the fundraiser that Andre and Trixie organized for the studio." Josie sighed and pushed the wrapper aside.

"Josie, what is wrong with that woman's face?"

"What are you talking about? Her face is perfectly— Crap." Josie had meant to remove a blemish from her client's chin but ended up creating a giant hole in her face.

The bell over the door rang, and Zoe breezed in. Her best friend always arrived in style. She wore a tight black ankle-length skirt with a thigh-high slit, knee-high boots, and a fuchsia satin blouse that resembled the upper half of a Vietnamese áo dài but with puffed sleeves. It was gorgeous and had to be one of her latest designs.

"Are you two ready for the fundrai—oh my God!" Zoe ran to the monitor to get a closer look. "What happened to that woman's face?"

"Josie is dreaming about you-know-who again," Tasha mock whispered to Zoe. "She doesn't want to talk about it."

"Hush. Spencer and I will video chat next week to go over our application," Josie grumbled as she attempted to undo the tragedy before her eyes. "Happy now?"

"When can I meet him?" Tasha's eyes flashed. "Come on, sis. I want to meet the man who got you to go wild in New Orleans."

"Tasha, we had fun. You don't need the details," Josie said, blushing.

Her sister gasped. "Did you have *s-e-x*?"

"Grow up!" Josie tossed the granola bar wrapper back at her sister. It was childish, but Tasha was getting on her last nerve.

"Tasha." Zoe held out her keys. "Why don't you wait in the car? I parked it in the loading zone. We'll be right out."

Her sister huffed but grabbed her purse and Zoe's keys. After Tasha left, Zoe pulled a chair next to the receptionist desk that Josie had commandeered. It was littered with empty cans of soda, chocolate bar wrappers, and mugs of cold coffee.

"You're pushing yourself too hard," Zoe said. "I'm worried about you. You gotta let us help you. You can't manage all this, finish your application with Spencer, *and* edit photos for your Stevens Gallery submission."

"I have my lists. I can manage," Josie lied. She couldn't juggle everything and had already rescheduled her upcoming client meetings. By keeping busy, she kept herself from second-guessing her decision to leave New Orleans. To walk away from Spencer.

"Yeah, that's why you put a hole in that woman's face." Zoe giggled. "Maybe that could be your new secret menu offering. 'Will erase exes from your pictures.'"

"If this boudoir thing doesn't work out, I'll do that."

"But for real, I'm worried. You're not even taking Ruby out for your evening photo walks."

Josie hadn't touched her camera since she'd returned. But that was because she was busy. She'd even considered leaving it at the studio for her staff to use until they replaced the stolen cameras, but her staff photographers insisted on using their personal cameras until the studio ones could be replaced.

"Look, once the insurance thing is settled and we can replace our equipment, everything will be back to normal." Josie said it more to convince herself than Zoe. "The insurance guy says next week."

"You miss him, don't you?" Zoe poked her arm. "Tasha's in the car. Spill the beans."

"I miss his energy." Josie clicked open a window on her laptop to reveal a group picture from their day at the co-op farm. "Look how happy he is with his grandmother. Bà Bà is so sweet, but sassy. You'd like her."

"Sounds like you got along really well. Who's that guy? He's hot."

"You know how to pick 'em." Josie snorted. "That's Jimmy, Spencer's friend from high school. He's a medical doctor."

"Jackpot! Handsome, Vietnamese, a doctor, *and* single?" Zoe zoomed in on the picture to study Jimmy. "What's wrong with him?"

"Why? I barely got to know him."

"I mean, how can a guy like that be single? I'm sure the aunties are salivating to set him up with their daughters." Zoe laughed. "So glad my mom doesn't do that."

"Maybe they are?" Josie clicked around until she found the photos of Bà Bà's dresses laid out on the bed. "You'll love this. She has a closet full of vintage áo dài. These are her favorites."

"Whoa." Zoe's breathing grew heavy. Beautiful fabrics and vintage clothing had that effect on her. "Can you send me that picture?"

"Easy now. They're just dresses." Josie loved seeing the light in her friend's eyes whenever she was hit with inspiration.

"Do you have more pictures of her dresses?" Zoe clicked on a folder marked *New Orleans*.

"No, wait. Those are—" It was too late.

"You have a special folder with pictures of Spencer? That's so cute." Zoe scrolled through them. "Look at this selfie!"

Zoe stopped at a photo of her and Spencer while they waited for their food at the sandwich shop. She'd found it while organizing her New Orleans photos.

"It's gross how cute we look," Josie said. Now it was her turn to pout, but it didn't last long. She couldn't look at the selfie of them without smiling. "Those are my favorite pictures from New Orleans. But they're not part of our project. It was fun while it lasted."

"If you like him that much, why don't you try the long-distance thing?" Zoe placed her hand on Josie's arm.

"What if we're only compatible in bed? We're in different parts of our life right now. He has no responsibilities, while I have a business to oversee. And family to take care of." Josie groaned. "That was vacation Josie in New Orleans. Now that I'm home, I don't have the luxury to be carefree."

"Who says you can't be carefree here? You don't have to put so much on your shoulders." Zoe rubbed Josie's arm. Her best friend had been so patient with her. "Now let's go to the fundraiser."

"You and Tasha go ahead without me. I want to get these proofs to my clients early so it's one less thing on my list."

Zoe wrinkled her nose.

"I promise that I will be there. I can't miss my own fundraiser."

"Okay. Come straight to Hazel's Kitchen as soon as you're done." Zoe hugged her friend. "I'll keep an eye on Tasha."

"You're the best."

Josie locked up after Zoe and returned to her desk. Instead of pulling up her client's photos, she opened the selfie again. Made it full-screen. Josie in New Orleans had had the time of her life. She'd been carefree for those four days. But keeping things professional was the best for both of them. He needed his family, and she needed hers.

CHAPTER 34

Josie flagged down a waiter to order one of the themed cocktails that Andre had created for the evening. "I'll have a Candid Cosmo," she said. "And whatever the special apps are."

The fundraiser was in full swing. The entire community had turned out to support Parks Photography. Her parents' friends from church were standing in the back—even a couple of elders who didn't approve of the type of photography she did. But they didn't say anything about it when she offered to take photos of their grandbabies. Josie was surprised to see so many of her clients had shown up at the last minute. Her friends had called on every favor and connection they had to organize the fundraiser in two days.

When everyone called for a speech, Josie was overcome with emotion and love for her community. Right before she could ugly cry, she turned the floor over to Tasha, who easily entertained the crowd, and found a quiet area in the back of the restaurant to compose herself.

"You found my favorite hiding spot, right behind the column. I set this small table here to do paperwork when I don't want to hole up in the back office." Keisha handed Josie her cocktail while balancing a tray overloaded with appetizers. "How are you holding up?"

"Exhausted," Josie said, then downed half her cocktail. "It's been a long week."

"You poor thing. Here, eat up." Keisha slid some food onto the small table. "How about I have the kitchen pack some food so you won't have to worry about cooking for a few days?"

"I won't say no. That sounds a hundred times better than all the soggy fries, burgers, and frozen dinners I've been eating." Josie dug into the appetizers.

"That's a perk of being friends with the owners of Hazel's Kitchen," Keisha said, and winked.

"Josie, there you are!" Trixie peeked behind the column and joined them. Behind her were the rest of the Boss Babes. Zoe and Reina each had two cocktails.

"We bring provisions!" Reina held the drinks up high to avoid hitting everyone's heads. "We barely have room for these, so you'd better drink up."

"I can pull over another table." Keisha scanned the dining room. "Never mind, they're all taken."

"We have a great turnout considering we planned it in only two days!" Trixie beamed. "I also peeked at the silent auction bids. It's going to be a successful fundraiser. Josie, people are bidding like crazy over your New Orleans photos!"

"My donation for a VIP booth for six with a two-hour open bar at my club is already at a thousand bucks!" Reina tucked a strand of red hair behind her ear and whispered, "I may have started the bidding at eight hundred. If you see the name Annie Position, that's me."

"Reina!" Trixie scowled but then laughed. "That's actually not a bad idea. Maybe I'll encourage the bidding on a specially curated sex toy collection."

"Annie Position." Keisha snorted. "I just got it."

"You all are terrible," said Zoe. "But I love you anyway."

"It's all for a worthy cause." Reina held up her glass for a toast. "Cheers."

"Cheers!" the other women chimed in.

"I've missed you all," Josie said. "I feel like I've barely seen you between planning for the New Orleans shoot and actually going there. I'll make it to our lunch at Phở-Ever 75 once we get this insurance stuff sorted out." Hanging out with all her friends energized Josie. The exhaustion from the day started to slowly melt away.

"I'm glad you said that, because we have missed you! Who else is going to make sure I'm using my spreadsheets?" Trixie teased.

"Spreadsheet formulas are sexy," Josie countered, "especially when they help me grow Parks Photography."

"No spreadsheet talk tonight." Reina pointed at Trixie and Josie like a schoolteacher. "We're here to have fun and support Josie."

"I can't believe you did all this for me and the studio." Josie placed her hand on her chest. "When Zoe called and told me that Tasha was hurt—I'm just glad you took care of her until I got back."

"I'd beat up those thieves if I knew who they were," Reina said, holding up a fist.

"Shush. You'll break a nail. I know how much you hate that," Keisha said. "We let Andre and Xavier do the dirty work." Xavier was Andre's best friend and had a thing for Keisha. Not that either of them was ready to admit it.

"Don't encourage those two! They get in enough trouble on their own." Trixie shook her head.

"Are you getting enough sleep, Josie?" Zoe's eyes bored into Josie's.

"What? Those bags under my eyes have always been there." She tried to play it off, but that took too much energy. "Sleep has been elusive. When I am tired, every sound or bump outside has me on full alert."

Her girlfriends exchanged concerned looks.

"I'll be fine. Just another week or so before—"

"Stop, Josie." Keisha put her hand on Josie's. "We want to help."

"It's okay to ask for help," Zoe reminded her. "It doesn't mean you're weak or broken."

"I've never said that—" Josie began.

"Babes, let's get to the point," Reina interrupted, setting down her glass. "I'm calling an emergency Boss Babes meeting right here."

Josie watched as everyone nodded. Why did she have the feeling they'd planned this?

"Fine. What?"

"You're going to kill yourself if you don't slow down," Reina began.

"I've got it under control." Josie knew she'd been working hard. Harder than before her impromptu vacation. But this form of busyness was temporary. Once Tasha was fully healed and they'd purchased new cameras and lights, everything would be fine.

"Reina, stop attacking her." Keisha tapped Josie's elbow. "What we're trying to say is that you're avoiding your feelings about Spencer by working your ass off."

"There are no feelings," Josie protested. "We're collaborating on an art project and he understands that I can't get back to him until next week."

"Which is not healthy," added Trixie, who ignored her protests. "You are headed to Burnoutville."

"I've got everything under control," she repeated.

"Twelve-hour workdays, no sleep, eating fast food for dinner, and smothering Tasha." Zoe held out a finger as she listed each of her concerns. "That's what you've been doing for the past two days."

Josie opened her mouth but snapped it shut. After Tasha's accident twelve years ago, she shifted to always preparing for the worst—just in case. For so long, she'd lived on edge, waiting to put out fires instead of focusing on how well things could go if she trusted herself. Now she found herself putting out fires again all by herself when she had friends and family to help her.

"If one of us were doing all those things, what would you do?" Reina asked.

Josie hung her head. Her friends were right. She was taking horrible care of herself. Even worse, she tried to control Tasha because her own life was out of control.

"I'm trying to stick to the plan," Josie said desperately. "How else am I supposed to know what I should do next? If there's no plan, everything will fall apart."

"Oh, sweetie." Zoe rubbed her back. "We'd never let that happen."

"Will you let us take some things off your plate?" asked Keisha.

"Thank you for helping even when I'm too stubborn to ask." Logically, Josie knew that asking for help didn't mean she was weak. If she were to balance her business and an art career, she had to learn how to delegate. Continuing to pile up her workload meant burnout was inevitable. The point of her vacation was to rejuvenate her energy and creativity. The little she'd manage to achieve had been undone in only two days.

"We can make a list of things if that helps," Zoe offered, and gave Josie a hug.

"You know how much I love lists." Josie sniffled. She was glad to have friends who called her out and kept her on track. She picked up her drink, but it was empty.

"I'm here just in time." Andre sidled up with a tray full of drinks. He kissed Trixie on the cheek. "You did a fantastic job organizing the fundraiser, babe."

"It was your idea," said Trixie. "We make a wonderful team."

"Yes, we do," Andre said before going in for a long kiss.

"Ewwww, Andre," teased Keisha. "Take that to the back office!"

"It wouldn't be the first time," he said, and winked at Trixie.

"I did not need to know that." Keisha wrinkled her nose but grinned indulgently at her brother. "Leave the drinks and get out of here. We're having a Boss Babes–only discussion."

Keisha took the tray from him. Andre held out his hands in defense and walked backward away from them. He blew Trixie a kiss before turning away.

Josie could barely stand how adorable they were. Andre had been such a jerk to Trixie when he made her choose between him or her career. Yet he'd convinced Trixie to give him a second chance. Well, three chances.

"So?" Zoe asked softly.

"Asking for help is easier when I have my Babes."

Josie had always set ambitious standards for herself and expected everyone to live up to her mostly unattainable expectations. Once she'd made a plan, it was meant to be followed. But plans were allowed to change, weren't they? Especially if inspiration or a once-in-a-lifetime opportunity presented itself.

"How about you start by letting Tasha take the lead in her recovery?" Trixie suggested.

"And let me help you with the insurance paperwork," said Keisha. "I have a lot of experience filling out forms after we had that fire. It can be a headache."

"Boss Babe powers, activate!" cheered Reina. They all laughed.

"You know what? Tasha has asked for more responsibility at the studio. It's time I promote her to senior studio manager." Josie's shoulders lifted as if ten times lighter. She should've asked for help long ago. Tasha practically ran the studio for the short time Josie had been in New Orleans. She could do it permanently.

Now that Josie had help, she could focus on the two things that mattered most to her right now: Stevens Gallery and her collaboration with Spencer.

CHAPTER 35

Spencer's mother opened his bedroom door and stuck her head in. "Can I come in? I want to talk to you about something," she said in Vietnamese.

"Mẹ." He scrambled to sit up in his bed. His heart raced and his chest tightened as if he were a kid again and had done something wrong. Whenever his parents wanted to talk, it usually involved mostly listening on his part as he was reprimanded for something. Up until recently, discussing their feelings and deep desires wasn't part of their regular family gatherings.

"Why do you look scared? I'm not coming to yell at you." Her forehead furrowed. "I guess I only talk to you when it's something bad."

Spencer didn't know how to respond. His mom wasn't usually so open. She sat on the end of his twin bed.

"That's our fault. Mine and your dad's. You're the oldest, so we were harder on you. I realize that now."

"It's okay. You and Ba worked hard to give us this." Spencer gestured at their home. "It's not a bad thing to work hard and get good grades. And take a stable job."

"So you really want to make this movie?"

"I do. Remember in middle school when I wanted to join the film club? You and Ba said I had to focus on my schoolwork." He swallowed hard. "I thought I wasn't allowed to try anything related to the arts."

That day had stuck with him. He'd spent almost a week working up the courage to ask, only to be denied the opportunity without the chance to plead his case.

"I don't remem— Oh!" Mẹ gasped. "That was sixth grade."

He nodded.

"You were eleven. That year was a horrible time for us. Fishing was not good, and your dad and grandfather took second jobs after they came back from the water. We had no one else to take care of your sisters. Your grandmother couldn't handle three young girls on her own."

"You never told me that." He'd gotten the wrong message, but it wasn't his fault. Why didn't his family ever talk about these things?

"We didn't want you to worry. As the oldest, we already asked too much of you."

"But, Mẹ, all this time I thought I wasn't allowed to do anything else. Whenever I took a painting or film class in DC, I could never finish it. I could hear yours and Ba's voices in my head telling me what a waste of time it was." Spencer breathed heavily. His cheeks were warm. He'd never spoken to his mother like this. Telling her how much she and his father had hurt him.

"That's why I'm here. Ba and I want you to work on your film." Her sad eyes were wet. "You need to stop worrying about us. We are doing fine. Our family has always managed no matter how tight our finances are. We're survivors." She scooted closer to him.

"I don't want to let you down." Spencer sniffed. "It's all I've done lately. How are you going to brag about me if I don't have a fancy job in DC?"

Mẹ laughed and tousled his hair. "Your elders worked hard so you could be happy. If you have to try a bunch of different things to find what makes you happy, then do it."

"Really?" Spencer couldn't believe his ears. His parents were giving him their blessing. "What if it takes me years to figure out what I want to do next?"

"If that's the case, maybe a part-time job before your savings run out?"

He laughed. Now, that was a response more in character for his mother.

"You've got a point." He'd seen some openings for upcoming Asian American film festivals. Working them would help him meet others in the industry.

"Your Bà Bà is right. We need to tell you how proud we are of you. We're proud that you're doing new things and trying to figure out what makes you happy." His mother smiled.

He'd been waiting to hear those words all his life. Spencer's eyes welled up with tears. He blinked them away. If she told him she loved him, he might pass out.

"Your dad and I will work on telling you and your sisters that more often. We're trying to do better. Be patient with us?"

"As long as you're patient with me."

"We'll all do better." His mother stood up and smoothed out invisible wrinkles in her shirt. She ran her hand through his hair again. "You really should get a haircut."

Spencer laughed quietly. Of course she had to end their deep conversation with a comment on his appearance. The entire talk had been hard for her, he knew, but it was momentous all the same. This was the first time she'd truly spoken to him as an adult.

His parents had given their blessing for him to pursue film-making. All the same, he didn't want to let them down. Telling the story of his family—his entire Vietnamese community in New Orleans—was a big responsibility. He hoped he could do it justice.

Five minutes after his mother left, Bà Bà flung open the door to Spencer's bedroom.

"Spencer!" she exclaimed urgently in Vietnamese. "I want to talk to Josie!"

He sighed. Alone time was hard to come by in his home, but he always made time for his grandmother.

"I already told you, we need to give her space. She's back in DC taking care of her sister," Spencer reminded her. His grandmother had gotten attached to Josie even faster than he had. Josie had been a tornado that had changed their lives forever.

He wanted to talk to Josie, too. He'd written her at least fifty texts. And erased all of them. What could he say in a text that would convince her to give him another chance?

"I want to invite her to my birthday party," she explained,

as if it were perfectly normal for her to call her grandson's ex-girlfriend. Or fling, or whatever they were.

He rubbed his forehead, avoiding the bruise on his temple. He couldn't look in the mirror without thinking of Josie. His skin had transformed from purple to an anemic greenish yellow. Soon the bruise would disappear from his life forever. The same way Josie would if he couldn't win her back.

"Have you called her?"

"Bà Bà, it's only been two days. She's taking care of her sister."

"You are too slow," she scolded in Vietnamese. "You're letting her get away."

Spencer fell back onto his unmade bed. "I'm trying to figure out how to get her back. I don't know what to say to her."

"Silly boy. Josie needs more than talking." His grandmother tsked. "You need to prove to her you're her equal. She's a woman who wants big things. Do you?"

Spencer groaned loudly. Why did Bà Bà ask such hard questions?

"Okay, I'm going to watch my shows." She turned and left, but not before Spencer caught a sly smile on her face.

He shut the door behind her, locking it this time. He wouldn't be surprised if one of his sisters barged in to meddle like his grandmother had. He climbed back into his bed. Flipping open his notebook, he scratched out all his terrible ideas on how to win Josie back.

Maybe Bà Bà was right. He was approaching this the wrong way. What *did* he want? When he first ran into Josie, he had no idea. He started—tried—to make films because he was bored and needed to get out of his parents' home. As Jimmy pointed out, he never stuck with any of his ideas. None of them stoked his passion. He gave up when he had to dig deeper or work harder.

Until Josie.

Her excitement gave him a purpose. She encouraged him to document his grandfather's legacy. The flyer for the Fifty States Exhibition was the perfect excuse to spend more time with her. Then something magical happened. The more interviews he taped, the more confident he grew. He started to believe that he could create something beautiful.

All because Josie encouraged him that very first day.

Yet he had disappointed her. She thrived on certainty, and he wanted to be open to possibilities until he found the right one. She didn't know that he had certainty for most of his adult life. This was the first time he had the chance to experiment and try things without making it a career.

What Josie didn't know—hadn't seen—was that he had big goals and would work his ass off to achieve them. He'd show her that he could see a project through from beginning to end. Then she would see what a great team they made, and how well they complemented each other. She'd understand how he fell in love with her in only four days.

Spencer sat up in his bed. He had to go to DC so they could finish their application together. Face-to-face. But first he needed some help.

CHAPTER 36

Y ou won't regret promoting me." Tasha threw her good arm around Josie.

"Of course not. You learned from the best." Josie winked.

"Hush, girls! I'm only two books away from taking this entire game." Their mom and three of her friends sat around their dining table. Their Sunday post-supper spades night was serious business.

The sisters broke out in giggles and ran into the kitchen before their mom could scowl at them again. Game night was a big deal in their home, as the winning team held bragging rights all week. Their mom despised how her friends gloated over her whenever she lost. Even their father retreated to a friend's home until the smack talk and sound of cards slapping against the table had long faded.

"Mom is handling the news well." Tasha turned on the tap to rinse the dinner dishes before placing them in the dishwasher. "It's about time you took more time for yourself."

"I'm decent at spades but not cutthroat enough for Mom." Josie grimaced, remembering the times she and her mom had lost because of her. "She only invited me to play because she thought I worked too much. Besides, she's much happier with Mrs. Harris as her partner."

"They're killing it!" Tasha agreed.

"We heard that," their competitors called out. The sisters' eyes widened before another burst of quiet laughter overtook them.

"Shhh, you're going to get us in trouble," whispered Josie. Her heart was light. Tonight was not unlike other Sunday nights when they were younger. The two of them cleaning the kitchen while eavesdropping on the adults' gossip. And getting caught.

Josie's shoulders had finally relaxed after the last three whirl-wind days back at home. Now that she'd turned over day-to-day operations to her sister, her brain was less cluttered. This was exactly the space she needed in order to focus on her art.

"You want me to pack up the rest of the crab mac and cheese for you?" Tasha held up the white vintage baking dish. "This is how much Mom missed you."

"I wasn't even gone a full week! And you both told me to stay in New Orleans." Josie took the dish from Tasha and scooped the leftovers into a container. "I'll never turn down her mac and cheese."

"So what will you do with all your free time?"

"I'm not sure exactly." Josie knew that she wanted to work on her portfolio but was unsure of her approach. "Maybe take time to just play with my camera for a bit?"

"Wait, did you say you didn't have a set plan?" her sister teased.

"I have a loose plan. Like figure out what I want to photo-graph outside of boudoir photos for a start." Josie shrugged. This must be what Spencer had felt like after he'd moved home. There were so many possibilities that she didn't know where to start. "Maybe finally learn to swim? That's one of the last things on my thirty by thirty list. I can't believe I only have three items left to check off!"

"What about your collab with Spencer?" Tasha asked hopefully.

"Who knows if he still wants to work together. I've had so much to deal with that I haven't even texted him since I got back. Things ended, well, weird." Josie had blindsided him by breaking things off.

Now that there was distance and a little time between them, the entire experience had been surreal. She barely recognized herself in her pictures from New Orleans. He'd known a version of herself that only existed for those few days. Would he even like the real her?

"Hey, stop overthinking it! You've been taking care of me for a long time. It's your turn to figure out things." Tasha passed containers of leftover baked chicken, mashed potatoes, and mac and cheese to Josie. "Here, put these in the fridge for me."

"You're trying to steal the mac and cheese!" Josie playfully swiped at her sister. She placed the container in her tote bag so she wouldn't forget to take it home.

"Josie!" her mom yelled from the dining room. "There's someone at the door."

"Got it!" Josie called back. She tossed the other leftovers in the fridge. "Whoever it is doesn't know how dangerous interrupting spades night is."

They knocked once more before Josie made it to the front door. She hurried before her mom yelled again.

"Hold on. I'm coming." Josie opened the door to find a man standing on the stoop under the dim porch light. "Spencer! What are you doing in DC?"

Spencer looked happy. She didn't know why she was surprised by that. After all, she'd been the one who broke it off. It didn't seem like him to mope over a four-day relationship.

"I thought it might be easier to work on our application if we're in the same metro area?" Spencer gave a small, hopeful smile.

"How did you even get this address?" Even through her shock, the corners of her mouth lifted as a grin spread across her face. He'd come all this way to see her!

"I texted Zoe. I had her number from your last day in New Orleans." He slipped his hands into his jeans pockets as if to keep them still.

"I asked a friend if I could borrow his couch," he continued. "Since I gave up my apartment when I moved home." He didn't want her to think that this trip was completely impulsive.

"I see," Josie finally said. "I'm sorry I haven't texted or called. It's been a little—"

"Josie, do you need help out—" Tasha stopped and darted her hand from behind Josie out to Spencer. "Well, hello. You must be Spencer."

"Tasha, it's nice to meet you." He shook her hand. "How's your wrist?"

"Even better now that I've been promoted to senior studio

manager." Tasha nodded at Josie. "She's turning over things to me so she can focus on her art."

"You are?" Spencer exclaimed. "That's wonderful news!"

"Girls! Close the door. You're letting out the heat!"

"Sorry, Mom," Josie called back. "Tasha, can you grab my bag? Spencer and I need to talk."

Tasha's eyes gleamed. "Only if you tell me all about it tomorrow."

"I'm not going into the studio tomorrow, remember? You're in charge now." Josie shook her head indulgently at her sister. "Go grab my stuff and tell Mom I'll call her tomorrow."

After Tasha left to get Josie's things, Spencer held up his backpack with his laptop and notes.

"I'm ready to work and nail our application for the Fifty States Exhibition."

"You mean right now?" Josie said, and looked over her shoulder. She didn't want Tasha to overhear and try to help. She wasn't ready to share Spencer with anyone yet.

"The deadline is next week." He flashed his biggest, most charming grin. "Are you up for a challenge?"

She wasn't sure how to respond, but he didn't push her. He simply stood there on her mom's porch and waited.

"Here." Tasha rushed back with some bags. "And before you even check, I did not steal your mac and cheese. You better call me."

Tasha gently pushed Josie out the doorway and onto the stoop. She winked at Spencer before waving them off. The door clicked behind them.

"You're full of surprises." Josie laughed and ran her fingers through his hair. "You got a haircut."

"Got tired of my sisters calling me a Keanu wannabe." He touched the back of his neck where his hair had been shorn closer to his skin. "Though now I'm worried I look like a K-pop star wannabe."

"You look handsome," she whispered as she ran her hand down his neck. "It suits you."

His eyes widened, and he shivered under her touch. She searched his brown eyes for—what? Hope, adoration—love? She had no right to expect any of those things after she broke up with him.

She bit her bottom lip and caressed his temple where she'd marked him with her beads. Spencer closed his eyes and leaned into her hand. She guided his head closer to hers until their breathing synchronized. His lips quivered with the heat of her mouth so close to his.

Josie closed the distance. Their breath intertwined as their lips met. He opened himself to her. She'd missed exploring his mouth and the way their tongues danced together. The kiss woke up other parts of her as heat began to blaze through her body.

As much as she disliked surprises, Spencer was exactly who she needed at this moment.

CHAPTER 37

Josie didn't mean to kiss Spencer on her mother's porch like a teenager. All the excitement from New Orleans rushed back when she touched his face. A familiar warmth filled her belly. She pulled away before things became too heated. They had too much to discuss.

"Wow, now, that's a kiss." Spencer blew out a long breath. His cheeks were flushed from more than the brisk January air. "Do you welcome everyone to DC that way?"

"Depends on if I knocked them in the head with beads," she said, swatting at his chest.

"How many of us are there?"

"You'll never know." Oh God, she had missed this. Missed him.

"Let me guess. You have a shrine of beads in your apartment. 'To all the boys I've knocked out with Mardi Gras beads.'" He waved a hand in the air.

"Close." She laughed. "Your beads are hanging on the wall in my living room. But I'll never kiss and tell about the others."

She caressed his cheek, and he leaned into her hand. "I'm glad you're here," she said.

"I know you're not a fan of surprises, but I couldn't wait until tomorrow to see you."

"You flew in today?"

He nodded. "Dropped off my things at my friend's place in Southwest and came here."

Josie had played out different conversations with him in her head, but she couldn't remember any of them. Of all the different scenarios, she hadn't expected him to come here. He was happy in New Orleans and tired of the DMV.

"Wait, I brought you something." He slid his backpack off and sat on the top step of her mother's stoop. Spencer patted the spot next to him. She sat down. He dug around and brandished a white bag with green print.

"What! Are those beignets from Cafe du Monde?" Josie's mouth watered even though she'd stuffed herself with her mother's cooking only an hour ago. She couldn't believe that he'd gone through all the trouble for her.

"They're a little cold. But hopefully still delicious." He pulled out another, similar bag. "Lucky for you, I asked for the sugar on the side so they didn't get soggy."

Josie gasped. "Those bags are the same size."

"Yes, there's as much sugar as there are beignets." He chuckled and handed her both of them.

She pulled out a beignet and dropped it into the bag of sugar. She folded the top of the sugar bag three times before shaking it.

"The perfect ratio," she declared.

Josie unearthed the beignet from the sugar bag, held her

breath, and took a bite. It wasn't as good as a fresh one hot from the fryer, but the sweet, chewy bread transported her right back to the first night they met.

"You remembered!" Spencer's face lit up.

She offered him one but he shook his head. "I can't eat all of these," she said. "There's gotta be at least six or seven in here."

"I got you two orders. They might reheat well in the oven to-morrow for breakfast. You have a little sugar—" He brushed the corner of her mouth. "There. I should've brought napkins."

Josie froze. Her heart thudded in her chest. It was too easy to fall back into their easy intimacy. She didn't want to repeat what had happened in New Orleans. He was here now, but for how long?

"Spencer, what is going on?" she blurted. "I'm glad to see you, but I thought you didn't want to come back to DC."

"I'm here to win you back."

Josie sputtered. Sugar flew into the air. Spencer grabbed a water bottle from his bag, opened it, and handed it to her. She sipped the water slowly to gather her thoughts. Working on their application together was more plausible, but she didn't expect him to hop on a plane for her. That kind of thing only happened in movies.

"I told you, there's no future for us. We're in different places in our lives."

"You said we didn't know each other well enough for me to fall in love with you. That's why I'm here. I want to know who Josie is when she's not on vacation. To see how talented and smart and driven you are when you're on your turf." He gave her a lopsided grin.

"What makes you think I want to know you better?" she challenged.

"Exhibit number one: that kiss you planted on me." He pretended to swoon.

"Spencer, I'm serious. You can't just show up and expect me to drop everything for you. I'm not on vacation anymore."

"Give me a week," he pleaded. "Give *us* a week. Once the week is over, if you don't think we have a future, I'll go back to New Orleans and never bother you again."

Josie's jaw dropped. "What are we supposed to do? Go on dates?"

"That's a good start. But I also want us to finish our application for the exhibition. If you still want to do it."

She'd been so caught up with the studio and Tasha that she hadn't thought enough about the exhibition. It seemed easier to focus on a project that didn't rely on someone else to complete. Like her portfolio for Stevens Gallery.

"It depends on if you've changed your mind about the topic again."

"I'm sorry I was wishy-washy. This is the first time in my life where I've gotten to try creative things. I had idea-itis." He waved his hands in circles on either side of his head. "But I know exactly what I want to do now."

"Idea what?"

"I had too many ideas and got overwhelmed. I wanted to

do all of them." His brows drew together. "Which I obviously couldn't manage and it frustrated you."

"I call that shiny object syndrome. I've been there plenty of times. Why do you think I make so many lists?"

"Finally, she reveals her secrets!" He bumped her shoulder with his. "I've started to make lists, too."

"And?"

"It's a secret." Spencer's eyes flashed. "But give me a week and you can help me check them off."

Josie's mouth twitched. He knew how much she loved checking off lists. Now that Tasha was running Parks Photography, she had more free time, which wasn't yet accounted for. She usually planned out her week on Sunday nights, and she looked forward to pulling out her pens, inks, and notebook for a session once she got home.

The universe was telling her to accept his challenge.

"You have one week." It was enough time for her to decide if she and Spencer had a future worth pursuing.

"Woohoo!" Spencer cheered.

"Shhh! You'll wake up the neighbors." She grabbed his arm and scanned the houses closest to them. "Mom's neighbors go to bed early."

"Woohoo," he whispered with a goofy smile. "Meet me at Hazel's Kitchen tomorrow at eleven."

"What? But they're closed on Mondays." What the heck did he have planned? The Boss Babes had to be involved.

"You told me I had to check it out. I'm only doing what you

told me to do. Bring your camera and laptop." Spencer stood up and slipped his backpack onto his shoulder. He practically skipped down the stairs. "And your notebook!"

He blew her a kiss as he walked off in the direction of the Metro station.

What the hell just happened? He'd returned to her life as abruptly as he'd first entered it. What else could she do but go along for the ride? Something had changed in her since she'd come back. Before New Orleans, she would've been annoyed about someone interrupting her plans *and* not knowing what came next.

When it came to Spencer, however, she was delighted. Whatever he had planned for her tomorrow, she looked forward to the surprise.

CHAPTER 38

"Keisha, thanks for letting us set up here," Spencer said as he slipped through the front door of Hazel's Kitchen the next morning. He was so nervous about this plan that he'd left his friend's apartment early. For once, the Metro didn't have delays, and he made it to the restaurant an hour before Josie was supposed to arrive.

"I couldn't say no after Zoe explained your plan." Keisha locked the door behind him.

She grabbed his arm before he stepped farther into the restaurant. "I hope you know what you're doing. If you hurt her in any way"—she squeezed harder—"you'll have to answer to me, my brother, and the rest of us Babes."

"Uh, um, I'll do my best." Spencer would do his best to win Josie over, but the decision was up to her.

"Good." Keisha dropped his arm and batted her eyes as if she hadn't threatened him a second ago. "Now, I've set up this four-top for you. I'll be in the kitchen prepping for community night if you need anything."

The table was tucked away in the back. Cozy. Romantic, even.

On the table sat a coffee carafe, mugs, and some takeout boxes. Everything they needed to work on their application. Keisha was rooting for him and Josie even through her threats.

Spencer unzipped his backpack and pulled out his laptop to put the finishing touches on the slides he'd stayed up late working on. Josie wasn't due to arrive for another hour. He stifled a yawn. Thank goodness there was coffee.

"Hey! Look who the cat dragged in." Josie stepped out from the hallway leading to the bathroom. She wore a long, purple dress that accentuated her breasts. A matching scarf was wrapped around her hair. Her purposeful strides kicked up the flowing fabric. She was even more majestic on her home turf. She belonged here.

"Josie! You're here early."

"Keisha let me in. It's weird not going into the studio in the mornings. I couldn't stand the quiet in my apartment, so I came here instead." She pointed to the chair across from him. How had he missed her bag right in front of him?

"Good, let's get to work on the application, then." Spencer pulled out the chair across from her.

"I've decided not to wait to submit my portfolio to Stevens," Josie announced.

Spencer's stomach lurched. Did this mean she didn't want to work with him anymore? She wouldn't have a reason to spend time with him otherwise.

"What about the exhibition?" he forced himself to ask. "You were entering to get more exposure for your work."

"That's only if we're finalists. It's time to shoot my shot with

Stevens. I've been using the Fifty States application to procrastinate." Josie's shoulders were squared in determination. "I've put it off for too long."

She continued to amaze him with her drive and confidence.

"Why are you looking at me like that?" she said. Josie's eyebrows drew together as she studied him. "You think it's a bad idea to drop out of Fifty States?"

"No, it's not that." He smiled so hard his cheeks hurt. "You're an inspiration. You know what you want and go for it."

"So are you." She tapped her pen on his laptop. "Look at how much you've accomplished in just a few days."

"No. I was fumbling along until I met you. You showed me that if I didn't finish a project, how would I know if it was any good?"

Josie snorted. "Spencer, I have no idea what I'm doing."

"You pull it off well."

"I've had lots of practice pushing through my doubts." She sat down in the chair across from him. "But doing something is better than nothing. Entering the competition was a way for me to procrastinate, and I don't want to put off Stevens anymore. I want to enter and move on with my life."

"Can I be like you when I'm a grown-up artist?"

"You mean doubting myself and my work? If you really want to."

"No, trying new things and kicking ass."

She blushed and tried to hide her smile in her coffee mug.

"I'm not saying that to get into your pants."

"I'm not wearing pants," she replied.

"Even better." Spencer froze as soon as the words left his mouth. He was determined not to jump into bed with her until Josie was sure she wanted to be with him. Not that he would admit that to her.

Josie's cheeks were flushed. She looked away.

"I'm sorry. I didn't mean to—" Spencer stopped. He had no idea what he meant to say. Of course he wanted to jump into bed with her. She was fucking sexy. And smart and funny and—

Josie broke their awkward silence. "I still want to help you finish your application."

"Thank God. I have no idea what I'm doing here." Spencer sighed in relief. He opened his laptop and turned it around so she could see his checklist.

"I made an outline of the story I wanted to tell with my film. And now photos, since you're focusing on your portfolio." He pulled out his notebook and flipped it open to his brainstorming notes. "The scope of our original idea is too big for a beginner like me."

"How so?" Josie poured them both coffee and pushed a mug toward him. "I can see where you got super excited, because it's hard to read your handwriting."

He nodded. "I can barely read it myself. I can't stop thinking about Crescent City Co-op and how these people from different backgrounds overcame their differences to create it. That's the story the world needs to hear."

"I thought the same thing when I was there. You're the perfect person to share their story."

"You believed in me since the beginning. You never even asked if I knew how to make a film. You just encouraged me."

She beamed. "Your passion is very evident when you talk about your work."

"Get this. I came clean to my parents about what I wanted and they're not disappointed in me."

He caught her up on his family meeting and how his parents encouraged him to continue with the film. And how they'd banked enough savings for him to explore for a while.

"Wow. All of that happened after I left?"

"I couldn't believe it, either. After the talk with my mom, I realized that I was never given the opportunity to try different artsy things."

"Now what?"

"After I submit this application, I want to try new things even if they're not going to pay the bills. It won't take long to finish. Since you're focusing on your portfolio, I'll update the sections you were in."

"Does that mean we're—I mean, is our collaboration over?" Josie's face fell.

He sensed the disappointment in her voice. His plan was working. She wanted to spend more time with him!

"Don't think I'm letting you off so easily," he said. "You promised me a week."

"I did." Josie bit her lip, but her eyes flashed with excitement.

"It means the application will be done soon. Can you look it over when I'm done?" Even though she wouldn't be his partner for the application, he wanted her professional eye on it. He gulped his coffee and began typing.

"I promised to help you, didn't I?"

"I can finish this later." He closed his laptop and notebook. A week wasn't very long. He didn't want to waste his precious time with Josie sitting in front of his laptop. "When we were in New Orleans, you let me set our agenda. Now that I have a good handle on this, what do *you* want to do?"

"You said you wanted to try new things, right?" She smiled mischievously.

The look in her eyes frightened him. What had he gotten himself into? This must be how Josie felt whenever he sprung a surprise on her. No wonder she didn't like surprises.

"You're going to say boudoir photos, aren't you?"

Her wicked grin was all the answer he needed. When Spencer had vowed to do whatever it took to win Josie back, he didn't expect this.

"Okay, I'm in."

CHAPTER 39

"pencer, there's no one in the studio but us. And I turned on the heat so you'll be comfortable." Josie bit off a giggle as she watched his feet pace behind the three-panel screen they kept in the studio for clothing changes. This was the point where her clients were most nervous. They had to get out of their head before the first photo could be taken.

She and Spencer had walked around her neighborhood until the evening, when they snuck into the studio after hours. Josie made a mental note to reset everything when they were finished. If Tasha found out, she'd tease her mercilessly about not being able to stay away for one day.

"I need a minute." Spencer's voice cracked. She'd never heard him so nervous. Before, in all their time together, he'd always been ready to dive headfirst into anything they did.

Josie ran toward the screen but stopped short. Maybe she'd pushed him too far. This was supposed to be fun and empowering. At least for her women clients. This would be her first shoot with a guy.

"You don't have to do this. It's okay if you change your mind."

She spoke softly through the screen. "It was just a silly idea I had."

There was a rustle of fabric as he shuffled behind the screen. A few seconds later, he walked out wearing one of the thick white terrycloth robes they offered their clients. His legs were bare. The robe was slightly open to reveal his smooth chest.

Spencer scowled as he padded around the room before settling on the velvet burgundy chaise, a client favorite. His robe slipped as he lifted his legs onto it. He quickly pulled the robe closed and tucked it between his legs to keep it from shifting.

Josie licked her lips. Hot damn. How could something that covered so much skin be so sexy? *Focus.* She wanted this to be a true boudoir shoot. She tamped down her arousal for now. What happened after the shoot was another story.

"Spencer?"

"Tell me again why you want to take boudoir photos of me."

Josie grabbed a bottle of water and placed it in his hand. She pulled up a stool next to the chaise.

"At first it was a silly idea. But the more I thought about it, the more I wanted to try it." She first mentioned it in fun, and teased Spencer since he didn't like being the subject of photos.

Her staff photographers had done a few dudeoirs, as they jokingly called it. Her studio didn't get very many requests, so her staff fought over them. It was a different way for her team to flex their creativity, so Josie always ceded the jobs to them.

He nodded and waved for her to continue.

"Then I remembered what you told me when we were in New Orleans. Actually, two things." She held up her fingers. "You asked me why I didn't add my boudoir photos to my portfolio for Stevens. And you said I needed to trust my intuition more. Maybe I'm overthinking this portfolio thing. Why am I ignoring what I'm good at? Making people feel beautiful when I photograph them."

He snorted. "I didn't mean boudoir photos of me," he said. "Not that I mind being half naked next to you. It's the photos I'm not so sure about."

"Say the word, and I'll shut it all down." Josie squeezed his hand to reassure him. "What I love about my job is that I get to show my clients how I see them. Beautiful. Strong. Brave."

"I feel the opposite of all those things right now." He pulled at his robe. "I feel naked. Vulnerable. Most of my life, I've been told that Asian men aren't sexy."

"Fuck those people. You're sexy to me, Spencer." The words flew out of her mouth. Josie inhaled sharply. When their eyes connected, it was all she could do not to rip open his robe and run her hand across his chest until she reached the waistband of his boxers. He'd know how sexy she found him.

She looked away and cleared her throat.

"Society expects you to be strong all the time. That's why we should do more boudoir photos of men. Why not show their— your softer side? I want to do a series with people of all genders. You're the first person I thought of."

"Because I was the only man around when the idea came to you?"

"No, silly. Because you're strong. And you have a soft side. I see it whenever you're with your Bà Bà. Or talk about her."

His eyes softened at the mention of his grandmother. His entire body relaxed. He slid into a reclining pose on the chaise.

"Did you feel that? Your entire body changed. You can still be soft and strong at the same time. Will you let me document it? Photograph you?"

"Is this how all your clients feel? Terrified?"

"Some, yes. They warm up. I don't take any photos until they give their enthusiastic consent. It's important that this is a good experience for both of us."

"You talk about it like it's sex."

"Taking photographs of someone in their underwear is just as, if not more, intimate than sex. They're letting me into their soul. The camera reveals so much."

"Not the camera. *You.* You see deep into people's souls when you photograph them." He took a deep breath in through his nose and out through his mouth. "Okay. I'll do it."

"You sure?"

"Yes. I trust you. And I believe in your vision for this series. I'm honored to be your first for something."

She snorted. "If you're making bad jokes, that means you're no longer scared."

"I'm still terrified, but at least I know you won't make me look bad. I'm ready."

There was the Spencer she knew. Cracking jokes. Except, this time, he wasn't using humor to deflect his fear. He was using it to bolster his courage.

"Keep talking while I take some warm-up shots." She picked up Ruby from around her neck and moved slowly to keep him from feeling overly self-conscious. "Tell me more about your application. What are you concentrating on now?"

She half listened as he laid out his vision and his plan to take his own photos. The more he spoke about his family's legacy, the more comfortable he became in his body. His legs stretched out on the chaise and part of the robe fell away to reveal his strong calves. His thighs parted as he bent one leg and rested his arm on his knee. Black boxer briefs peeked out from under the white terrycloth. His arms floated to rest behind his head.

Josie kept her finger on the shutter. She was in a flow state similar to his. He was reveling in his skin now. She walked around him to capture him from as many angles as she could.

"I wish you could see how focused you are right now." He held up his hands to form a frame with his fingers. "I'm taking a photo in my head."

"That's so cheesy." She burst into laughter.

"You can count on me for cheese." He winked. They both cracked up.

"Okay, you ready for a clothing or location change?" Josie's concentration had broken, but it was time for a short break anyway. She'd taken so many photos in rapid succession that her camera was running hot.

"Where should I go?"

She'd chosen their largest studio with the most furniture options because she didn't have a clear vision of her series at first. Now she realized that her intuition had been guiding her all along. Her most successful shoots were the ones where her clients chose the props and furniture that called out to them.

"Let your intuition guide you."

He slowly spun around the room as he assessed his options. His robe came open and the bottom of it twirled. She couldn't grab Ruby fast enough to capture this impromptu moment. This man was an absolute natural. It was hard to believe that he was shaking in terror an hour ago.

He'd done this all for her. Spencer believed in her vision enough to face real fear. He encouraged her to explore an idea in its infancy without knowing the outcome. No one except her best friends had supported her dreams in this way.

Josie's heart pounded. She loved him. She almost couldn't believe it. The one least likely to make a decision without researching it to death had fallen in love with a man she'd known less than two weeks.

Goose bumps broke out over her body. She was as terrified as Spencer looked earlier. But it was the truth. As different as they were, they complemented each other. She loved Spencer.

Spencer stopped spinning and pointed at the bed. He shrugged off his robe. It fell around his feet in a half circle as if guiding him toward the full-size, wrought iron bed draped with crisp white sheets.

His back was to her, and what a view. The way his ass stretched the knit of his boxer briefs begged for her hands to grab it. She remembered how she grabbed it as he thrusted into her. Was that only last week?

Well, fuck me. First realizing how much she loved this man. And now was she supposed to concentrate on photos with him in that bed? She didn't have enough willpower for that.

"Is this okay?" he asked shyly.

"Yes, it'll do." Her voice cracked. "I want you to be comfortable."

She tried to clear images of him splayed out on the bed with his cock at attention from her mind. This was supposed to be a boudoir shoot. Where the suggestion of nudity created sensuality and eroticism. Her image of him formed from pure lust.

Josie didn't want to take any more photos. She didn't want to share this part of him with anyone else. Jealously flared through her at the thought of other women or men staring at photos of Spencer in bed. *Her* bed.

She set down her camera. "I think I've gotten enough pictures."

"Oh, we're done already? I was starting to get warmed up." He slid backward onto the bed. The bulge in his shorts was hard to miss. "I enjoy posing for you."

"I didn't say I was done with you." Josie walked up to the edge of the bed and ran her nails down his thigh. His cock twitched. "As long as that's what you want, too."

Spencer's eyelids dropped, and he threw his head back as she claimed his other thigh with her nails.

"Yes, please," he whispered.

CHAPTER 40

As you wish." Josie climbed onto his lap, straddling him.

Their lips crashed into each other. She explored his mouth, committing everything about him to memory. He tasted of coffee and cake from their stop at her favorite bakery.

He groaned into her before pulling away to catch his breath. She traced small circles on his neck with her nails. Each completed circle became a landing zone for her lips to caress and her teeth to further claim him as hers. His chest heaved with each kiss and bite.

He pulled her back for another kiss. He searched for her tongue hungrily. She wrapped her hands around his head. Right now, she didn't want to think about the future.

Tonight she'd savor every touch, every kiss. The last time they'd been together, she fought for control and focused on only her needs. This time would be different. She wanted to explore every inch of him and learn what touch made him sigh and which ones elicited moans.

She pushed him onto the crisp white sheets. Grunting, he grabbed her hips and pulled her down with him. The quick movement knocked her breathless. They laughed when she fell on top of him, but the heat of his hard cock drew her attention back to his body.

His fingers dug into her hips as he flipped her over so he was on top.

"My turn," he whispered before sliding down between her legs. He pulled off her underwear and dove under the skirt of her dress.

Moaning, she opened her legs for him, offering herself, her love to him. His mouth landed on her thighs as he kissed his way to her throbbing pussy. His tongue darted between her swollen labia and hit the jackpot. She hissed as his tongue circled around her clit. Pleasure shot through her body. Heat pooled inside her as her muscles clenched. She needed more.

She twisted his hair in her fingers and pulled him closer, but he held firm. Each time his tongue brought her to the brink, he pulled back, leaving her gasping. Spencer only laughed when she tugged on his hair.

"My cock gets even harder when you're so needy and demanding," he growled.

"You're trying to make me beg." She wiggled her body out of her dress and tossed it aside. Her bra followed suit. "Maybe I'll distract you instead."

"Fuck, distract me all you want." He kicked off his boxers. He climbed back up and turned his attention to her breasts. Even with the heat on, her nipples hardened under his gaze. He always made her feel like the most beautiful woman in the world.

Spencer licked his lips and gave her a hungry grin. Her back arched when his hot mouth enveloped her nipples. He bathed them with his tongue, each swipe sending lightning bolts of pleasure through her body.

His cock lay heavy on her thigh. She reached down and wrapped her palm around his hard heat. He grunted and shifted so she could reach him more comfortably.

"I can't wait any longer, Spencer." Her chest heaved and her pussy ached for him.

She rolled out from under him and grabbed a condom from her bag. He pulled himself up to sit against the wrought iron headboard. Another photo series flashed in her head. One that involved satin ties and a blindfold. A rush of heat spread over her naked body. She filed the idea away for another time and dashed back to the bed to slip the condom on him.

"Ready?" She straddled him and hovered until his cock was at her entrance. Her breathing was ragged.

"I'm all yours," he whispered. His fingers trembled as he caressed the swell of her breasts.

He loved her. She could see it in his eyes. She wanted to tell him how she felt, but she wasn't ready. Once she uttered those words, she couldn't take them back. Everything would change. They'd have to talk about the future and what she wanted from their relationship. She didn't have any answers, but she realized that it didn't matter while they were in this bed.

She could enjoy this moment between them without letting the infinite possibilities scare her away.

Josie eased herself down his cock. His silky hardness stretched her. Filled her with so much pleasure that even her ears flushed. She wanted to give all of herself to him. As much as was possible.

Spencer's eyes rolled back in his head. He grabbed her hips and thrust into her. She reached for the headboard behind him and matched the roll of his hips into her. Her entire body tingled. Their bodies had found a rhythm that increased with each thrust, each buck of their hips. Josie's body tensed. She was so close. She squeezed her thighs around his.

"I need—" She gasped as he rocked into her. He nodded and reached between her legs. He pressed the pad of his thumb on her clit. She ground herself against his thumb, against his cock. Faster and faster until she exploded in pleasure, crying out his name.

"I'm yours always," he cried out as he grasped her hips with both hands and found his own pleasure.

Josie kissed him and swallowed his cries of pleasure. She wanted to hold every touch, every part of him close for as long as she could. She loved him so much it hurt. No matter what happened after this, she vowed not to hold him back from finding his purpose and happiness.

CHAPTER 41

"Josie, wake up," Spencer said as he shook her shoulder. She was angelic all wrapped up in the white sheets. He didn't want to wake her up but he had to. "It's eight in the morning."

She opened one eye and swatted at him.

"Too early," she mumbled. She pulled the covers over her head.

"We fell asleep in your studio," he whispered.

"Shit!" Josie sat straight up. The sheets fell to her waist. "We have to get out of here."

Her bare breasts caught his attention. He recalled how sensitive they'd been last night. He wouldn't mind revisiting that memory.

"Stop staring at my boobs!" She pushed him out of bed. "If Tasha finds us in here together, she's going to have a field day."

She ran around the studio to collect their clothes. She tossed his clothes at him piece by piece as she grabbed them. Most of his things were still behind the screen, so he was able to dress quickly.

"What time does she get here?" Spencer asked as he buttoned his jeans.

"Studio opens at ten, but she likes to get here early to catch up on emails and paperwork." Josie dug around in the sheets for her panties and slipped them on. She grabbed her dress off the floor and threw it over her head.

"You make the bed and I'll reset the studio." She ran around and fiddled with the umbrella lights.

"I forgot how cranky you are in the morning," he teased as he tried to remember how the bed looked before they made love in it. "Shouldn't we change the sheets?"

"Dammit. Yes. Sheets are over there." She pointed to a wire shelf where they stored various bedsheets and other soft goods. "Hurry!"

Spencer hadn't seen Josie so flustered before. He found it endearing that the woman he loved had learned to pivot from her plans so quickly. Fifteen minutes and a clean studio later, they were both out of breath.

"Did we miss anything?" Spencer had been so nervous last night that he barely remembered what the room looked like.

"Hush and give me a second to wrap up my hair." She stood in front of the long mirror and adjusted her scarf.

He wrapped his arms around her waist from behind and kissed her neck. She sighed and rested against his chest.

"Last night was more than I ever hoped for." *I love you, Josie*, he wanted to add. But he didn't want to scare her away. He'd give her as much time as she needed.

She turned around and kissed him. "It was great for me, too. But we really need to go because I'm not ready to explain anything to Tasha. Or my staff!"

They grabbed their bags and snuck out the back door. They walked as quickly as they could without drawing attention. It was early enough in the day that they easily blended in with people walking to work.

"That's the first time I've done the walk of shame *with* the person I shamed with," Spencer said, and clasped her hand.

"It's a first for me, too." She swung their hands as they walked to the Metro station. "So where to?"

"I know you're awake because of the adrenaline rush, but it'll be safer for both of us if I get some coffee in you."

"Thank God. I need—"

"A triple shot espresso with a shot of mocha," he finished.

"You remembered."

"You know how I feel about you. I'll do whatever's in my power to make you happy." He squeezed her hand. "I know just the place for breakfast."

They snagged a booth at Busboys and Poets to enjoy a laid-back breakfast. An hour and a few espressos later, Josie cozied up with Spencer, his arm draped around her shoulder. Her limbs were languid, as if last night's afterglow refused to let her go.

"I haven't been to Busboys in ages." Josie pushed away her empty plate and rubbed her stomach. "I forgot how good the food is."

"I used to come here for lunch. My old office was about five blocks away. I also discovered a bunch of new-to-me authors thanks to this place." He pointed to the shelves in the café bookstore.

"I didn't know you were a reader."

"Gotta keep you on your toes so you don't get bored with me."

"I don't know if that's possible." She pointed to the extra side of bacon he'd ordered with his Oaxaca omelet. "You're not going to finish that last piece of bacon?"

"All yours."

"Any man who gives me his last piece of bacon is a keeper."

"Is that so? I'll have to remember that for our next brunch after we make a run of shame out of the studio you own."

"Ha! Next time we'll go to my place." Josie wanted there to be a next time and another one after that. "No walk of shame needed."

"I'd like that very much." He pulled her in for a side hug.

As she chewed on her bacon, she wondered if he was ready to talk about their future together. He'd declared his love for her in New Orleans, but he hadn't brought it up again since he came to DC. She didn't want to lose the easygoing familiarity between them. Not yet.

"Do you want to look at books? Or do something else?" He waggled his eyebrows. "Because I have an idea."

"You know how to bring out my adventurous side. I'll take door number two: something else."

"Since we're so close to Chinatown, why not check out Stevens Art Gallery? We can pretend to be art collectors and see if they're worthy of your art." He turned up his nose and pursed his lips to impersonate his version of a snobby art dealer.

"Art dealers? Dressed like this?" They were still wearing the same clothes from yesterday.

"No, really, we should scope it out. Maybe you can pose next to some art and we'll photoshop your work into it. For inspiration."

Josie didn't want to reject his suggestion, since she often suggested something similar to the Babes. Envisioning her work on the Stevens Gallery walls was one step toward her dream.

"Let's do it. But you have to be on your best behavior. It's an art gallery, not the streets of New Orleans."

"I can't believe you think so little of me. I have manners." His lips turned up in a wide smile.

They paid their bill and started a leisurely walk toward the Chinatown art gallery. Josie shivered. Though the sun was out, the mid-January air was still chilly. Spencer placed his arm on her shoulder and pulled her close to him.

"Why don't we cross the street so we're in the sun. That way you won't get too cold." He smiled brightly as he rubbed her shoulder to warm her.

Josie wrapped her arm around his waist and inhaled his deep, masculine scent. She couldn't help but think ahead. How long would he stay in DC? As much as she wanted to, she couldn't bear the thought of holding back his carefree spirit by asking him to stay here.

CHAPTER 42

We're close to Stevens Gallery," Josie declared after she double-checked her maps app. She still wasn't sure about Spencer's idea, but they were mere blocks away. It was silly to turn around now. It's not like she had any other plans today.

Josie took a few steps before realizing that Spencer wasn't next to her. He stood on the corner of 7th and H Streets, where the majestic Chinatown Arch stood watch over the city. People milled around the Metro escalators. A guy with a sizable afro was busking with his five-gallon paint bucket and drumsticks. This corner was always hopping with activity.

"It's sad how Chinatown is full of chain stores and restaurants," said Spencer. "Just because the drugstore has signs in Mandarin doesn't mean they're not erasing its history."

He wasn't wrong. Many of the original Chinese American families had moved out to the suburbs due to the rising rents. Gentrification was happening all over the city, including the neighborhood where Hazel's Kitchen was located.

"You're thinking about your family, aren't you?" Josie slipped her hand into his. "Your community is thriving. You're doing your best to preserve its history. And your film will make sure everyone knows how they've come together to create the co-op."

"You're right. Sorry to be a buzzkill." He squeezed her hand. "You said Stevens was that way?"

Josie nodded and led the way. Her stomach twisted. Why was she so nervous when they were going only as visitors? It wasn't as if she were trying to get a meeting with their curator or gallerist.

"Do I look okay?" She checked her head scarf for flyaways.

"You're beautiful. Like a free-spirited artist."

She scowled. "You're only saying that because we spent the night together."

"Wrong. I thought you were hot from the moment you knocked me out with your beads." He winked.

She shrugged off his compliment. "Stevens is one of DC's premier art galleries. They focus exclusively on photography."

Spencer pulled her off to the side. He placed both hands on her shoulders and looked into her eyes.

"I know I'm not a fine art expert, but I can tell that your photos are different from any I've seen. If they can't appreciate your work, I know you'll find a way to get it out there." He leaned in for a soft kiss. "You don't have to do it alone. I'll help you."

"I've been dreaming about this for so long that I've made it into a huge thing," Josie said. Then she straightened her back and nodded. There would be more galleries after this one. "I'm ready."

Stevens Art Gallery was small and minimalist. It was mostly

empty except for a staff member and two women in very expensive pantsuits who were discussing a photograph in the back. A selection of black-and-white and color photographs hung on their walls.

"Welcome to Stevens Art Gallery." A tall brunette greeted them. "Let me know if you have questions about the artist or their pieces."

The woman returned to her desk. Josie appreciated her low-key sales approach. Choosing artwork for your home took time. It was a big decision to invest in something a person looked at every day.

The photos in front of them were ethereal landscapes. The artist had gone for a soft focus on the background with one or two eye-catching flowers or trees in the foreground. She didn't care for landscapes but she could appreciate the artist's technique and composition.

"What do you think so far?" Spencer whispered in her ear.

"Very good technique here. See how the background is completely out of focus?" She pointed at the photograph of a field of sunflowers. "That's called bokeh. I use it during my shoots when I want to evoke a more sensual mood."

On the adjacent wall were black-and-white photos of different DC monuments and historic buildings. All the classics were represented: the Washington Monument, the Lincoln Memorial, the Vietnam Veterans Memorial, even the Supreme Court Building. On each photo was one hazy figure colored in purple or blue. The figure was different in each one.

The composition and storytelling in these photos were top-notch. The first set were soft and dreamy, perfect for a small office or living room. The monument ones evoked dominance and influence. Perfect for a politician's office.

The work managed to have commercial appeal and artistry. Of course, any artwork in a gallery should have some commercial appeal if the gallery were to sell it. Her approach had been all wrong. What if her work wasn't good enough? How could a boudoir photographer compete for coveted space on these walls?

"Doing okay?" Spencer asked as if sensing her self-doubt. He squeezed her hand.

"I'm good. Let's check out the next artist." She avoided his worried glance and led him around the back.

Landscapes at night. These were dark and moody. These were the exact opposites of the photos she'd taken in New Orleans. Next to them were the most gorgeous portraits she'd ever seen. The photographer had captured each person's essence so well, she could get lost in their eyes. One person's eyes were full of joy and hope, while another photo captured despair and longing.

The skin across her chest tightened and began to tingle. The walls began to close in on her. Her work wasn't good enough to belong here. *She* didn't belong here.

Josie pulled Spencer's arm. She must've looked panicked, because he hooked his arm through hers and walked her out the door. He even managed to wave good-bye to the brunette on the way out.

She gulped the brisk air as soon as they stepped outside. Spencer kept them moving until he found an empty café table.

"Josie, what happened in there?" His thumb drew slow circles on the back of her hand.

"My work isn't right for Stevens Gallery." It hurt to say the words, but the truth hurt sometimes.

"You don't know that."

"Maybe I don't, but my gut says no. My portraits aren't good enough to set foot in the door of Stevens. I'm only a boudoir photographer with no formal training." Josie rubbed her eyes and ran her hands across her face.

"I'm not a gallery curator, but I know your work is good enough to be there. You see people's hopes and dreams and capture them. You can't give up before you've even tried."

"Maybe the universe is giving me a sign." Josie sat up.

"Yes, it is. The universe is telling you to shoot your shot. Right now they have nothing but boring plants and monuments. And a few portraits. They need *your* portraits to add some energy to their gallery." Spencer's chest heaved from defending her work.

"Yeah, the landscapes were a tiny bit boring," she admitted.

"You gotta save them," Spencer said, shaking his head in pity. "They need so much help."

She laughed. "I'm pretty sure Stevens Gallery doesn't need saving." He'd kept her from spiraling into self-doubt. "Thank you. For talking me off the ledge."

"You weren't even close to the ledge." He pulled her to standing. "How about we work on our respective applications and take over the art world?"

"Maybe we should keep our expectations more realistic," Josie suggested, but his confidence was contagious. And extremely sexy. She kissed his neck and whispered, "Let's go back to my place, where we won't be disturbed."

"We're not talking about art anymore, are we?"

"You'll have to wait and see."

CHAPTER 43

After their emotional visit to Stevens Gallery yesterday, they'd curled up in her bed and binged on reality baking shows. Which led to more lovemaking. Who says baking isn't sexy?

"You weren't kidding about your mom's crab mac and cheese," Spencer said the next morning as he stuffed another forkful into his mouth. He was stretched out on Josie's couch wearing only her floral silk robe. Josie sat opposite him so their legs were intertwined.

Her one-bedroom apartment was warm and feminine. She'd decorated her walls with paintings, sculptures, and photographs. Most of the art wasn't hers. Josie's collection was so diverse, yet they all fit together because each piece celebrated people. Humanity.

"I'm carb-loading you. So you have energy to do that thing with your tongue again tonight." She tickled his feet. He kicked playfully at her.

"Ah-ha, ulterior motives!" Spencer held up the half-empty plastic container. "If pleasuring you with my mouth is the payment for the creamiest, most savory mac and cheese I've ever had, it's a sacrifice I must make."

"What should we do while we wait for your clothes to dry?"

Spencer had never made it back to his friend's apartment to pick up a change of clothes. Josie offered him use of the small washer and dryer in her apartment. She also offered her robe to wear until his clothes were done.

"No plans for today?" Spencer narrowed his eyes and arched his eyebrows. "I'm leaning toward earning my keep as stated earlier."

"I'm afraid to jostle you, considering the amount of my mom's leftovers you've eaten," she teased. "Since I already submitted my portfolio and show proposal to Stevens Gallery after we got back here yesterday, I want to see how your dudeoir photos came out."

Spence sputtered. "*Dudeoir*? That's gotta be the least sexy term ever."

"Can you think of anything better?"

"Anything without *dude* is a vast improvement. *Male boudoir* is too awkward and unsexy. What about *bootydoir*? That's gender neutral."

Josie snorted. A reward for his bad joke.

"*Boudoir* can be gender neutral. Your suggestions are awful."

"You wound me."

"You'll survive. Now let me get some work done." She untangled her legs from his and walked to her dining table where they'd left their laptops. "Don't you need to finish your application?"

"I'll go check on my clothes. As pretty as I feel in your silk robe, it's a little short." He stood up and stretched. Yep, definitely a cool breeze on his butt cheeks. At least she'd appreciate the view as he walked to her laundry nook.

"Hey, I got a reply from Stevens Gallery already." Josie froze in her chair. Her fingers hovered over the track pad. "Is a fast reply good or bad?"

"No clue." He stepped into his boxer briefs and tossed the shirt over his head as he made his way to her table. Her forehead was lined with worry, and she tapped her foot against the leg of her chair.

"Do you want me to read it for you?" he asked.

She bit her lip as she considered his offer.

"No. It's just an email." She clicked and read aloud.

"Dear Ms. Parks, on behalf of Stevens Art Gallery, I thank you for trusting us with your work. We are afraid that we are not able to select your work for exhibition at our gallery. Each year we receive an unprecedented number of high-quality submissions. Unfortunately, not all the work that we like can be shown. As you are an emerging artist, we suggest you explore less provocative subjects and further hone your craft before submitting your work to other galleries. We wish you the very best in your pursuits, artistic and otherwise. Sincerely . . ."

Josie shut her laptop. Her eyes were wet and dull. The joy she'd shared with him earlier had been snuffed. "I really thought I had a chance."

"Hey, it's okay. That's just one gallery." He hugged her. Her body trembled. She held on to him in silence.

"I'm taking some time off to figure out what I really want to do," she said when she finally let go of him. "I was already burnt out when I first met you."

"What are you talking about? You can't give it up." Spencer searched her face for a sign that she was joking but found none. "Josie, you're scaring me."

"For years I've set my hopes on that art gallery, but I never stopped to consider if it was the right place for me. I've wasted so much time trying to fit my work into a mold, only to realize I've been using the wrong mold." Tears welled up in her eyes. "I was a fool to think a boudoir photographer could sell her work in a gallery like that."

"They're the ones who are missing out!" Spencer was angry on her behalf. How dare they imply that her work wasn't good enough. "Your photos would liven up that place. It was so stuffy. How many more photos of sunflower fields does the world need?"

She chuckled through her tears.

"I'm taking a break from photography," Josie declared. "I'll be like you and explore my options. Maybe change careers."

He cringed as she tossed his words back at him. He must have sounded so lost when he told everyone about exploring his options. Josie was anything but aimless.

"Of course you should. But please don't give up on all the amazing work you've done so far. All the women you've helped fall in love with their bodies. That's better than any art gallery in the world."

"Maybe my work isn't meant to be in a gallery. There are people who don't consider boudoir photos art." Josie closed her eyes. "But it is art."

Spencer's gut twisted. The woman he loved was hurting and words were not enough to make her feel better.

"You don't need me to say this, but I will anyway. You do something better than making art. Josie, you transform people with your camera and your words. They turn into beautiful butterflies."

She opened her eyes. Incredulity covered her face.

"I know because you did it for me the other night. After all these years, I've learned to ignore women who rejected me. They told me that Asian men weren't attractive or sexy enough to date. Seventy-five percent of my confidence is bravado. Fake it till you make it. But in that studio, you gave me the chance to feel comfortable in my body. To feel masculine and sexy."

Spencer hadn't realized how transformative that night was until now. He desperately needed her to know how special she was. How much she'd changed him.

"Josie, you see the beauty and strength in everyone you photograph. That's the most important thing you could ever do."

"I love you, Spencer Pham," she whispered.

He froze. Had he heard her correctly?

"You love me?"

She nodded. Her sadness transformed into joy. No, love.

"Me, too. I mean, I love you, too." Spencer picked her up in a giant bear hug and swung her in a circle. His chest swelled with joy. "I've loved you from the moment I met you."

She rolled her eyes.

"It was a different level of love, but this right now—I love you, Josie." Spencer repeated his declaration because he could finally say it without scaring her away like last time.

"What does this mean for us?" She gestured wildly between them. "You're going back to New Orleans eventually. I don't want to stop you from doing what makes you happy."

"I want to stay, Josie, but there're too many variables. I can't make any promises right now." Spencer chewed on his bottom lip. "Can you give me a few more days to sort things out?"

He had too many balls in the air right now to be certain of his next steps. What he did know was that he loved Josie and he couldn't stand to see her sad. He knew her well enough to know that her giving up photography wasn't the answer.

Spencer would figure out a way for Josie to share her work with the world, with people who would appreciate her. Then he'd find a way for them to stay together.

CHAPTER 44

S pencer, you've been sneaking around for the last three days. What is going on?" Josie touched the scarf he'd tied around her eyes while they were still in the rideshare. A few minutes later, Spencer helped her out of the car.

"Soon, I promise." He kissed her and hooked his arm through hers. "Thanks for being a good sport. I know how you hate surprises."

Spencer had given her the space to stew over and then become angry about the gallery's rejection. She'd focused her energy on helping him finish his application, which they'd submitted yesterday. It would be at least three months before he received a response.

In between the hours they'd poured into it, he'd been on his phone, texting. But she wasn't sure with whom. She would've been jealous if he hadn't just declared his love for her.

Now he'd dragged her somewhere. She heard cars idling at a stoplight and people calling to their dogs. A familiar smell hit her nose. With the blindfold on, she couldn't quite place it.

"When can I take this off?"

"Someone's very impatient today," he said, and tsked. She could hear a smile in his voice. "We're here. You can take it off once we're inside."

He opened a door and guided her inside.

"Surprise!"

Josie pulled off the scarf and opened her eyes to see a crowd in Hazel's Kitchen. She had smelled their food! She spotted her mother and Tasha, the Babes, her staff, and more friends. It was almost everyone she knew! They all smiled and cheered.

"Spencer, you threw me a party?" She slipped her arm through the crook of his.

"Look harder." He pointed to the walls.

She followed his finger to find large, framed photographs. They must've been at least poster size. When did Andre and Keisha start showing so much art in their restaurant?

Her jaw dropped. Wait, those were her photos from New Orleans and her neighborhood around her apartment near the Wharf. And some from their walk together in Chinatown and Penn Quarter.

"Welcome to the opening of the Josephine Parks Exhibition," Spencer announced. Everyone clapped and cheered. No one used her full name except for her mom, but she liked the sound of it for her debut.

Her very own art show. Josie blinked rapidly to keep the tears from falling. Andre and Keisha had even set a table with wine and cheese. Next to it was another table heaped with the restaurant's signature appetizers.

"You did all of this?"

"I had help. A lot of it." He nodded at her friends and family. They all waved. "You don't need a snobby art gallery to show off your beautiful work. In here, your photos can be appreciated by the people you capture. The everyday folks with unusual stories."

Her heart swelled. She had no idea how he'd managed this in just a few days. It must have taken so much time. Spencer *planned* this for her. She'd been unmoored after her rejection, but he never gave up on her. He put all of this together to show her how her work made a difference in people's lives.

Josie puffed out her chest. All these photos told the story of how she'd found herself again. She fell back in love with photography in New Orleans when she began looking at people differently. He'd helped her rediscover her passion when he introduced her to his grandmother. Capturing Bà Bà's joy at Crescent City Co-op was the turning point.

"This is the best surprise I've ever received. Thank you," Josie whispered, and tugged him close for a kiss. She meant to offer only a peck on the lips with a promise of more. When she sighed into his mouth, he delved deeper to claim her. She had no choice but to clutch his shirt and thank him by tasting him. Everyone around them cheered even louder.

Josie pulled away. Her cheeks were warm. For a minute she'd forgotten where she was.

"I should throw you art shows more often." Spencer smiled.

"I'll thank you properly later," Josie said softly.

"I'm counting on it," Spencer said, and offered his elbow.

"You did this in three days? It must've been so much work." Her photos hung in floating frames and cast dramatic shadows on the wall. Where did he even get them printed? The printer her studio used had at least a week turnaround time. Wait—how did he get access to her files?

"The Babes handled all the framing and hanging, plus the food. Tasha helped edit the photos and get them printed. I swore everyone to secrecy. Even your mom."

"You talked to my mom?" She gasped. "And Tasha actually kept a secret!"

"I'm this close"—he held his index finger and thumb together— "to convincing your mom to give me her crab mac and cheese recipe."

"If my mom gives it to you before me, I'll never talk to you again!"

Spencer threw his head back and laughed. Of course he'd charmed her family and friends. He'd charmed her that very first day.

"We can't let that happen. How about I give you a tour of your own work?"

Josie chuckled. Now, that was something she didn't hear often. She intertwined her fingers with his.

"This wall is what I call your *I'm Hungry* phase." Spencer pointed to a photo of Mrs. Vargas holding a tray of freshly baked conchas inside the bakery near her apartment. "I have no idea what these are, but I want some."

He'd curated a selection of images from the sandwich shop in New Orleans, photos she'd taken of Keisha and Andre during the restaurant's community nights, along with shots from diners and other places with food.

"On the surface, this series is all about food. But if you look more closely, you can see how the artist has captured joy and pride in these people. They're proud of their food and their culture. So they use food to bring their community together."

A small crowd had gathered around them. He motioned for them to step back so they could appreciate the series as a whole. Spencer guided her to the next wall. "This series is what I call *Better Than Fucking Sunflowers*."

Josie cackled. "You didn't!"

"I didn't. But I wanted to. Zoe convinced me to call it the *New Orleans Series*."

He'd chosen her photos from Crescent City Co-op. In the center was her favorite photo of his grandmother. The one where Bà Bà tossed her flowers into the air. She looked much younger than her almost one hundred years. Josie wished his grandmother were here to see herself in the show.

"Josie!"

Could that be? No way. She followed the voice.

"Bà Bà!" Josie ran to his grandmother and enveloped her in a hug. She wore a light blue áo dài. "Now, this is my kind of surprise. You flew all the way here for me?"

"You made me famous! Look at all the people who came to see me." She waved at the crowd around them. Everyone laughed, already charmed by the older woman.

"Don't forget about us." Three younger women stood close behind Bà Bà. She recognized his youngest sister, who now sported an adorable pixie haircut.

"It's good to see you again, Nina." Josie hugged her.

"I'm Rose, the favorite sister." This sister wore a thin head-band in her shoulder-length hair.

"You are not the favorite!" a stern woman exclaimed. "I'm Cynthia. Pleasure to meet the woman who convinced Spencer to get his act together."

"Now you've met all of my sisters," Spencer said to Josie. "Be careful, they're very nosy. My parents couldn't make it, but they send their congrats. Now the rest of you shoo while I finish my tour."

His sisters and grandmother headed to the snack table.

"I still can't believe you did all of this for me."

"There's one final stop on the tour. The most important one." Spencer handed her a glass of champagne he'd grabbed from a nearby waiter. "You ready?"

Even after so many surprises, she couldn't wait to see what else Spencer had prepared for her. Spencer gulped down his champagne and set the glass on a nearby table. His breathing hitched and the confidence he had earlier seemed to leak away. She wasn't used to him feeling so nervous.

"Spencer, are you okay? You drank that a bit fast." Josie touched his arm and added encouragingly, "I love everything so far. I can't wait to see what else you've done."

"I'm great. Come this way." His voice perked up, and he guided her toward the bar in the back of the restaurant.

A series of seven or eight frames were displayed on the wooden bar. At least that's what she assumed, since each one was cov-ered with a black piece of fabric. These were smaller than the ones hung on the wall, probably measuring around eight by ten inches. Whatever photos he'd chosen for this part must have a strong meaning for him to be so nervous.

"Ooh, mysterious." She sipped her champagne to hide the twitch of her fingers. His apprehension was rubbing off on her. While the other photos were joyous, they were also uncovered. What made these different enough to receive special attention? She tamped down the desire to unveil them one after the other. This was his idea, so she forced herself to be patient.

"Before we start, this series is all my doing. So if you hate it, the blame is on me." Spencer took a deep breath and removed the fabric from the first photo. Then the next five, each with a flourish.

Josie gasped.

"These are all my clients." She stepped up to the first photo. Josie touched each photo gently as her sessions with each woman flashed in her mind. "Quita, Joyce, Mai, Lizzie, Padma, and Sheila. How did you convince them to share these?"

"Tasha and I asked all your past clients to tell us how your photos transformed them," he said. Spencer pointed to the card below each photo. "Quita used to hate photos. Before you, other photographers could never get the lighting right for her dark skin. You gave her tips during the shoot, and she's shared them with her friends so her beauty shines even in their selfies."

Josie exclaimed in delight as she read each card. "Joyce. She was my first client who brought her own props. Whips and a leather mask. Plus the sexiest pair of thigh-high stilettos I've ever seen. This says I gave her the courage to release her inner domme."

He'd chosen each one to show Josie how she'd touched all these women. Each person came to her studio for photos but left with a new way of seeing themselves. Deep down, she'd known that the photoshoots had changed them. She hadn't realized how much until now.

"These are beautiful." She didn't want to ugly cry, but her eyes were welling up. "I mean, I knew they walked out of the studio taller, more confident. I had no idea their experience made such a huge impact."

"Josie, we had *hundreds* of responses. I didn't have room to include all of them here, but Tasha saved all the emails for you to read later." He handed her a napkin for her tears. "Do you see why this world needs your photos?"

"Dammit, Spencer, you're making me cry." She wiped her eyes. "And there're still two more photos."

"These are the most important to me. And hopefully to us." Spencer shifted his weight from one foot to the other. He took a deep breath, released it with a whoosh, and whipped off the covering.

"This is you at Cafe du Monde." She laughed. "Our first date."

How could she forget the night they first met?

Powdered sugar floated in the air as he took a bite of the beignet. Someone with an eye for detail could see the bruise forming around his temple.

"But you didn't want anyone to see your bruise. I haven't shown anyone this photo because of that." Josie caressed his bruise in the photo. Looking at him now, she could barely make out where the beads had hit him.

"I chose this one because you humored me with my rules for eating beignets. It's also the moment when I knew I couldn't let you walk out of my life."

"You were the one that walked out that night," she teased.

"I didn't want to! That was Nina and Jimmy's fault." Spencer peered into the crowd. "He's around here somewhere. You can yell at him if you want."

"Stop stalling," she said. "What's the last photo?"

His earlier nervousness now held a tinge of excitement and fear. He breathed in through his mouth and exhaled quickly. Without taking his eyes off her, he grabbed a corner of the fabric and slid it down.

Josie's eyes widened. Her hand flew to her mouth.

The last photo was Spencer, reclining on a velvet chaise with his robe half open. It was from his boudoir shoot. He was so beautiful and vulnerable in this shot, yet there was a hint of the freedom he displayed only moments later during his session. She hadn't told him yet, but Josie didn't want to share his boudoir photos with anyone else. Yet this private moment between them was here for the world to see. All to prove to her how much she meant to him.

"Spencer," she whispered as she traced the frame with her finger. "You didn't have to include this."

"I did." He cleared his throat. "Because you've changed my life forever. You believed in me even though I didn't believe in myself. I had no idea how to make a film, much less finish one."

He took her champagne glass and set it on the bar. Spencer grasped both of her hands and looked into her eyes.

"You are the bravest woman I've ever met. Your idea for an inclusive boudoir series will empower so many people. I'm proud to be your first model for it. I will sit for as many photos as you need to achieve your goals. I love you, Josie Parks."

His love for her was etched deeply on his face, and his eyes were wet. Josie's chest heaved as she absorbed what he'd done and his declaration. *Spencer loved her.* So much that he organized a solo art show for her in only a few days.

"What about your family and New Orleans?" Her voice broke. "You've been away from them for too long."

"I have a plan that I hope you'll go along with."

"Okay, I have changed you." She chuckled. "Tell me."

"I'm applying for jobs at film festivals here and in New Orleans. I'm not even remotely qualified, but I don't care. If you were brave enough to submit your work to Stevens, I can handle the rejections. I can travel between both cities. We'll make the part-time, long-distance thing work."

Josie opened her mouth, but he held up his hand.

"But I think we should open a gallery together."

"What? Do you know how much work that is? Where would we even—" Josie shook her head.

She'd never considered opening her own gallery. She immediately begin creating two lists in her head: Why Opening a Gallery Is Too Much Work and Why Starting a Gallery Is the Best Idea Ever.

"Let me finish. I've seen the art in your apartment. You have a knack for curating pieces that tell a story about everyday people.

It would be a cooperative gallery where everyone has a voice in how their work is shown. We can do it together."

"I love your idea! There are so many great artists in DC who aren't getting the attention they deserve." Josie grabbed his face and pressed her warm, soft lips to his. "And I love you, too, Spencer Pham."

Everyone in the restaurant cheered as he returned her kiss. Josie's first art show was a success.

CHAPTER 45

One week later in New Orleans

I'm gonna puke." Spencer ran his fingers under the collar of his shirt. "I shouldn't have worn a tie."

"They're going to love your film. Now stop messing up your tie." Josie straightened it and smoothed out the shoulders of his jacket. They were in a classroom at his church, where his grandmother's birthday celebration and Tết festivities were being held. "Remember that everyone cares most about the story your film tells."

"That's what I'm worried about. I don't want to accidentally embarrass my elders."

"You worked your ass off on this short and everyone will love it." She pushed him against the door. "And it's the first time I've seen you in a suit. It's incredibly sexy."

Their bodies were mere inches apart. His familiar scent tinged with fresh soap and hair gel sent a tingle through her body. His eyes, his face—the way he bit his lip when he was nervous.

"Did you ever sneak girls in here to make out?" She arched her eyebrows. "I know what would relax you."

"Fuck—I mean, shoot." He groaned. "As much as I want to

devour you right now, I can't do that in the same classroom that I took catechism classes. It's sacrilege."

"Ooh, a hard limit," she teased. "I was only kidding. But at least you're not as nervous."

"Thank God, because my anxiety went through the roof at the thought of it." He laughed and hugged her.

"Though I'll have to take that off my Places to Have Sex with Spencer list."

"Wait, you made a list of places to have sex without consulting me?"

"I just created it in my head. Your input is required, of course."

"I'd be delighted to help you make the list *and* check it off." He kissed her deeply, doing that tongue thing that made her toes curl. She was panting when he finally pulled away.

"We can start both when we get back to our apartment," he suggested.

"I packed red lingerie for the Lunar New Year. *And* Trixie tucked one of her special sex toy care packages into my suitcase. It's your reward for surviving your first film showing."

"I hate to admit it, but lust is a good motivator." He laughed.

They were staying in a much less extravagant rental for her return to New Orleans. She'd helped him interview his grandmother's friends and his family to make a tribute video for Bà Bà's birthday celebration. They'd stayed up late last night to put the final touches on it.

"I couldn't have done it without you. Thanks for coming down to New Orleans with me." He kissed her forehead.

"Bà Bà would never forgive me if I missed her birthday party.

Besides, I've never celebrated Tết in New Orleans before. Something to cross off my bucket list."

After the solo art show that Spencer had organized for her, she'd crossed out Stevens Art Gallery from its number one spot and replaced it with *Follow your dreams wholeheartedly*. Josie then turned her 30 by 30 list into a Badass Experiences to Try list and expanded it using Spencer's suggestions. The thirty-year-old time limit had been arbitrary. She'd been so focused on crossing things off that she'd lost sight of why she even wanted to accomplish those things. Her new list was even more meaningful, because she was sharing her new experiences with the man she loved. Like the artist collective Spencer had suggested. They planned to start on it once they returned to the DMV the following week.

"I love you, Spencer." She smoothed out his hair and straightened his tie again.

"I've never loved anyone as much as I love you, Josie." His eyes bored into hers.

If she kissed him again, it'd be more than a kiss. And he'd be late for his own showing. She brushed her lipstick off his lips.

"Are you ready?"

He took a deep breath and nodded.

"Let's start our next adventure together." She opened the door.

"Any adventure that includes lucky lingerie is a good one for me."

Always the joker. At least he had his nerves under control.

He offered her his arm. She slipped hers through it and pulled him close until their shoulders touched. With Spencer at her side, Josie could tackle whatever surprises came her way.

A NOTE FROM THE AUTHOR

The New Orleans you know isn't the same New Orleans I visited as a child. The biggest city in Louisiana is known for Mardi Gras, po'boys, and jazz. What many people don't know is that the Vietnamese community has made its imprint on the city's culture as well. I hope to show you a different part of the city than mainstream media focuses on because it's the part I connect with the most.

My family fled Vietnam in the late 1970s at the end of the war. After being separated and shuffled around various refugee processing centers in Asia and the United States, they settled in Louisiana. I grew up in a small town about two hours northwest of New Orleans.

Back then, there weren't many places to buy Vietnamese groceries in my hometown. About once a month, we made the drive down to New Orleans, specifically to Versailles. The Vietnamese community there was so big and exciting to young me. Not only did my mom stock up on fresh produce and pantry staples, but she also browsed the fluorescent-lit shop next door. The rows and rows of Paris by Night convert videos, cassette tapes of Vietnamese American pop music, and bootleg Chinese dramas dubbed in Vietnamese were her happy place.

I didn't care for the "uncool" V-pop music playing in the shop, but my patience was rewarded by a xe lửa phở (very large bowl of phở) and freshly wrapped gỏi cuốn at one of the nearby restaurants afterward. On the return trip, I often caught myself bopping to my mom's new music blaring through the car's speakers. Those memories evoke so much joy for me.

While I took some artistic liberties about New Orleans in *Full Exposure*, there are many truths. Many of the Vietnamese immigrants found work in fishing and shrimping. Others, both in New Orleans and the rest of the state, worked as laborers in jobs that didn't require a good grasp of English.

The cooperative farm that the Pham family is part of is loosely based on VEGGI Farmer's Cooperative (Village de l'Est Green Growers Initiative). Like VEGGI, my imaginary co-op farm was founded when so many Vietnamese Americans lost their income after the Deepwater Horizon oil spill. Look up VEGGI and help them support the New Orleans community with fresh produce. I can't keep plants alive to save my life, so apologies to VEGGI for anything I got wrong.

All of the named places that Josie and Spencer visit are real, though I might have tweaked a few details to serve the story. If you're ever in the area, check them out! Yes, I tried a phoritto at the Pythian Market food hall and was surprised by how much I liked it.

I hope this book inspires you to learn more about the Vietnamese American community in the South. I'm proud of my Vietnamese and Southern heritage and hope to pass it on to my kids and generations to come.

BÁNH MÌ SLIDERS WITH SRIRACHA MAYO

Prep time: 20 minutes, plus time to marinade
Cook time: 20 minutes

Hawaiian rolls evoke memories of picking up greasy but delicious Church's fried chicken (a Southern fast-food chain). I inhaled the rolls they tossed in with our take-out orders. The sweet, soft bread complements the savory pork and pickled carrots to give you the typical Vietnamese salty, sour, and sweet flavor combo.

The dry rub also works well on other proteins, such as tofu and chicken. If you substitute with tofu, I recommend deep-frying or air-frying it before adding the seasoning for optimal flavor.

1½ tbsp five-spice powder
1 tsp each garlic powder, onion powder, ground black pepper
3 tsp of kosher salt
2 pounds country-style pork ribs, boneless
1 tbsp sugar

308 BÁNH MÌ SLIDERS WITH SRIRACHA MAYO

½ cup of white vinegar
1½ cup of matchstick or grated carrots
1 tsp cilantro leaves, finely chopped
2 tbsp of mayonnaise
sriracha chili sauce
Maggi seasoning (to taste)
12 small sweet rolls, such as Hawaiian rolls

Combine the five-spice powder, garlic powder, onion powder, ground black pepper, and 2 teaspoons of kosher salt (you'll use the rest later) to make the spice rub. Sprinkle generously on the pork. Place in zip-top bag and let it marinate for at least 4 hours (overnight is good too).

Preheat broiler for at least 15 minutes. Place country-style pork ribs on rack inside a roasting pan and broil for 8–10 minutes per side, until pork is golden brown and cooked to 145° F. Remove from oven and let rest for 5 minutes before cutting into ¼-inch slices.

You can also grill the pork.

CILANTRO CARROT SLAW

In a medium bowl, combine sugar, 1 teaspoon of kosher salt, and white vinegar. Stir until salt and sugar are dissolved. Add carrot and chopped cilantro leaves. Mix well. Let sit for at least 15 minutes. Toss it halfway through. Squeeze out any excess liquid before adding to the slider.

SRIRACHA MAYO

In a small bowl, combine mayonnaise and sriracha. Stir until well mixed. Keep refrigerated until ready to assemble sliders.

ASSEMBLE SLIDERS

Cut rolls in half. Spread sriracha mayo on each side of the roll. Place the sliced pork and carrot slaw on one side of the roll. Drizzle with Maggi seasoning and sprinkle with more cilantro leaves if desired. Top with other half of roll and enjoy!

ABOUT THE AUTHOR

THIEN-KIM LAM writes stories about Vietnamese characters who smash stereotypes and find their happy endings. A recovering Type-Asian, she guzzles cà phê sữa đá, makes art, and bakes her feelings to stay sane. Thien-Kim is also the founder of Bawdy Bookworms, a subscription box that pairs sexy romances with erotic toys. She's been featured on NPR, BBC America, and NBC.